Montana DESIRE

JOSIE JADE

This a work of fiction. Names, characters, places, and incidents are the product of the author's imagination or are used fictitiously, and any resemblance to actual persons, living or dead, business establishments, events or locals is entirely coincidental.

Cover created by Deranged Doctor Designs.

A Calamittie Jane Publishing Book

MONTANA DESIRE: RESTING WARRIOR RANCH

Chapter 1

Cori Jackson

Note to self: never check your email when you're in a hurry to get out the door.

I'd been stupid enough to do just that, despite knowing I had an entire family hell-bent on making me miserable. I had thought our phone conversation last night—same old song and dance about what a disappointment I was, *cha-cha-cha*—had covered it all.

I was so wrong.

And they'd sent it in an *email.*

Now I was late, and my line of work didn't wait for when things were convenient—or when your family wasn't threatening to disown you.

I heard the cow in labor as soon as I got out of my truck. She was already in the thick of it. I ran to the barn. Jerry Rushdan, owner of the ranch and the lady in labor, was looking in on her, anxious.

This calf was big and he was concerned, as he should

be. But I had faith that nature would take its course, and if anything went wrong, then I would be here to help.

My problem was that I was going to have to get the anger and the frustration in my head under control long enough to actually focus.

My family was a real piece of work, dropping this on me. In an *email.*

"Hey, Jerry."

He smiled. "Hi, Cori. You all right?"

"Sure. And she'll be okay too. Don't worry."

His face already told me that he was still going to.

Jerry was one of my favorite clients. He cared about every one of his animals as if they were family. That made it difficult when things went wrong or animals got sick, but it was also nice to see. Sometimes in industries like ranching, animals were treated a little more expendably than I was comfortable with. But for the most part, I considered myself lucky to be here and to have the practice that I did.

If only my family felt the same.

Jacksons were surgeons. That was just the way it was. Everyone in my family was a surgeon. Grandparents, parents, siblings, spouses. The whole medical field knew my family, and the name was synonymous with talent and prestige. I did appreciate that.

But I didn't want it.

I'd never exactly been a model child, and I'd known from an early age that I didn't want to be a surgeon. But that was the expectation. It was what we did.

After all, Jacksons didn't defy the family legacy.

That was basically what my parents told me this morning in an email that sounded as though they'd run all the language through their lawyer. At first, it had been nice enough, even sympathetic. They understood getting my veterinary license had been a passion of mine, but now, it was time to come home.

Translation: We're done letting you sow your wild oats. Time to become a surgeon. You're a *Jackson*.

Fine. They'd said it to me before, and it was easy enough to dismiss. But that was before the ultimatum.

Apparently, as the heads of the Jackson surgery dynasty, they were getting pressure and questions about why their youngest daughter hadn't joined the family business. Prominent members of the medical community were asking about me and when they'd get the chance to observe my skills.

It was flattering, and if any of them wanted to make the trip out to Garnet Bend to see me surgically remove a blockage from a cow's intestine, I wouldn't say no.

But their eagerness to mentor a Jackson meant nothing to me. I didn't have any interest in the complications or politics that came along with working on people. Or being in the hospital environment, where I knew from years spent in my family that gossip, rumors, and cliques ruled the day.

Animals were simpler. They told you where they hurt, and then you fixed it. And though most people wouldn't love that I thought this, the appreciation that an animal gave you after you helped them was far more gratifying than anything a human could say to me.

"How long has she been in labor?"

"Not sure," Jerry said. "She wasn't last night, and when we woke up this morning, it looked like it was starting. Went out to the fields for a bit, and when I came back, she sounded like that."

I knelt next to the cow. Her name was Mel, and Jerry wasn't wrong. She was in some distress. Not to the point where I needed to intervene, but it was good that I was here. "I'm glad you called me."

Cattle births weren't uncommon, and Jerry alone had probably seen hundreds. Even with his soft spot for his animals, he knew what sounded right and what didn't.

"You sure you're okay?" he asked. "I don't think I've ever seen you without a smile on your face."

I couldn't manage to summon that smile right now. "I'm fine, thank you. Just some family stuff."

"Ain't that a bitch?" he asked with a snorted laugh. "Well, I hope you get that sorted out. There's nothing that can get under your skin like family."

"Tell me about it," I muttered.

Jerry laughed. "You need me to stay out here?"

"No, I'm good. Thank you, though. I'll call you if I need something."

"Gonna be heading back out to work on one of the fences, but I've got my phone on me."

One more thing that I appreciated about Jerry. He didn't hover. Some days, I was in the mood for company. Today? Not so much.

I had a lot of thinking to do.

My family…wasn't poor.

I nearly snorted like Jerry. That was an understatement. An entire family of surgeons? Yeah. They were loaded. I was a trust fund baby. It wasn't something I advertised, but I couldn't do anything about where I came from.

That was the point of the email. I was supposed to receive that trust when I turned thirty in a few weeks. But they'd changed the terms of my trust. Receiving it at all was now contingent on my getting accepted to and actually graduating from medical school. Human medical school.

After all, I was a Jackson, and I already had a medical degree. I could have my pick of any school in the country.

I tried to throw water on the anger that came racing to the surface. How was it that they didn't see the hypocrisy? I *already had* a medical degree. But that wasn't good enough for them.

Nothing ever was.

Mel let out a long cry and I stroked her head, providing comfort the best way I could. She wasn't far enough along yet. But she would be soon. Until then, I was stuck with myself and my thoughts about my ridiculous family.

Maybe I should have made Jerry stay so he could distract me from it.

It wasn't really about the money. I didn't feel as if I'd earned it or deserved it in any way. But being a small-town vet wasn't exactly lucrative. I'd been making ends meet for a long time, and I would continue to do so. But I'd been looking forward to the trust as a buffer. It was enough to keep both me and the clinic in the black for *years* without even counting my current salary.

My phone vibrated in my pocket. That brought a small smile to my face, at least. It was Joel, my boyfriend. "Hello?"

Mel chose that exact moment to let out a brutal sound of labor, and it almost made me laugh.

"Jesus, that's some kind of greeting," he said.

"Sorry. Cow in labor."

I could practically see him rolling his eyes. "You sure? That's not really what it sounds like."

"Yes," I said with a sigh. "I'm very sure."

"Because—"

"Because it sounds like animal sex? I can send you the

video of the calf's feet coming out if that's something you'd like."

I heard the sound of fake vomiting on the other end of the line. "No, thank you."

For a rancher's son, Joel had a pretty weak stomach. But that was all right; I had one that was strong enough for the both of us, and he had other things that I liked about him.

Although, sometimes I was hard-pressed to remember that. "You still coming over tonight?"

"Was planning on it. What are we eating?"

"Could you pick something up?"

Joel made a noncommittal sound. "I would, but I'm not coming from a direction that actually has any food on the way. Can't you just cook something?"

I sighed and did my best to tamp down my frustration. It was just a reaction in response to my parents' letter and nothing more. Joel worked hard, and I knew he was driving a long way to be with me tonight. The least I could do was cook him dinner.

The store was on the way home. I could stop and pick up the ingredients for something simple. "Sure."

"Thanks, babe."

I gritted my teeth at the endearment. I'd asked him not to call me that, but he'd thought I'd been kidding. I didn't want to fight about it.

Mel lowed again, and I saw the movements I was looking for—she was getting close. Time to get my gloves on and get ready to help her.

"Think I could make you sound like that tonight?" Joel asked.

"Jeez, Joel."

"What?"

I pulled a pair of gloves out from my medical bag and

put them on, pushing up my sleeves while I had the phone between my cheek and shoulder. "You understand that literally no woman wants to be compared to a cow that's giving birth, right?"

He laughed.

"I have to go. Things are starting to happen here."

"Okay. Ditch me for a cow. I get it." Was it my imagination, or did he actually sound annoyed?

"I'll see you soon. Bye." I ended the call before he could keep me talking. Nature wasn't waiting for Joel to get the last word in.

The water bag spilled out of Mel, and things were about to get juicy—literally. Quickly, I called Jerry. "She's ready to start delivering if you'd like to be my backup?"

"Sure thing. Be right there."

Most people couldn't imagine loving something like this. It was messy, raw, and more than a little gross. But I never got tired of it. It was the coolest thing in the world to me to help bring something new and living into the world. If I'd followed my family's path into traditional medicine, I still probably wouldn't have been a surgeon, but an obstetrician.

It wasn't an easy birth. Mel labored, and I supported as best I could. But an hour later, she heaved one last push, and the calf came spilling out into the world. "There you go," I said. "Good girl."

You could feel the relief in the air. She was exhausted, but her night wasn't over yet. The placenta wouldn't be delivered for another few hours, but that was easier, and Jerry could be the one monitoring.

I stayed another half an hour to make sure the calf was up and walking before I left. All the vital signs were good for mom and baby, and now I couldn't stop the smile on my face. Turns out this was exactly what I needed today. "You'll monitor her for the placenta?" I asked Jerry.

"Yeah, I got that. If anything looks strange, I'll give you a call."

I checked the time. I needed to get going if I was going to get to the store and make dinner before Joel got to my house. "Thanks, Jerry. If everything's fine, I'll come by in a couple of days to see how they're doing."

He waved me off with a smile, and I headed to my truck.

I loved this job. And when I'd finally taken the plunge into this field, I'd promised myself that I would never go back to human medicine. I hated it there. And it wasn't something I ever wanted to consider again.

But I had to now. Not because I wanted to, but because there was a hefty part of me that was a realist, even if I was also an optimist and a romantic. I needed help if I was going to keep the clinic afloat. I had one part-time vet tech, who was a total sweetheart. But as much as I liked Jenna, it wasn't enough.

I didn't have funds to hire anyone else without that trust fund. And if I couldn't do it alone, I would have to go back, no matter how much I loved my practice and Garnet Bend. At the very least, I still had a few weeks to think about it.

Starting the truck, I sighed. This was a choice I didn't want to make. And there was nothing I hated more than feeling trapped.

Chapter 2

Grant Carter

I leaned against the fence and watched as Lucas Everett and Noah Scott, my friends and former Navy SEAL teammates, lifted the horse they'd been working with into the trailer.

The animal wasn't fully mobile and needed extra help, but she'd be a perfect therapy animal. After some training, she would be on her way to helping someone with PTSD make the most of their life. But the horse wouldn't be doing any heavy farm work. She could barely move this morning.

Just like me.

I was actively trying to push back the anger seething under my skin, but it was hard when I was watching my friends do things that I wanted to with the same ease they did. Instead, this fence post was holding me up.

When I woke up this morning, I knew this day was going to be shit, and I'd predicted correctly.

Some days were fine, and I was able to move and do whatever the hell I wanted without any pain or effort. And then there were the days when my lower back ached and I was limited, but relatively okay.

Then there were days like today, when it felt as if someone were pressing a white-hot knifetip into the base of my spine. Even the smallest movement blew fire up my back. It sucked.

Even worse, the others knew. That was the problem with being family.

We all knew enough about each other's demons to help fight them when we could and, more importantly, to make sure we were a collective team here on Resting Warrior Ranch.

Wanting to help fight emotional and mental demons was part of the reason a half dozen of my former Navy SEAL team members and I had started the ranch—to assist with our own PTSD, while also being of service to others.

We provided the wide-open space of the ranch for people who needed a chance to unplug and wanted to come stay. Various cabins were located all over the property. But mostly, we raised and trained emotional support and service animals—horses, dogs, hell, even alpacas and sheep.

Resting Warrior was a full ranch with long days and a lot of work, but we all loved it.

Knowing I was the guy on the team who wasn't pulling his own weight and whom everyone had to cover for…that *sucked ass*.

Dr. Rayne Westerfield, Resting Warrior's resident psychiatrist, would tell me that considering myself a suck-ass burden wasn't a great way of thinking—she had told me that more than once when I met with her—and I should *reframe*.

After all, I didn't control the shrapnel that sat in my spine.

But reframing and good thoughts and singing "*Kumbaya*" didn't help anything when you were in pain and feeling useless—especially pain that couldn't be helped by taking anything. The basic painkillers wouldn't touch this, and I wasn't about to start taking the hard-core pain pills. Then I'd be useless and high rather than just useless.

I was so damned tired of not being able to do what I needed to do, no matter how much everyone around me was understanding and supportive. It might have been childish, but there was only so much I could take of the warm and sympathetic looks and the immediate offers to step in and help.

Right now, I wanted them to get as mad at me as I was frustrated at myself. Because at least that would feel real.

The sound of the trailer being closed brought me back into the present. Noah looked me up and down before coming over, and Lucas waved before hopping into the cab of the truck. "You all set here?"

"How could I not be? You both did all the work."

He smirked. "Yeah, your lazy ass was just watching like a benevolent duke from days of old."

I rolled my eyes, careful not to move and send any more pain through my body. "You've got to stop watching the historical romance channel." But I appreciated Noah's willingness to give me a little shit.

"You all right to get up to the lodge?" Lucas asked from behind the wheel.

"I'm good," I said. "But you guys need to get going if you're going to make the delivery on time."

Noah bumped his hand on the fence next to where

mine rested. Because he knew even the slightest touch would hurt me. Damn it. "See you tomorrow?"

"Yep." I said it through gritted teeth but tried to sound cheerful.

He jogged around the trailer, and that was enough for me. I needed a drink. The lodge had a fully stocked bar, and even though it was a touch on the early side, I was going to make use of it.

Fuck. Even shifting my weight away from the fence sent searing pain down my legs and up my spine. Whatever that little piece of goddamn metal was doing today, it needed to stop.

The walk to the lodge from the stable took me ten minutes on a good day. It was nearly half an hour before I dragged myself up the porch steps and inside, sweating like I hadn't worked out in a year, despite the cool weather. It would be great if someone could just hit me over the head until this little session of agony was over.

All I wanted was to do something. Go for a run. Work with one of the horses. Go to the gym. Anything. Frustration was the only fuel I had now—and it was a pretty shitty power source.

Daniel Clark and Harlan Young, also former SEAL teammates of mine, were sitting at the kitchen table, talking about something I was choosing not to care about at the moment. They both turned and looked at me. I felt and ignored it as I walked straight to the bar in the corner.

"That good a day, huh?" Harlan asked.

"Yup."

Whiskey. That's what I needed.

"How's the pain?"

I glanced over my shoulder and instantly regretted it. The twisting motion was one of the worst. And yet, years after the injury, I *still* couldn't seem to train myself out of just…moving like a human.

I downed the first two fingers of the alcohol then poured myself another. "It's in the *mind your own business* range."

Daniel chuckled, unoffended. "You know it'll pass. You'll be back at full speed before you know it."

Making my way to one of the chairs near the fireplace, I sat, conscious of the fact that they were watching me way too closely. "I'm sure it will. I'll just sit here being useless until it does."

"Grant, it's fine," Daniel said.

No, it wasn't. But I didn't bother to argue.

Harlan stood and came over, leaning on the back of the couch. "Anything we can do to make it easier?"

"Go back in time five years and make sure I don't get blown the hell up."

Daniel rolled his eyes. "Anything more along the lines of actually possible? Something we can do to help?"

Daniel had been our team leader in the SEALs—an excellent one. The man liked to be able to fix the problems at hand and was fantastic at planning a course of action that ended missions in success.

But I wasn't a damned mission.

"Yeah, I get it. Everyone wants to fucking help. But it doesn't change the fact that you all have to keep picking up my loose ends. And there's nothing I can do about it."

"We all need help sometimes, bro," Harlan said quietly. "That doesn't make you weak."

He knew that statement intimately due to recent events. His fiancée got on the wrong side of a greedy son of a bitch and ended up nearly dead in an abandoned mine because of it. We'd had to pull them both out of it before it exploded.

"This is not the same. Nobody can pull me out of my own body in a stunning one-time rescue and make everything okay."

"When was your last appointment with Rayne?" Daniel was scrolling through his iPad, no doubt multitasking ranch business with this discussion. The man's brain never stopped. It was no wonder that we kept him in charge of everything here like he'd been in the SEALs.

I let my head fall back on the chair. "Seriously?"

"Yes."

"A couple weeks ago."

He looked up at me now. "And your physical specialist?"

I felt tightness in my chest, a fuse getting ready to burst. I needed to leave before I said anything stupid. These were my friends, and I knew their intentions were good. But I just…couldn't right now. "I don't need a mom, Daniel."

He raised an eyebrow. "You want to be pissed? Fine, that's your right. But if you're not actually taking care of yourself, this isn't going to get better, and you're just going to end up in a spiral. That affects us all."

I forced myself out of the chair and walked toward the door. The normal stride almost broke me out in a sweat, but there was no way I was going to show them how bad this hurt right now. "Fine. I'll take care of it. I'll see you both tomorrow."

"Where are you going?" Harlan asked.

"Home."

They didn't stop me, which was good. I made my way carefully down the stairs to my truck and slid into the driver's seat. I rested for a moment.

Shit.

I was going to need to apologize to them later.

But that was tomorrow's problem. Today, I was going

home, and I was drinking. The one problem with that was that I didn't have any booze at home. Fine. I could make it to the store.

Maybe I was stupid. It would be smarter to go straight home and lie down, but my pride and stubbornness were in full force. I wasn't going to let this beat me, no matter how hard it tried.

The store was on the way home. I would get in and out as quickly as I could. Pulling up to the tiny store, I smiled. There were a couple other grocery stores nearby, bigger and more traditional, but I liked this one. Arrowhead Grocer had been in the town of Garnet Bend since it was founded. Over here on the older side of town where everything was a little smaller and worn-down, it fit right in.

The owners were an older couple who cared about their shop like it was their pride and joy. And it was. They remembered their customers and joyfully filled any special requests.

Taking a deep breath, I shoved open the door to the truck and swung down. The hardest step. Absorbing the impact of any elevation change was painful when my back was like this.

The door opened, and a woman rushed out of the store, her hands full of bags. My heart skipped a beat, and I froze. It was Cori. Her hair was in a messy ponytail, the streaks of turquoise she kept in it peeking out. She usually rotated through colors, but I was partial to this one. It suited her.

She lived next door to my small house, and we saw each other regularly. All the guys at the ranch teased me about her. I'd never admitted it, but they were right. I couldn't help it. She was fucking beautiful and sweet—and also completely off-limits since she had a boyfriend.

I wasn't that kind of guy. No matter my personal

opinion of the boyfriend, I didn't cheat or help anyone do it. Though from what I knew of her, that thought would never even cross her mind.

"Hey, Cori."

She looked at me, and her face broke out into a smile. It made me realize that she *hadn't* been smiling. And, for her? That was strange. She was bubbly and bright, and it was rare for her to appear to be anything but happy. But people had their own shit to deal with that they didn't want anyone else to see. Lord knew I understood that.

"Hi, Grant. How are you?"

I placed my hand on the hood of the truck to brace myself. "Just grabbing a couple things before heading home. You?"

"Dinner." She lifted the bags in her hands. "Joel's coming over."

"I hope you have a nice time."

A shadow passed over her face, so fleeting that I almost thought I'd missed it. "Me too." Her phone lit up in her hand, and she glanced down at it. "I'll see you around?"

"Sure will."

On any other day, I would have already been putting her groceries into her truck for her. Today, I probably couldn't get there before she would have pulled out of the parking lot.

I watched her pull away before heading into the store and grabbing the whiskey and a couple other things to eat. Thankfully, the people here saw me enough on bad days that they didn't comment on my slowness or the way I limped.

Cori's truck was in her driveway, along with Joel's. I didn't like him. Shaking my head, I pushed the thoughts away. It wasn't my business.

As soon as I got inside, I realized I had made a mistake.

I'd decided to come home so I could avoid being under the constant scrutiny of too-helpful former SEALs. There was only one problem with that: home was lonely.

People around me were falling in love left and right. Lucas had Evelyn, Harlan and Grace were getting married soon, for real this time—not a fake marriage to save her ranch. Even Cori had someone in her life. And I was happy for them. I really was. I didn't begrudge anyone falling in love.

It didn't erase the sting.

The guys would mock me if they knew, but I was a bit of a romantic. I'd always known that. I had the dream of falling in love and being with that one person for the rest of our lives. Maybe kids, if that was what they wanted too. There was something beautiful and comforting about finding that person who made you better and accepted you for who you were.

Dragging myself to the kitchen, I shoved the food into the fridge and opened the whiskey. Whatever ray of light Cori had used to blow away the black cloud over my head, it was back.

I filled a glass and drained it. Poured another.

Usually, if I got a little sentimental and sad that those things weren't happening to me, a hot shower and my hand could take care of the problem. Now, that would only make my problem worse. Because that hurt too, and not even an orgasm could erase that kind of pain.

Now that I was here, I didn't have to mask the agony, and I made my way to the couch with my glass and the bottle, not bothering to turn on the lights. Darkness suited me right now.

Who would want this?

Clearly, I was a ray of fucking sunshine. My friends knew I was an asshole when I was in pain, but they'd gone through just as much as I had. Some of them worse.

But I was the one with the most obvious physical scars. Daniel's mothering needled at me. I hadn't been to my specialist in months. Because the last time I was there, he told me the truth that no man wants to hear—there was nothing that could be done.

That piece of shrapnel in my spine was too close to my nerves to be operated on safely, and any surgery was as likely to paralyze me as heal me. But either way, there would be a point where it dug too deep and cut too much and then no more walking for Grant Carter.

I sighed and took a sip of whiskey. Hopefully tomorrow would be better. They weren't wrong. I needed to keep seeing Rayne if I wanted to get off this roller coaster, no matter the status of my injury.

But the question echoed in my mind again. Days that I could barely walk or move, and a guarantee of someday losing what mobility I had. Who would want any part of that?

Chapter 3

Cori

Being home soothed my thoughts a bit.

Not completely. I didn't think there was anything that could stop my mind from circling the demands in that email and everything that came along with it, but being in my own space was a small comfort.

I decided on pasta. There wasn't enough energy or motivation in the world to make something more complicated tonight. But hey, over the years, I'd mastered the art of quick and delicious pasta sauce, so this would be good either way.

I'd been annoyed about having to cook, but as I chopped up tomatoes and added herbs and tomato paste and a few other things for the sauce, I felt my shoulders relax. Cooking was something I enjoyed most of the time, but being a vet often meant long and odd hours, and a good portion of my days—especially with a rural practice—those calls were either stressful or exhausting or both.

Setting the water to boil, I checked my phone. Joel was due in about twenty minutes, and that was perfect. We didn't live together, which was okay with me. I loved this little house, but Joel didn't. He'd talked about us getting a place somewhere else, but that wasn't what I wanted.

Or maybe Joel wasn't what I wanted.

When I'd come to Garnet Bend to fill the empty veterinarian position, this was the first place I looked at. Two stories, tiny, and painted a sunny yellow with white trim, it was the complete opposite of the houses my family favored.

I was renting. My vet salary was nowhere near enough to buy. I'd made it my own, regardless. The landlord was an easygoing older man who didn't care what I did as long as I paid the rent on time. So I'd painted the house a plethora of colors. The houses I'd grown up in were all cream and beige, and I wanted none of that.

The kitchen was a cheery yellow that matched the exterior. My bedroom was a shade of violet that trended toward blue, and the rest of the house was a smattering of the rainbow. And I couldn't be happier with it.

Water for the pasta boiled, and I turned on some music. This day was ending better than it started. I was more relaxed, even though I was tired, and I was hoping maybe Joel and I could have some fun later. That I could talk him into branching out a little in our sex life.

The door opened behind me as I was straining the pasta. "Babe?"

My jaw tightened, then I forced it to loosen. "Kitchen," I called.

I heard his footsteps make their way through the house until he entered the kitchen. He hugged me quickly from behind and kissed my cheek. "Smells good."

"Thanks."

This was comforting too. Even though we hadn't been dating very long, he and I had known each other forever. Our parents were friends, so we'd run in the same circles when we were younger. He'd never shown any interest in me until I'd moved to Garnet Bend, but it had been nice to have someone from my old life support me in this new venture.

And my parents, for once, had actually approved of something I did where Joel was concerned. I had to admit, that was one of the reasons I was still dating him. If I was going to disappoint my family in my professional life, at least my personal life gave them hope.

I smiled at him. "How were the races?"

He pulled out a chair and slouched down into it. "Not great. A couple of the horses were really slow. Might have to have you come out and look at them."

"Of course." Joel's father was in the horse racing business. And Joel worked with him, taking the horses to and from races all over the country. They had their own traveling veterinarian on retainer. Not sure why they would want me.

I waited for Joel to ask me about my day, but he was already looking down at his phone.

"That calf today was delivered safely," I told him. "The owner is going to call me if the mom has any problems delivering the placenta."

He laughed. "Well, he better not call while I'm making you sound like that cow in bed."

I turned away to stir the sauce so he couldn't see my displeasure.

"Hey," he said. "I'm kidding."

"I know." But it was still in poor taste. Not to mention,

Joel had never even come close to making me get loud in bed.

Nothing about our sex life was exciting to me. The things I would like to try with Joel seemed eons away from the ten minutes of missionary position he favored. I kept promising myself I would bring it up, but it never seemed to be the right time. When he was in a good mood, I didn't want to spoil it. And when he was in a bad mood…I just kept my distance.

Problem was, he could run hot or cold with no warning. He'd been that way even when we were kids—he'd even gotten kicked out of a couple of private schools because of his temper.

I stirred the sauce and listened to the soft sounds of him typing on his phone. He didn't try to engage with me or help with the meal. But I knew from experience that asking him to would just make him pout.

I wondered if my parents had talked to his father about what they were trying to get me to do.

"Did you see your dad today?"

"For a couple minutes, why?"

I cleared my throat. "Did he say anything about me?"

Joel looked up. "No. Should he have?"

"I got an email from my parents this morning."

"Is that weird?" He got up and grabbed a wineglass and retrieved an open bottle from the counter, pouring himself a glass.

When it was clear he wasn't going to pour me any, I poured my own glass before going back to the sauce. "Weird isn't the word I'd use. More like blindsiding."

"What happened?"

"They changed the terms of my trust."

"*What?*" Joel was a trust fund kid, too. But his had

kicked in at twenty-five. He knew what it meant to have something that you thought was guaranteed pulled out from under you. "What did they change?"

I didn't answer, turning off the sauce and plating up the pasta for both of us. It wasn't until I was safely seated at the table that I took a sip of my wine and told him. "I now only get my trust if I get accepted to and actually *graduate* medical school."

There was no way they hadn't consulted their lawyer to make sure I didn't exploit a loophole by just being accepted to the school and then never going.

"Technically, you've done both those things. Vets go to medical school too."

"That's not what they want."

He knew the whole situation already. We both ate in silence. The pasta wasn't fancy, but it was good. Joel was shoveling it down. "Hungry?"

"Starving," he said. "There wasn't any catering today. Bunch of idiots screwed up the schedule."

"Why didn't you order something? Or have someone pick something up?"

Joel shrugged. "To make a point. They need to be on top of their shit and have things like meals ready for people like us. Besides, I like it when you cook for me."

I stared at him, having so many problems with what he'd just said. *People like us*—as if he and his father were more important than anybody else. The fact that he'd gone on some sort of mini hunger strike—probably to get some poor soul fired—didn't sit well with me either.

But what really stuck in my craw was that lunch had been *well* before he called me to ask what we were doing for dinner. He'd decided that he wasn't going to pick up any food before I even asked.

I took another sip of wine, knuckles white around the glass stem. "I'm glad you like the food."

"I like it when you do things for me. So—" he took another bite "—what are you going to do about your parents' demands?"

"I have no idea." I could feel my stress coming back.

"Let's list out the pros and cons."

He loved a good pro/con list. I let out a sigh. "Which side am I starting with?"

"Telling them no."

I savored my wine for a second, resisting the urge to gulp it. "I don't have to leave Garnet Bend or my friends."

"True."

"Or you."

He grinned. "That is a con."

If only he knew how true I was coming to think that to be.

"I get to keep a job I love and this rental place. Cons—it's not as easy as I was hoping to keep the clinic afloat. I won't be able to hire a full-time technician or a second vet."

Joel sat back. "Another con, you won't be able to buy a house."

I shrugged. "That doesn't concern me."

"It should."

Buying a house was low on my priority list. "Saying yes is the opposite side of all those things. There's always the option of going to medical school, getting the money, and coming back here. But that's four years away. Plus, I pretty much hate everything about the medical field."

"Did they say that you had to be a surgeon?"

"No." I shook my head. "But you know them. That's the only path they'll accept. If I try to do anything other than surgery, then it would be unacceptable for a Jackson.

Hell, they'd probably change the terms again if I tried another specialty."

"True. They really do want you to be Ms. Surgery."

"Yeah..." I drained the last of the wine. At least he was on my side. That made a difference. He understood my wanting to stay here.

We finished our meal, and I got up and carried our plates over to the sink. I was ready to put all talk about my parents' demands behind us and get on with our evening.

"I think you should do it."

"Do what?" I rinsed one plate.

"I think you should go back to medical school. Do what your parents want and get your money."

My head snapped around so fast I almost gave myself whiplash. "What?"

Joel shrugged, looking down at his phone. "Let's be real. You need the money. You want funds to expand your practice, and, more importantly, you need to get out of this shitty rainbow house."

"I like this place." It wasn't fancy, but it more than suited my needs. Joel and I had been over this before.

"You only think that because you've forgotten what it's like to live someplace nice."

I resisted the urge to slam a plate down in the sink. "If you hate my house that much, why do you even come here?"

"Cori." He let out a long sigh. "Don't be mad."

"Why would I be mad? My boyfriend just told me he wants me to give up everything I love, *including him*, and go do something I hate, while simultaneously insulting my home."

"I'm just being realistic. I know your family. They're going to make your life hell until you do what they want."

"So, I should just give in?" He sighed again, the look

on his face telling me that he thought I was being particularly difficult. "It's my *life* they're messing with, Joel."

He gestured with his wine. "Yeah, it is. But even if you tell your parents to fuck off and don't take their money, do you really think that's going to be the last of it? It won't be. Your parents are some of the most intense, single-minded people I've ever seen, and they want you to do this. I'd be willing to bet they have about sixty backup plans in case this doesn't work."

"Like?"

"Like, finding someone in whatever vet organization you have to be licensed by and getting you reviewed. Like calling your landlord and informing him you're emotionally unstable and really need to come home. Or any other number of things. They have great minds and great lawyers. If I thought of those things in fifteen seconds, they'll have thought of fifty more."

I hated that he was right. In their minds, the family legacy was at stake, and they sure as hell weren't going to let me deviate from it without a fight, trust or no trust.

Joel was staring at me, and I didn't speak. I didn't speak for so long that he finally got up and went into the living room to turn on the TV. "Fine. Whenever you decide to stop living in your own little fantasy world, let me know."

"I don't want to ransom four years of my life to be able to do what I want. When I'm already *doing* what I want with my life."

I heard the soft sounds of some kind of sitcom, the studio laughter a completely inappropriate background for this conversation. "I think you did it backward, actually. You should've gone to normal medical school *first* to get them off your back and then gone to vet school."

I finished the dishes and put them in the dishwasher.

Joel laughed at something on the TV, and I gritted my teeth.

"I fail to see how that's better. That's still four completely useless years. And a lot of debt."

The garbage was full too. I grabbed it to take it outside.

"As if any school you wanted wouldn't give a Jackson a full ride." He barely looked at me as I passed by with the bag.

The screen door banged behind me as I went out. The sun was setting, the beauty of Montana all around me. I took a long breath after I tossed the garbage bag into the can, trying to force stress out of my body.

This wasn't the evening I'd been hoping for. But I could still turn it around. I wanted some physical time with Joel. Getting frustrated with him for not understanding my point of view wasn't going to get us there.

Across the small lawn that separated our houses, Grant's house was dark. His truck was in the driveway, but I didn't see any lights on. Maybe he'd gone to bed early? I hoped he was okay. When I'd run into him outside of Arrowhead, he'd had a heaviness to him I didn't usually see.

Grant was kind and a good neighbor. He was my favorite of the Resting Warrior guys. I liked all of them, but he had a gentleness that I appreciated, especially with the animals.

When I saw him again, I would make sure to ask how he was doing. But for right now…Joel.

I slipped back into the house and went to the kitchen to retrieve my wineglass. "I don't want to talk about my parents anymore," I told him. "This was not what I had planned for you coming over."

That got his attention. "What did you have planned?"

He looked me up and down and gave me a knowing smirk.

God, did he have any idea how boring I found our sex life? If he and I were going to continue—which, honestly, I was having more and more difficulty seeing—something was going to have to change.

And I wasn't even talking about my secret fantasy stuff. The stuff I knew I really needed if I was going to truly let go. That was for a much later day. Right now, I was merely talking about something more than ten minutes of him on top of me every time we had sex. It was nice, but never much more than that.

Sitting down and curling up next to him, I snuggled close and took a sip of my wine. This was no big deal, right? Couples tried new things in bed all the time, and it was okay. It didn't have to be that serious.

I took another sip. "I thought we could talk about our sex life."

Joel shut off the TV. That was at least encouraging. "What about it?"

I swallowed. "I was wondering if you were interested in trying something new. Different."

He stiffened. "Why?"

I smiled over at him, keeping my body language relaxed. "I feel like we're in a little bit of a rut. There's a lot of stuff we haven't tried that we might like."

We hadn't been dating long enough to be in a rut, but that wasn't the point.

"Like what?"

"You know." I smiled, wishing it weren't so stiff. "Sex in the shower. Or in a chair with me straddling you. The kitchen table or my desk. Just let the passion overtake us."

"I see." He wasn't relaxing.

"Come on, Joel. These aren't unreasonable requests.

Don't you want to do more than just vanilla missionary every single time?"

As soon as the words came out of my mouth, I knew they were the wrong thing to say, but it was too late to take them back.

Besides, this talk was necessary.

Evidently, Joel didn't think so. He slid over on the couch until we were no longer touching at all. "So you're saying I'm inadequate in bed."

"No." Sort of. "I'm saying there's so much more, and I'd like to explore it with you."

If wanting to have sex in the shower was setting him on edge, mentioning what really turned me on probably wasn't in the cards ever.

I reached for him. "Don't overreact. Let's talk this out."

Definitely the wrong thing to say. He shot off the couch like he was on fire. I was just about to backpedal, tell him to forget the whole thing, when he spun back toward me and I saw his face.

He wasn't embarrassed. Wasn't irritated.

He was *furious*.

I scrambled off the couch and away from him. I'd never seen Joel look like this before, especially not at me.

But in the back of my mind, I remembered the rumors that had gone around about him in high school and college.

Temper. Unstable. Violent.

Things I'd written off as rumors spawned by people jealous of his family's money. There wasn't any way the stories could be true. I'd never seen behaviors from Joel suggesting he was any of those things.

Until now.

I held my hands out in front of me. "Whoa, why are

you getting so upset? I'm just trying to have a discussion with you."

"A discussion. Right. Yeah, I know all about discussions. Everybody wants to have *discussions* when they think I'm out of line."

I had no idea what that meant. "I just want to explore new things with you. You're being unreasonable."

"You think you're better than your family," he spat out, face red. "Think you're better than me in bed."

"I don't think either of those things! My family has nothing to do with this conversation, and I was just trying to ask you if we could change things up a little."

The fury slid from his face as quickly as it had arrived. "You were criticizing me and my performance in bed."

God, I felt like I was talking to Jekyll and Hyde. "No. I was just trying to point out that I'd like to be a little more adventurous. A lot more adventurous, if you want me to be honest."

"Like what?"

"All the other stuff I mentioned and more. It's not unreasonable."

"More, like what?"

I rolled my eyes. "Forget it. If sex in the shower causes you to freak out, there's no point in talking about the other things."

"No, I want to know."

"No." I shook my head and finished the last of my wine. "There's no point in even discussing it."

Honestly, I wasn't sure there was any point in discussing anything at all with him anymore.

"Just fucking tell me, Cori."

How dare he take that tone with me. As if *I* were the one being unreasonable.

I did something I rarely did. I lost my temper.

"Toys. Us using my vibrator while we're having sex, Joel. Other positions…*all* the positions. Standing up, sitting down, you behind me pulling my hair as you pound me hard. Oral. Anal. Everything." I didn't yell, even in my fury. It was ingrained in me. Nobody in my family *ever* yelled.

Whatever tiny hope I'd had that he might be on board with what I desired once he heard it disappeared at the look of disgust on his face.

"You're a Jackson," he spat. "You shouldn't want those things."

Suddenly it was clear that was why he'd been with me all along. He wanted to be connected to my family, and I was the easiest link. "Right. Because Jacksons aren't human. We're surgical machines. Well, not me, obviously."

"You can learn to be normal. To want normal things in bed."

I set my wineglass down before I got tempted to throw it at him. "I don't want normal. And I sure as hell don't want *your* normal. I want to be blindfolded, tied up, spanked, *more*."

His eyes narrowed, and his face turned a mottled red. "You're nothing but a whore. I can't believe I ever wasted my time with you."

That was a slap in the face. I knew he wouldn't want the same things I did in bed, but all he had to say was that wasn't what he was into.

Instead, he was looking at me like I was a piece of chewed gum on the sidewalk—used, worthless, gross. My anger—not an emotion I used often or knew how to hold on to—fled, leaving me feeling small and repulsive.

"Joel…" I stretched out a hand toward him.

"We're done." He strode away from me and started up the stairs. "I'm getting my stuff and I'm leaving, and I'm never coming back to this shitty house ever again. You pervert."

"Joel—"

"*No!*" he yelled down the stairs. "We're done. Don't call me. Don't text me. Don't even look at me when I leave. You're disgusting."

Chapter 4

Grant

I never bothered to turn on any lights. The semidarkness of the fading sun suited me. Instead, I just sat on my couch, nursing that second glass of whiskey.

Time passed, though I wasn't really paying attention. Pain could do that to you—rip away any sense of self or time.

At some point, I heard the door to Cori's house open, and I saw her through my darkened windows as she put out her trash. She was so casually beautiful; I couldn't stop the thoughts I shouldn't be having.

The boyfriend was there—I'd seen his truck out front.

He'd never given me any reason to dislike him the way that I did. It was a gut-level thing. Joel and I were never going to get along, and I chalked up my dislike to plain old jealousy.

I was a big enough man to admit that I was, in fact, jealous.

She looked over at my house, and worry crossed her expression. Why? What was there in my direction that caused her to worry? That was the last thing I wanted her to feel when she looked at me.

It only lasted for a second, and then she went back inside.

A long, slow sip of my whiskey, and I laid my head back on the couch. The drink was helping. But so was just…not moving. Hopefully this and a full night's sleep would relieve the pressure and tomorrow would be better.

I closed my eyes, and a noise brought them open again, along with my instincts singing to life. Something was wrong, but I hadn't been listening closely enough to identify what it was.

There. Raised voices coming from next door. Or just one raised voice. Male.

My body went entirely still.

Cori might be off-limits to me because of her relationship, but I was still her neighbor. And I wasn't the kind of neighbor that would just let something like this happen without making sure she was okay.

Heaving myself off the couch, I ignored the pain and went to the window. Nothing *looked* wrong, but I still heard him yelling. It didn't take more than a minute for him to come storming out, looking as if he'd just run a marathon.

The look on his face made me tense. That wasn't just a man upset about something; that was pure rage. It was an expression I'd only seen on the faces of men about to lose it entirely.

What the hell happened in there? There was nothing I could imagine Cori doing that warranted the aura of hatred and near violence pouring off that man. He was carrying a bunch of things. What looked like clothes and a toothbrush.

My eyebrows rose. Were they breaking up? If that was what was happening, then I shouldn't be intruding on their privacy. But I didn't trust Joel. And Cori's safety was more important to me than her privacy.

"You're a pervert. I can't believe that you would *ever* ask me for that," Joel bellowed. He went back inside, and I heard Cori's voice, though I couldn't make out what she said.

"Yeah," Joel yelled. "You're disgusting. That stuff is unnatural."

Cori came out on the porch. She was flushed too, but even from here, I could see she was miserable. Joel carried a couple of books to his truck and tossed them through the cab window. Never pegged him for much of a reader.

"If someone enjoys it, who are we to judge as long as it happens between two consenting adults?"

Wait, *what*?

"I don't think about that sort of thing because I'm not some perverted *freak*," he said, voice echoing off both our houses.

Cori wrapped her arms around herself. "Jesus, Joel. It's not like I asked you to cut me up or beat me. This is not completely out of the norm."

Hmm. Evidently Cori had wanted to get a little adventurous, and ol' Joel had said no. Although, calling this temper tantrum "saying no" was kind of an understatement.

And hell, this man was an even bigger idiot than I'd originally thought.

My mind was now racing with the possibilities of what she'd asked him for and finding *plenty* of interesting options. She could ask me for each and every one of them, and none would make me react like Joel.

I'd dabbled in that world a little bit. Not nearly as

much as some of my friends, but I wasn't ashamed to like it. And Cori shouldn't be either. The fact that this man was telling her what she wanted was shameful burned me up inside, no matter what it was.

"You're disgusting," Joel said, walking up the stairs toward her. "Perverted, and I cannot believe that I was ever with someone like you."

The way Cori shrank into herself was something I would never forget. Her eyes were fixed on the ground, and her voice was steady, though her tone was miserable. "Just leave."

"I'll leave when I'm good and ready, after you forcing me to listen to your perverted fantasies." He pulled open the screen door and went inside, letting it slam behind him.

Cori swiped at her face, brushing away tears that I couldn't see at this distance in the deepening evening.

"You know what?" Joel said, coming back out of the house with a bunch of random shit in his hands. It looked like a picture and a stuffed animal. A couple smaller things.

Fuck, those were gifts he'd given her. What an asshole.

"You'll be lucky if I don't tell your whole fucking family the kinky shit you're into. Wonder what they'd do if they knew their daughter was a freak? Even more than not following in the family business, that their precious little girl wants to—" He cut himself off as if he was too disgusted to even say it.

Cori was fully crying now. Even I could see that. But she straightened her back. "You've made your point, Joel. Now, leave. Get the hell out."

Brave girl.

Joel's face contorted into anger, and as soon as he took a step toward her, I was moving. Pushing open the front door to my house and making sure I wasn't limping in the slightest. It only took me a few seconds to make my way into the light.

He froze when he saw me appear.

I crossed my arms. "I think the lady asked you to leave."

"What are you going to do about it, cowboy?"

Joel and I had met a couple of times, but I'd seen more of him than he had of me. Because my training had made sure I was aware of potential threats. Even before tonight, my subconscious had labeled him as one.

I knew by the way he held himself that he was more of a bully than a trained fighter. He was all talk.

I casually walked down my steps, holding my breath against the pain. "Not a cowboy," I said. "Just a good neighbor. One who will use his SEAL training to make sure you leave. Because the minute she asked you to and you didn't, you became a trespasser."

"Well, aren't you a Boy Scout," Joel said with a sneer. "This is none of your business."

I leveled a stare at him. "Your fight isn't my business, but if you think I'm going to let you intimidate or hurt a woman while I'm around, you'd best rethink that strategy."

He snorted in disgust. "Fuck you." Then he looked back at Cori. "And I'll definitely never fuck you again."

I didn't look to see her reaction. I wanted to know if she was okay, but I sure as hell wasn't taking my eyes off an opponent while he could still do damage. Joel was still angry. It was written in every line of his body. But he got the message, and he pulled out of the driveway, burning rubber as he took off.

I stayed there for long seconds, making sure he wasn't going to come back, before I looked over at Cori. She was still frozen on the porch, eyes locked on me. Her arms were wrapped around her middle as if they were the only thing holding her together.

Shit.

My concern for her physical well-being had been so prominent, I hadn't thought about whether Cori would be embarrassed to have a witness to an intensely personal argument. Of course she would be. That asshole had just spilled one of her most vulnerable secrets, and I'd shoved myself right in the middle of it.

"Cori—"

She shook her head and turned, fleeing back into the house, door closing behind her with a brutal finality.

Guess we wouldn't be talking about any of this tonight.

I limped back into the house and went straight up to my bedroom, leaving the remnants of my unfinished whiskey behind.

Chapter 5

Cori

The Pearson ranch was the last place I wanted to be driving to right now.

Guess that was what happened when your boyfriend's father became a client and then that same boyfriend dumped you in the cruelest, most vicious way imaginable.

It had been three days, and every time I thought of it, everything in me still burned with shame. Which meant I was pretty much constantly blushing because I couldn't stop replaying that awful night over and over again in my head.

How had I not seen that coming?

Should I have been able to?

Joel never struck me as the kind of person that could be that angry. It was a side of him I'd never seen before, but now that I had, and the immediate pain of losing the one steady thing in my life had dulled a fraction…I was glad.

All Joel had to do was say no, that it wasn't really his thing. That maybe we could find a different thing that interested both of us. If his reaction was that bad over something that small, who knows what else could have set him off?

I hated the small voice in the back of my head that questioned whether it really *was* small. That maybe I was all those things he said and that the fantasies I had made me some kind of deviant, bad person.

That wasn't true. I knew it wasn't. But it was hard not to think it when the person you should be able to trust most told you that you were. Not to mention what Grant must have thought of me after hearing all that.

God, Grant.

I'd had to avoid him like the plague over the last few days. I was grateful for what he'd done, but also mortified. The thought of seeing him again and seeing the pity in his eyes made my soul shrivel. Or worse.

Grant was a good guy. He probably felt exactly the same way Joel did and was just too kind to say it. I would have to face him eventually if I didn't want to move, and I loved my house enough that I wasn't planning on it.

But I wasn't ready to see him yet.

The only saving grace was that Joel hadn't repeated what I'd asked him about loud enough for Grant to hear. So even if he'd heard more than when he stepped out onto the porch, he still wouldn't know what I'd asked for. That was good.

My gut flipped as I pulled into the Pearson ranch. Please let Joel not be here. *Please* let Joel not be here.

I hadn't gotten any furious calls from my family yet, so I assumed he hadn't followed through on the threat to tell them about my fantasies, or the fact that we'd broken up at all. That was fine with me. My parents were already too involved in my business anyway.

The last three days had been so emotional that I wasn't any closer to a decision on the whole trust fund thing. Thankfully I still had a little time, though I was sure my parents were chomping at the bit waiting for a response.

Relief flowed through me. Joel's truck wasn't here. Only his father's. Graham Pearson wasn't the friendliest man in the world, but he paid me well and I thought he was polite enough not to fire me because his son had decided we couldn't be together anymore.

Parking the truck, I grabbed my vet bag and headed toward the stable. This was a routine trip, and I didn't expect to see anyone. I'd be sending an email to Graham and his trainer later, regardless.

But when I walked into the stable, Graham was waiting. He looked like the classic idea of a cowboy. Suit and boots, hat and cigar. That hat tipped in my direction. "Cori."

"Afternoon, Mr. Pearson."

He smiled. "How many times have I told you to call me Graham?"

"It still feels too strange to me," I said with a laugh. "Didn't expect to see you out here. Everything okay?"

"Not exactly." He gestured for me to follow, and I did down the long length of the barn. "It's Sunrise," he said, stopping in front of a stall that contained a beautiful dappled brown horse. Of course I was already familiar, and I reached out to touch the horse's neck.

"What's going on?"

Mr. Pearson shrugged. "Damned if I know. She's been sluggish, lying down more often than not. But she's not showing any other signs that something's wrong. Shoes are all good. She probably just ate something that disagreed with her, but since you were coming out anyway, figured I'd let you know."

"Thank you. I'll do an examination and update you."

"Sounds good," he said, turning on his heel. Before he disappeared around the corner, he turned back. "Oh, and I just wanted to say that I'm sorry you and Joel didn't work out."

I smiled wanly. "Thank you."

"If you ever change your mind, I'm sure he'll take you back. Poor boy is heartbroken. But I understand that sometimes you just need something else."

My mouth dropped open, and I stared at him. Joel had told him *I* was the one who ended it? I shut my mouth and blinked. "Yeah," I said. "Thank you."

What else was there to say about that? He left without another word, and I turned back to the horse. "This, Sunrise," I said, "this is why animals are easier than people."

The gentle horse whickered in response and nudged my arm with her nose. "You okay?"

Of all the horses in the stable, this one was usually a ball of joy. Energy and jitters and prancing in place. She seemed strangely subdued.

I made my rounds with all the other horses, and all of them were fine. I was monitoring a sprain in the foreleg of one, and the pregnancy of another. They all passed with flying colors. It took forever, because if there was one thing the Pearsons had, it was horses. This was the biggest stable I'd seen outside of an actual racetrack or stud farm.

When I'd finished with the rest, I came back to Sunrise so I could spend more time with her, and just like Mr. Pearson had mentioned, she was lying down.

"Hey, girl."

I did an examination, but other than a racing heart,

there didn't seem to be anything wrong that I could diagnose externally. If I brought her to the clinic, I could figure out what was wrong a lot faster.

"We'll find out what's wrong with you. Okay, sweetie?"

Because something *was* wrong. I felt it with the gut instinct that years as a vet had given me.

Mr. Pearson was sitting on his porch smoking another cigar when I came out to my truck. "You were right, Mr. Pearson. There's definitely something up with Sunrise. Nothing wrong that I can see, but if you can bring her by the clinic, I'd like to do some tests."

He shrugged. "I'm sure she's fine. If you can't see anything wrong, then there's no point in wasting a trip."

"Still," I said. "I'd like to do some blood tests. Maybe some X-rays."

"She got out of the fence a couple days ago. Probably ate a weed that disagreed with her. She'll be fine."

I frowned. If he didn't want me to actually treat the horse, then why had he bothered to draw attention to her condition in the first place?

"Okay," I said. "But I plan on coming back in a couple of days to see how she's doing."

That horse was sick, and I wasn't going to let her wither if the man didn't want to bring her to me.

"Fine."

We both waved, and I pulled out of the ranch with an odd sense of relief. I was glad Joel hadn't been there or arrived while I was still in the stable. After the other night, I wasn't sure I would be able to remain calm around him, and I sure as hell didn't want to find out what kind of reaction he would have.

It was late enough that I didn't have to go back to the clinic, and I was tired. Coffee. I needed coffee, and Deja Brew was on the way home.

Lena was behind the counter when I pushed through the door, and she lit up. "Well, hello. Long time no see."

"I know," I said. "I've been busy."

She looked me up and down. "Or something's wrong, and you're lying to me," she said.

My heart stopped. Grant. The Resting Warrior guys were all in here. Could he have told Lena out of concern? Or to let her know that the breakup had happened?

"He told you?"

"Nobody told me shit, but you just did."

Damn. "I walked right into that one."

"Yes, you did." She came out from behind the counter and flipped the sign on the door from open to closed. "Evelyn! We're closing early."

My other friend peeked her head around the corner. "What's up? Oh hey, Cori."

"You really don't have to do that," I said. "I'm fine."

"Bull*shit,* woman," Lena said. "What do you want to drink? We're having a dish session, and I'm not taking no for an answer."

I couldn't help but smile. That was who Lena was. She was a tornado wrapped up in kindness and coffee. We shared a love of fun hair colors, and she'd been one of the first people to make me feel comfortable when I'd moved to town. "I just came in for coffee."

"Coffee it is. Go out on the patio. We'll be there in a second."

Evelyn smirked at me. She'd been at the mercy of Lena's aggressive kindness, too. Especially when her life fell apart. I'd heard most of that story after the fact. Evelyn still had the scars, but she was doing better. And even though she hadn't been in town very long, I was glad she was here. She and Lena were both good friends.

I sighed and did as I was told, following Evelyn out to

the small brick patio behind the shop. It was mainly for staff and friends, with pretty lights strung up for summer evenings. Though as it got later in the year, it was starting to get a touch too chilly for it. We were almost to that point when we wouldn't be able to use it, so I might as well enjoy it before the snow hit.

Lena appeared with a tray and three cups of coffee before sitting and fixing me with a stare. "Okay, what the hell happened?"

Briefly, I thought about lying, but there wasn't any point. Lena had an internal lie detector that was more sensitive than an actual polygraph. She would figure it out eventually, and that would be worse than my brief embarrassment.

"Okay," I said. "But this doesn't leave the patio."

Lena crossed her heart. "I swear."

Evelyn nodded.

"Joel and I broke up. Or rather, I should say, he broke up with me."

"Oh no," Evelyn said. "Are you okay?"

I shrugged. "No, but that's more because of how the breakup happened rather than the breakup itself."

"Wow," Lena said. "It must've been bad."

The coffee was good, and I focused on sipping that to give myself some time before I had to admit the truth to them. "So, we were having dinner, and I was tired and I… wanted to try something new."

Evelyn looked confused. "Okay."

"So, I got up all my courage and asked him if we could change things up a little. You know, new positions, toys, whatever. Just be a little adventurous."

Lena gasped. "*Girl*. Hell yes."

I laughed. "Really?"

"Really. I've always wanted to try different stuff too.

Especially ropes and the bossiness, it all seems really hot." She shrugged when Evelyn started giggling. "I'm not sorry."

"Well, Joel didn't feel that way. He said a lot of things, but the central points were that I was disgusting and a pervert for even thinking about that. Let alone asking him for it."

They stared at me blankly.

Lena set down her coffee cup. "Are you serious?"

"He got his stuff and left. Wouldn't stop yelling the whole time." I flushed red. "He was so angry, I wasn't sure what would have happened if—"

I cut myself off before I mentioned Grant's name.

"If what?" Evelyn prodded.

Oh well, they were going to know anyway. "You know Grant is my next-door neighbor? He came out of his house when Joel wouldn't leave. I'm glad he did, but I don't know how much he heard of what Joel said. He probably… I don't know what he thinks."

"Grant is a sweetheart," Lena said. "I doubt he thinks anything but that Joel is an *asshole*."

I laughed but didn't feel it. "I hope so. I've been avoiding him since it happened."

"You shouldn't. He's not only a sweetheart, but a gentleman. I doubt that he would even say anything about it other than to make sure that you're okay."

"Yeah…" I sipped my coffee and looked at the mountains in the distance.

Evelyn pulled her legs up into her chair and wrapped her arms around them. Perfect to help with that hint of autumn chill. "Clearly, that's not the only thing that's bothering you," she said.

"No. I mean…" I cleared my throat. "There's some family stuff that I'm really not ready to talk about, but mostly it's just Joel. I can't get it out of my head that maybe he's right and I've gotten this all twisted up in my head as something that I want, but it's not something I should actually go after. If it were something that was okay, then I just feel like he wouldn't have reacted that way."

Lena stared at me for a second. "Yeah, you're going to have to retract every part of that statement before I smack it out of your brain."

Evelyn and I laughed, but the discomfort remained in my gut. "Really?"

"*Yes,* really," she said. "Unless you think the millions of people who read kinky novels, consume kinky porn, and you know…actually participate are disgusting and perverted people. In which case, we need to have a very different conversation."

"No." The answer was immediate. "I've never thought that."

"Then why do you think it about yourself?" Evelyn asked, picking up her coffee so she could cradle it between her knees.

I shook my head. "You didn't see him. I've never seen him—*anyone*—that angry. Ever. It was scary." She shuddered, and I bit my lip. Damn it, I shouldn't have brought up angry men. Evelyn had lived through too much of that. "Sorry."

"No, don't be. I can't live my life with everyone trying to think about whether every single thing they say is going to remind me of Nathan."

"Cori, Joel's anger says more about him than it does about you," Lena said. "It tells me he's insecure and your requests endangered his ego and self-esteem."

"I wasn't trying to say he wasn't enough. I just wanted to try some new things."

Evelyn shrugged. "Sounds like you dodged a bullet to me. Good riddance."

They had a point. The fact that I wasn't more destroyed over the breakup itself was a sign. Maybe we'd just been coasting because we were comfortable and had known each other since we were kids. I'd glossed over the parts of our relationship that weren't working in favor of ease.

Like the fact that he hated my house. I ignored that because I loved him. Or, I thought I loved him. Joel was a reminder that not everything from my family's world was awful.

So much for that.

Evelyn's engagement necklace glimmered in the evening light. "How are wedding plans going?"

She laughed. "Slow. I'm keeping most of them on hold until after Harlan and Grace's wedding. We're all hands on deck for that."

That was coming up fast. With everything else going on, I'd forgotten that the wedding was next week. "Guess I'll have to find another date."

"No kidding," Lena said. "That asshole isn't welcome."

Lena was the planning machine behind Harlan and Grace's wedding. As far as I knew, Grace had hardly made any of the decisions.

"Can I ask something weird?"

"Sure," Evelyn said. Her eyes told me that she probably already knew what I was going to ask.

"Why are they getting married first?"

She laughed softly. "Yeah, I get that a lot. Mostly because Lucas and I aren't in a hurry. We'll get there. And because Grace and Harlan should have been married a long time ago, and they deserve it."

That was true. The couple had been to hell and back

multiple times, and their wedding was like a breath of fresh air throughout our whole community. No more watching the pair of them to see whether they'd end up kissing or fist fighting.

"Is there anything I can do to help with the wedding?" I asked. "You've got to be going crazy with the cake and the food."

"You want to be a makeup guinea pig? I need someone to practice on, and, go figure, Grace conveniently scheduled a dress fitting down in Missoula that day. I think she did it on purpose."

"Sure," I said. "As long as there's coffee."

"There will be an overwhelming amount of coffee," Lena confirmed. "Day after tomorrow."

I nodded. "Works for me. So you're not stressed out with all the preparations?"

"Oh, I totally am, but if you tell that to Grace, I know where to hide a body."

Evelyn and I both laughed, and my shoulders eased. It was good to have someone tell me that I wasn't crazy. I wasn't disgusting, and I deserved better than what Joel had done.

Lena dove into the wild story of how she was chasing down ingredients, and I smiled, grateful to have friends like this.

Chapter 6

Grant

The treadmill miles disappeared under my feet, and it felt good. For the most part. It was easier than outdoor running for the consistency and the evenness it offered as far as terrain.

The last few days had been better, pain-wise. Not excellent, but better. And getting a workout, finally, made me feel like I wasn't just sitting on my ass and being lazy.

I knew I wasn't, and I knew I was doing the best I could. But I still couldn't change the restlessness that prickled under my skin when I couldn't do things. Or the feeling of guilt and uselessness.

All those things meant that I should probably schedule an appointment with Rayne sooner than later. That, or one of the guys was going to end up doing it for me.

It was part of the deal, being a part of Resting Warrior. You had to deal with your shit, or the rest of us would hold that person accountable to do what they needed to do to get better.

Of course, that was a far easier policy to live under when it wasn't you who was about to have their balls busted. And it was a lot easier when you thought those things were actually helping. Right now, I wasn't completely sure that they were.

Cori popped into my head. Again.

She hadn't left it since the other night. I wanted to apologize whenever I had the opportunity, but I felt as if she was avoiding me. We'd lived next door to each other for years now, and I didn't think I'd ever gone this long without at least seeing her in passing.

But the scene the other night still didn't make sense in my head.

I wouldn't claim that Cori and I were close in any way, but I knew her well enough to know that she was kind. Generous. Sweet and bubbly with a giant heart. None of those things that Joel had been hurling at her.

What I'd heard didn't give me the complete picture of what had happened between them, but I'd heard enough to scratch my head. Even in my kinkiest, wildest dreams, I couldn't imagine Cori doing or asking for anything that warranted that kind of response.

Scratch that. Nothing warranted that response. Ever.

What Joel had done wasn't just fight. Fighting was one thing. It happened in relationships, and you dealt with it. Now that Evelyn and Lucas had been together for a few months, there had been a few knock-down drag-outs between them. But they worked it out and were in bed together no more than a day later.

God knew how often Grace and Harlan fought. But their fighting was half of the reason they loved each other.

They matched each other in ways that made me jealous. But I'd never admit that to them.

That wasn't what Joel had done. He'd torn her down and intentionally hit her where it hurt. I saw it in those tears and in her entire demeanor. It wasn't a fight; it was an all-out assault. No matter what happened, that wasn't something you did to someone you claimed to love.

Anger burned in my chest, reliving the memory of that small step he'd taken toward her. I didn't know what he'd been planning on doing, but if there was even a sliver of a chance he was about to hit her?

I stopped the treadmill, catching my breath.

If there was even the smallest chance, then I wasn't sorry for the interruption, no matter the embarrassment that I caused.

Moving to the stretching area, I pulled out one of the exercise balls. Might as well try to do some of the exercises assigned by the physical therapist, though they hadn't done much for me. The reality was that stretching didn't fix shrapnel.

I was draped inelegantly over that same ball when Noah came in and laughed, seeing me. "Having fun?"

"Not particularly."

"Want to spar? It's been a while."

It had been a while, and given the path of my thoughts, I could use something to whale on a little bit. "Sure."

We taped our hands and stepped onto the mat. This was familiar. All seven of us knew one another well enough that sparring was mostly an exercise in blocking the other's favorite attacks. But it was still fun.

Noah came at me, and I dodged to the side, spinning to make sure that I was still facing him. I blocked the next punch with my arm, and the impact reverberated through my body, followed by a sharp blast of pain.

"Fuck," I said, my voice echoing off the walls.

I turned away, trying to work through that burst of pain. Noah let me do it, and I was grateful for that.

"Guess that's the end of that," he said.

"I'm fine."

Facing him, I caught the tail end of his eye roll. "You're clearly not."

"Yeah," I sighed. "It's been a while since I've been to the physical therapist. It doesn't feel like it works."

"Well, clearly it does something," he said. "Because you've been a lot worse lately. And I don't say that meaning that we're tired of helping you or whatever kind of shit your brain is going to try to feed you."

I smiled at that. He wasn't wrong.

"I say that because we can see that you're in pain. And it's not fun for anyone."

"No kidding."

Noah swiped a hand over his face. "Don't be a smartass about it."

"I'm not trying to. I'm frustrated as hell, and being told to bend over and touch my toes doesn't help the actual cause of the pain."

"No," Noah acknowledged. "But unless you got your medical degree since I last saw you, you're not a doctor, and you don't actually know how much it's helping your body adjust to it."

I hated that he was right. Because it brought up the frustration that buzzed under my skin almost constantly now. "Fine. I'll go."

"Look at that," Noah said with a grin. "I didn't even have to threaten to drag your ass to the appointments."

He would do that, too.

Time to change the subject. The last thing that I

wanted to talk about and dwell on was my fucking pain. "You find a date for the wedding?"

Noah laughed. "No. It's a little late for that."

The wedding was next week. But that was still enough time to ask someone and for them to say yes. "I don't know, I'm sure you could find someone."

"Nah." He shook his head. "I've already accepted and said I'm going solo. I'll just deal with it."

"When was the last time you had a date?" I asked.

I was walking a fine line here, and I knew it. The things Noah and Jude dealt with were darker and less straightforward than pain. I hadn't seen Noah with anyone or even attempt it in the time I'd known him.

"I'm fine," he said. "And you're one to talk. Do you have a date for the wedding?"

With a laugh, I pulled the tape off my hands. "I deserved that. No, I don't right now. But I do have an idea."

"Oh? Who?"

"Mind your own business," I said.

"You know we'll find out if she says yes."

I grabbed my bag and looked back at him. "Yeah. And?"

He grinned. "I can't wait."

I shook my head and pushed out the door. The others were absolutely relentless the minute that one of the guys became involved. Which was fair; I was too. Different being on this side of it.

My main concern was that if Cori did say yes, I wanted to shield her from the questions that would come with that. It wasn't a secret that she had been with Joel. And being on a date with me? People would know that something had happened. It was entirely possible that she wouldn't be ready for that. But I was going to try anyway.

Ironically, despite that sharp blast of pain during the short-lived sparring match, my back actually felt a lot better. Later I needed to thank Noah for knocking it back into a good place.

It was earlier than I usually got home, and for once, the universe was smiling down on me. Cori was definitely avoiding me, because she was pulling into her driveway exactly at the same time as I was, clearly hoping to be inside and ensconced in her house before I got here.

She saw, and she blushed so hard that I saw it while she was still in her truck. That was fine—I wanted to show her that avoiding me was unnecessary, regardless of the wedding and what I wanted to ask.

"Cori," I called, slipping out of my own truck and catching her before she made it to her stairs.

Freezing, she turned, but her eyes were fixed on the ground as she fiddled with her keys. "Hey, Grant."

"I was hoping to catch you," I said, making sure there wasn't any sign of the other night in my voice.

"Oh? Why?" Cori's eyes flickered over me, catching on my arms and down the length of me and back. I was in my workout gear. Shorts and a sleeveless shirt. Not what she usually saw me in.

If I were a bigger man, I would say that I didn't notice the way she looked at me, and that it didn't matter. But I did notice, and I liked the way she took me in. I would gladly let her look if that was what she wanted to do.

"I was hoping you could stop by the ranch tomorrow and check on one of the new arrival horses. If you have the time? He's got something going on with his leg."

"Oh," she said again, and I saw the way her mind refocused into her professional space. This was work. It was familiar and not at all embarrassing. "Let me double-check my appointments."

She pulled out her phone and flicked through her calendar. "Yeah, I can come by tomorrow afternoon. Around two. Is that okay?"

"That's perfect," I said. "I'll see you tomorrow?"

"Yeah."

An awkward moment passed in which neither of us moved, as if there was more to say even though the conversation was over. Finally, she broke away, hesitating as if she might say something else and then changed her mind. I watched her make it into the house and waited until the door was closed behind her before I returned to my own side of the property line.

She wasn't in danger, but my instincts wouldn't let me do anything else.

This was a good icebreaker to get us back to what we were—friendly neighbors. If I'd asked her to the wedding tonight, I didn't think she would have said yes. But I was going to see her tomorrow, and for the first time in what felt like forever, I was actually looking forward to finding out what tomorrow would bring.

Chapter 7

Cori

The wind cut through my shirt before I had a chance to pull the sweater over my head on the way to my truck. It was definitely fall. This was the first day we'd had that was actually *cold.* A precursor to the long, snowy Montana winters. They weren't for everyone, but I was used to them by now. There was just as much beauty here in the winter as there was in the summer. You just needed better boots in the winter.

I started the truck and pulled out, heading out of town toward Resting Warrior. My stomach gave a little flip, knowing that I was going to see Grant. I was so worried about him, but yesterday had been fine. And whatever he thought about Joel and that night, not one thing had showed.

He'd never know how grateful I was for that.

The wind picked up as I left town, blowing hard enough that I could feel it in the steering. The flat, gray clouds that hung low in the sky were ominous. Not only was it cold, it looked like it was going to snow or storm or make life hard for everyone somehow.

I hoped that the weather held out just a little longer so that Grace and Harlan's wedding wouldn't have to deal with the extra hassle. Lena didn't need to deal with driving the cake to the venue on snowy roads—she was stressed enough as it was.

But after that? Bring on the cold. I was ready for sweaters all the time, curling up with tea and hot chocolate, and enjoying being cozy in a way that simply wasn't possible in the summer.

Pulling up to the main Resting Warrior lodge, I grabbed my medical bag and hopped out, waving to Lucas sitting on the porch with coffee and a laptop. It was nice that I was enough of a fixture here that I could just wave and make my way to where I needed to go. Some of my clients, even though they trusted me, felt the need to stick to my side like Velcro when I was on their property.

The stables were quiet and empty of people. The paddock was empty, too. No sign of Grant or Noah or any of the Resting Warrior guys. I checked my phone. No, I was right on time, so where was the horse?

I started to walk back toward the lodge when I spotted Mara carrying some food toward the dog pens. She could probably tell me where Grant was.

"Mara," I called, jogging to catch up to her.

She smiled when she turned and nodded. Mara didn't speak. Or rather, she did, but it was rare. Resting Warrior was a safe place for her to work and live with people who weren't going to judge her for that. She was a near-invisible force that kept the ranch looking beautiful and made sure that the more menial tasks were taken care of.

"I'm looking for Grant," I said. "He wanted me to look at one of the horses, but I don't see him anywhere."

Gesturing, she pointed toward the wild portion of the Resting Warrior property. The whole place was far larger than the portion that was developed. They had plans for it, but right now, it was mostly used as a safe place to train the animals. "He's walking the horse?"

Mara nodded.

"Thank you."

She smiled again, and I moved past her toward the fields. Hopefully he wouldn't be too far. He might have lost track of time trying to get the horse to move around.

He was pretty far out, but I spotted him some distance away, so I didn't have to wander. And as I got closer, I saw why he'd asked me to come. The horse was having trouble —favoring its front left leg. It didn't look overly painful, but I needed to get closer to see what was going on.

Grant saw me and waved. "Hey." He was smiling as we met in the middle. "Thanks for coming."

"Happy to. Though I had to ask Mara where you were."

He laughed softly. "I should have left you a note. This is Ginger." He stroked his hand down the horse's neck. "New arrival. Really sweet, but you can see something's happening with her leg. I wanted to give it a little exercise to keep it warm."

"Let's see."

Grant held on to the bridle and kept the horse still while I ducked down and started my examination. She shied away from me when I touched her leg, and Grant spoke to her softly to calm her down. "It's okay," I said, using my vet voice. "I'm not going to hurt you."

When I ran my fingers over the leg, all the bones felt

okay. No signs of serious swelling, no cuts, and her shoe and hoof were fine.

But when I gently squeezed, she shied away again, and the same when I bent her leg at the knee. "Okay," I said. "Seems like it's a sprain. I'd like to get her into the clinic for an X-ray just in case there's something we can't see, but I'm pretty confident. So, gentle work and walking like this is actually perfect." I smiled at Grant. "You've got good instincts."

"I like to think so," he said quietly, and though I was looking at the horse, I could feel that he was looking at me when he said that. Standing this close, I found it hard to ignore that he was right there. And my stomach gave that same little flip that it had when I started on my way here.

I needed to know what he thought about the other night. If I didn't find out, it was going to drive me mad. I opened my mouth to ask, and pain sparked on the top of my head. "Ow. What was that?"

Another ping of pain, and a second later, I saw the little white ball hit Ginger's back. Grant cursed and grabbed my arm. "Hail."

Now I was cursing too. He pulled me away from the main ranch. "Where are we going?"

"We have a few emergency sheds across the property. Small, but it'll work."

That wasn't remotely surprising. A bunch of former SEALs like the Resting Warrior men wouldn't chance being taken by surprise or unprepared, even on their own property.

"There."

He pointed, and I had to squint to see it. With the hail starting to come down and the way the building was cleverly camouflaged in a copse of trees, it was nearly invisible. "Well, damn," I said.

Grant laughed.

I pulled the neck of my sweater up over the back of my head to ward off the hail that was coming down faster. The stones weren't huge, but they were enough to sting. Never very fun.

Opening the door, Grant guided Ginger inside and then me before following and closing the door behind us. The shack was so small, there was barely any room. I was pressed against the wall, and now that Grant was inside with me, we were in each other's space. Even more than when we were standing close outside.

This close, I could feel the warmth coming off him. Smell the faint pine scent floating around him, along with something sharp and clear like snow.

Last night when he'd stepped out of the truck in workout gear, it was like a punch to the gut to see pieces of his body on display. I'd never seen him like that before. Or if I had, I'd never noticed because I was with Joel. But now that I wasn't…

It was all that I could see. How had I missed how attractive he was all this time? Attractive wasn't even the right word. *Hot* was the right word. Especially this up close and personal when he was looking at me and I could see the green of his eyes.

Outside, the hail dropped. It was loud on the wooden roof of the shack, but it seemed like a background to whatever was happening between us right now. The air in the empty space separating us was taut with something magnetic.

All I could see was the way he'd made Joel leave. Coming to my rescue even though I hadn't asked him to. And then he hadn't made me feel lesser because of that. The breath in my chest felt shallow.

Grant's eyes dropped to my lips, and all of that air

disappeared. He was going to kiss me, and I didn't hate that idea. Screw that. I wanted him to kiss me. Right now, I wasn't going to feel guilty for moving too fast after a breakup or think about what could go wrong with kissing the man who lived next door. All I wanted was to know what it would feel like.

He leaned in slowly, as if he was asking for permission. There was plenty of time for me to ask him to stop. I knew that he would have. But I didn't.

Slowly, gently, his lips brushed across mine. It wasn't a kiss yet. It was the moment before a kiss, breathless and endless.

Grant exhaled and pulled back, clearing his throat. My stomach dropped in disappointment, but that was okay. That was smart. Probably better, given that the breakup was only days old and we were neighbors. That was fine.

But it didn't feel fine.

"I wanted to ask you something," he said quietly. "We're both invited to the wedding."

There was no reason to clarify which wedding.

"I don't have a date. And since I'm hoping the asshole is no longer invited, maybe we could go together. Neighbors. So we're less lonely or awkward being single at a wedding. Or maybe we could be those things together."

I opened my mouth to respond, but before I could move, Grant did. He reached around me and slid a hand up my spine until one hand rested on the back of my neck. "And I want to make myself clear. I am dying to kiss you. But before anything like that happens, we need a better foundation than being caught in a hailstorm."

A shuddering breath left me, combined with relief that I didn't know I needed. He wasn't blowing me off. Not completely.

"You want to kiss me?" I asked.

"Yes," he said without hesitation. "I do."

Biting my lip, I leaned farther into the hand that was on my neck. "I want you to kiss me."

A small smile broke out on his face. Heat rose between us, and he leaned in. His lips brushed my temple, and my stomach fluttered with about a hundred butterflies. "Come to the wedding with me?" he asked softly.

"Yes."

He relaxed. I hadn't even noticed that he was tense, but I felt the relief. It was in me, too. I wanted more than his lips on my skin, but at the same time, this was everything that I wanted. I wasn't willing to move from this spot.

Neither was he.

We were frozen there until the hail faltered and silenced outside. But it wasn't awkward. It was easy. It felt safe. And when the hail stopped completely, he slowly pulled away from me to let us out of the shed. I almost wished the hail would have lasted longer.

The ground was covered with a crusting of icy pellets that crunched under our feet as we exited. Ginger was fascinated by it too, licking some of the icicles.

"I guess I'll see you at home at some point," I said.

"Definitely."

Both of us wanted more than this. I could feel it. I would wager to say we both felt it. But he had a point. And if it was more than just this moment, it would wait.

That's what I told myself as I forced myself to turn and walk away. It would wait.

Chapter 8

Grant

"You had an idea, huh?" Noah pushed into the barn with a smirk on his face. "I bet you did."

The ice from yesterday's hailstorm had melted, but it left the roads of the ranch and the stable muddy as hell. The horses were going to need extra attention and a bath later with the way that mud was coating their legs.

"What are you talking about?"

Of course I knew what he was talking about, but I wasn't about to admit that to Noah. He was going to have to work for it. I continued brushing Ginger down as if nothing in the world was different.

"I'm talking about the fact that you left me in the gym two days ago telling me you had an idea for a date to the wedding, and now you and Cori are going together? All this time, you've been telling us to go to hell, and we were right."

I looked at him and raised an eyebrow. "We're going to the wedding together. I didn't ask her to marry me."

Noah was still grinning from ear to ear as if that didn't matter in the slightest. "Still. This is a step. I thought she had a boyfriend?"

The very mention of that asshole made me see red, but I straightened and squared my shoulders. "Not anymore."

"That's good. I'm happy for you."

"Wait," I said, pausing the brushing. "How do you even know about this?"

He shrugged. "Cori told Lena and Evelyn. Evelyn told Lucas."

I sighed. "So, everyone knows."

"Yup."

Not that it mattered. It wasn't like we were going to show up to the wedding and be completely invisible. But if all the guys knew, these next few days were going to be absolutely unbearable.

"So, when's your wedding?" Noah asked.

I pointed at him. "If you say that shit around Cori, I don't care how my back is feeling, you'll be in for an ass-kicking."

He laughed. "I'm just joking, man. But I thought you liked her. Didn't take you for a guy who's scared of commitment."

"I'm not scared of that," I said evenly. Then quieter. "And I do like her. But I'm not going to rush this. She just had a breakup. I don't want to be the rebound guy. So I want to keep it easy and light for a while. And you all asking when we're getting married is the opposite of 'easy and light.'"

Noah held up his hands in surrender. "Fair enough. I'll make sure that I keep my mouth shut when you two are present and together. But I can't make promises for everyone else."

"I'll tell them."

The truth was that my stomach had been in knots since yesterday. The line on my control had been so thin that if I had moved an inch from the way we'd been frozen together, I would have pushed her against the wall and kissed her like I really wanted to.

I believed Cori when she said that she wanted to kiss me. Her eyes showed it, and I felt it between us. But it was also true what I told her and Noah. Rushing this wasn't a good idea. In no world did I only want to be a replacement for Joel.

No. If Cori and I were together, then I wanted to give it an actual try. Deep down, I already knew that she was too special for me to mess this up. So I was going to do everything in my power not to. And to show her that she was safe with me, and that I would never do what he'd done.

"Seriously, though," Noah said, the teasing gone from his voice. "I know that you've liked her for a while, and I'm happy for you."

"Thanks." I tried and failed to stop the smile that crossed my face. She could have said no, and she didn't. More than that, she *wanted* me to kiss her. I could still smell the mix of vanilla and cinnamon that seemed to waft away from her. As if she was constantly near freshly baked cookies.

I saw the flashes of teal in her hair and the way they shone even in the dim light of that tiny shack. Big hazel eyes that looked at me like I was the only person in the world.

For her, I wanted to be the only person in the world.

Shit, I was already half gone.

But she said yes, and the satisfaction that went along with that filled my chest and the rest of my body. It was primal, profound, and purely male. She wanted me.

Noah clapped me on the shoulder before heading out of the stable, and I finished with the horses. A few of them needed to be rinsed down, but on the whole, not as bad as I'd expected.

The weather today was chilly in the wake of yesterday's spontaneous ice storm, and the breeze had a bite to it that heralded winter. It was about that time. It was rare for Montana to make it all the way through October without any snow. If we had a Halloween that wasn't white, we were lucky.

I needed to pull out my heavier jackets for ranch work now.

Jude was coming down the stairs from the lodge. "You want coffee?"

"Headed to Deja Brew?"

He nodded, and I changed my direction to meet him at his truck. Jude made the weekly run to the bakery and coffee shop so that we could keep the lodge kitchen stocked with bread for sandwiches and other goodies that weren't the healthiest, but they were fucking delicious, so none of us was about to say no. Lena Mitchell was a hell of a baker.

Jude had done this same task every week for the last… more than two years. As soon as he'd met Lena, he started doing it. Eventually the rest of us stopped offering, because we knew that he was going to say no.

But tagging along was always fun. If only to watch the way our friend tripped over himself with the woman he was clearly in love with.

Given that I didn't want them to give me a hard time about Cori, I was currently more sympathetic than normal, as far as giving Jude a hard time. Still. At this point, everyone in the entire town of Garnet Bend would break out into spontaneous applause if they just kissed.

The ride to town was quiet. Jude was almost always quiet. Of all the guys, he was the most stoic. We pulled up to the front of the coffee shop, and Jude parked the truck. I could see some kind of commotion happening through the windows, and Jude and I walked into the middle of chaos.

Deja Brew looked like what I imagined the behind the scenes of a fashion show might look like. There was makeup everywhere. On tables and balanced on chairs and on the floor. Some dresses were draped over the backs of the overstuffed armchairs. A hair-dryer was running, and women were everywhere.

Lena looked over as we came in and immediately started laughing. I imagined the looks on our faces made it clear this was the last thing we were expecting.

"Trial run for wedding hair and makeup, boys. Don't worry, I still have your order. Just give me a minute."

"Take your time," Jude said, and as soon as he spoke, Lena's eyes dropped. She blushed. Shit, if I was noticing how much they needed to get together, it was long overdue.

I was so overwhelmed by everything in front of me that it took me a minute to realize Cori was sitting in the middle of it all. And everything else fucking disappeared.

Her hair fell in soft curls around her shoulders, the teal parts shining out like beacons. Darker eye shadow than I'd ever seen her wear was smudged across her eyes, and they looked bigger and deeper than normal. Shining lips reminded me way too much of us pressed together in that shed yesterday.

Cori was beautiful every single day. This was so much more than that. I'd never seen her like this, and it felt like a punch to the gut in the best way. Holy shit.

She looked over at me and startled. I guess she hadn't seen me either. But she saw me now, and God, I couldn't stop looking at her. I was having a hard time controlling my body right now. If I wasn't careful, I was going to be hard in front of half the women in the town.

The wedding was going to be way more difficult than I thought, if she looked like this. This didn't make me want to take it slow. This made me want to take her hand and pull her outside and *thoroughly* finish the kiss we had put on hold.

She stood and came over, giving a small wave to Jude. "Hi."

"Hey."

"Grace had her final appointment for her wedding dress, so I'm a stand-in for the bride as far as makeup."

Jude stepped away from us so that we were as alone as we could be in a room full of people. "You look beautiful," I said quietly, and I watched her cheeks go pink the same way Lena's had. That reaction tugged at my gut, pulling me toward her. It took everything I had in me not to step closer. Because we were being watched.

"Thank you." She glanced behind her, and at least three heads, including Evelyn's, snapped in a different direction. "How's Ginger today?"

"She's good. Had to spray her down because of the mud from the hail."

She laughed quietly, and I could listen to that sound all day. "Good. Keep me in the loop. I'll make sure to make time to check on her."

"We appreciate it."

When I looked toward the counter, Jude was collecting the bags of bread and pastries and paying Lena for them. She nearly always included more than we had paid for, and Jude did his best to sneak more money to her because of that. They each succeeded about half the time.

"I never asked," Cori said. "Where should we meet? For the wedding?"

I grinned. "Well, since we live so close, I can drive."

"We do live close," she said with a smile. "That would be perfect."

Jude appeared at my side. "Ready?"

"Sure." I smiled at Cori. "See you soon."

"Bye."

The other women bursting out into shrieks and squeals as soon as we left the shop wasn't something they bothered to hide. "Was it this bad with Harlan and Lucas?"

Jude shook his head as he slid into the truck. "No, I don't think so. But then again, they weren't dating someone the whole town knows."

I didn't bother to correct him to say that we weren't dating. It didn't matter at this point. Besides, after seeing her like that, I didn't want to deny anything. That image of her was going to live in my mind for a long fucking time.

A laugh entered my thoughts, and Jude shook his head. "I know you're already going to get this from everyone else, but it's about time."

"I am going to get it from everyone else," I said, laughing with him. "But you only get to give me a hard time if you finally take the last step with Lena."

That did the trick. He straightened in his seat and sent a glare my way. I'd never had the chance to ask, and now I felt like I needed to. "What's going on there? If it's this bad with me, it has to be worse for you. Everyone can see that you're practically in love with each other."

I glanced over at him, and I caught the sadness that crossed over his face. Not just sadness, but the deep sorrow that came from things that haunted you and no one else. I was familiar with that feeling and that expression.

He didn't respond with words, but the way he looked was answer enough. Whatever was going on with him and his hesitancy with Lena, it was darker and more complicated than anyone realized, and now I had no doubt it was wrapped up in his past.

We rode the rest of the way to the ranch in silence, and that was fine for both of us.

Chapter 9

Cori

Grant was in my head. Ever since the almost-kiss, I couldn't get him out of it. The way that he'd looked at me yesterday wasn't helping. It made dreams about him suddenly spring to life without even trying.

Now that I was single and free, my brain was catching up with me. The breakup with Joel didn't even feel that recent. With every passing day, I realized how much we'd been coasting for way too long.

Even when I'd been dating Joel, I hadn't had fantasies about *him*. The fantasies I had—even about expanding our sexual repertoire—hadn't featured Joel at all. My subconscious had known he wouldn't ever do it.

But now, I *was* picturing Grant. In any and all situations involving him and me and our mouths meeting and clothes disappearing.

But the more I thought about it, I felt that Grant was right, too. He was a good guy, and I didn't want to rebound off him. And yet the way his gaze filled with heat yesterday made me want to explore faster.

God, the wedding tomorrow was going to be something else. I already had butterflies thinking about it.

There were butterflies of a different kind in my stomach as I drove into the Pearson ranch. I didn't exactly feel welcome here, but I wanted to check on Sunrise. I didn't need to check on any of the other horses yet.

No trucks in the driveway. That was good. Easier, honestly. With the wedding tomorrow, Joel was the last person I wanted to see.

At first when I got to the stable, I didn't think Sunrise was in her stall. Until I saw that she was. Lying on her side in the hay. "Hi there," I said softly, getting myself into the same space. "How are you?"

A soft sound, fairly pitiful.

I didn't need to listen to her lungs to see that she was struggling to breathe. Her side was heaving, breaths irregular. When I did listen, there wasn't anything obstructing her lungs. No other injuries. Heart rate was high but not irregular.

This horse needed to come to the clinic. There wasn't any other way to put it. I pulled out my phone and dialed Mr. Pearson. It was clear that he was driving when he answered. "Hello?"

"Mr. Pearson," I said. "It's Cori Jackson."

"How can I help you?"

I cleared my throat. "I came out to check on Sunrise, and she's really having a hard time breathing. At this point, tests are necessary if I'm going to figure out what's going on."

"No," he said. "We've been working them hard training. Maybe a bit overworked and tired, but the animal is fine."

"Mr.—"

"Look, I don't have time to talk about this right now. You don't have permission to remove that horse from my property, do you understand?"

"Yes."

He hung up without another word, and I stared at the phone for a second. Mr. Pearson had always been gruff, but in the past, he'd been a little easier to work with. Why wouldn't he want to find out what was going on?

I'd left my sample kit at the clinic. But I'd thrown a steroid shot in my bag on the off chance the horse needed it. And it did. The shot would give her system a boost and make it easier for her to breathe. And hopefully allow her to hold on until I found out what was wrong with her. Because I *was* going to find out.

There was no chance I was going to let an animal suffer just because the owner was being a stubborn ass about it. But there was nothing I could do today.

"Cori."

The voice made me freeze as I was closing the gate on Sunrise's stall. I took one long breath before I turned. "Joel."

"Here for a horse?"

I fixed him with a stare. "Well, I'm certainly not here for you."

"Oh, Cori," he laughed. "You know I've always loved you when you're sassy."

What? He was talking to me like he hadn't screamed all sorts of profanities at me last time I'd seen him.

"On the contrary. I don't think you really loved me at all, Joel. And now that we're over, I'm realizing that we've been over for a long time." I turned and walked away from him toward the exit.

His footsteps softly crunched behind me. "I was going

to call you today. Talk about when to pick you up for the wedding. You're still going, right?"

"Are you serious?" I whirled on him, and the words were out of my mouth before I fully processed them. "You even *imagine* that you're welcome at the wedding?"

Joel looked confused. "You RSVPed with my name as the plus-one. So, obviously, I'll go."

I laughed. I, honest to God, laughed out loud. Courage surged up my spine, and I glared at him. "No. You gave up that privilege when you decided to verbally assault me. You are, under no circumstances, welcome at the wedding. I have another date, and you can go to hell. Goodbye, Joel."

The look on his face made me feel better than I had since that night. The combination of shock and utter disbelief gave me whatever closure I needed.

I was almost at the door when I heard him behind me again. He grabbed me, and I nearly stumbled as he gripped my arms and spun me around, backing me into the corner by the door. My back crashed against the shelves of equipment, knocking off a couple of bottles and brushes. One shoulder blade ached with a hook pressed into it.

"What are you doing?"

The look on his face wasn't shocked now. It was dark and terrifying. Fear struck deep, and I regretted the way I'd spoken to him. He'd already snapped once without much provocation. No reason to think he wouldn't do it again.

"You know, I thought more about the ideas you proposed," he said in a low voice. "And I think I've come around to them a little bit."

"What—"

He forced me back again, sliding me off the shelves and deeper into the hooks…where there was rope. My mouth instantly went dry.

This was *not* what I wanted. "Joel, I need you to let me go now."

"Why? You were asking for something new and dirty a few days ago." He grabbed a piece of rope and wrapped it around me.

I dropped my bag and shoved him, but he was ready for that, thrusting his hips into mine and locking my body against the wall while he managed to wrap rope around my arms.

He was stronger than I was. "Joel." I heard the panic in my own voice as I pushed at him. How did I let him put me in this position? How did I end up here?

Something unlocked inside of me, and I fought him. I used every part of my body to force him away from me. Every bit of energy went to trying to stop what was happening. So much effort that I couldn't even scream.

It wasn't enough. He had me. And every second, he had me a little more tangled in the rope. I could barely move my arms.

Emotion strangled me. This couldn't happen. This couldn't be happening to me. "Please stop."

Joel looped a piece of rope around my neck and drew it tight. "Why do you want me to stop? Isn't this what you wanted? Experimenting with something new? Your kinky sex?"

This wasn't the same. Wanting something new in bed didn't mean that I wanted *this*.

He reached for my jeans, and I fought him again. Kicked. Pain cracked through me when I accidentally hit my head against the wall.

Gravel crunched, and Joel backed away and released me at the last second before one of the ranch hands walked through the stable door.

Joel yanked the rope with me in it. Still off-balance, I

fell in a heap on the ground, heaving in air now that my throat was free. Above me, Joel laughed and made a comment about me being clumsy.

The employee kept walking. From his point of view, it would look as if I'd somehow tripped and gotten caught in the rope. But I wasn't going to waste any time. I ripped off the rope, grabbed my bag, and leaped for the door.

Joel caught my arm before I made it and yanked me back. I could still see the man down the hall of the stable, and he looked back at the two of us. I hoped that he could see my panic.

"You seem to have a misunderstanding," Joel whispered in my ear. "I've decided I want to keep you. To teach you about normal sex and that it can be what you want."

"Get away from me," I croaked in a hoarse voice. "I'll scream."

He just smiled. "I'm in your life whether you want me to be or not. Our families are connected. So, I'll be the one who decides when this is over. Not you." His grip on my arm tightened so much that I knew it would leave a bruise. "Got it?"

I said nothing, just stared at the ranch hand, who obviously couldn't decide if he should intervene or not. Finally, Joel released me.

He slapped the rope in his hand. "If you try getting kinky with anyone else, you'll be sorry."

I turned and ran out of the barn. My hands were shaking as I pulled my keys out of my bag and even worse when I tried to get them into the ignition.

Joel was watching me from the door of the stable. I hit the gas. The truck sprayed gravel as I turned too quickly.

I drove just slightly out of sight before I had to pull the truck over. I barely made it out of the cab before I was heaving up everything I'd eaten today.

My breath wouldn't even out. Sheer panic was still racing through my limbs, and my legs wouldn't hold me. Shit. *Shit.*

I was lucky that guy had walked in when he did.

Rage followed that thought. I shouldn't have to be lucky. I couldn't believe what had almost happened.

Should I be crying? There weren't any tears, though I could feel the potential there.

Joel was still too close, and I had no guarantee he wouldn't come after me. I forced my legs under me and braced myself on the cab of the truck in order to get inside.

There was a part of me that wasn't processing what happened. I didn't feel like it was real. Being…almost raped. My mind shuddered against the word. That was a thing that happened to other people. It was a scary story. That was all.

Clearly not.

My stomach heaved again, and I breathed through it. I just needed to get home. Be home. Surrounded by comfort and nothing that would make me think about this. All I wanted was to make it go away.

I started the truck and forced myself to drive.

Chapter 10

Grant

I heard the rumble of Cori's truck and the lurch as she stopped too fast in her driveway. It hadn't even been ten minutes since I'd arrived home, and I'd barely gotten my coat off.

Stepping out onto the porch, I was about to wave to her and froze.

Something was wrong. Cori was so pale, it looked like she'd seen a ghost. Or worse. The way her hands shook as she was sorting through her keys was enough to make me pause.

"Cori?"

She jumped so fast it was as if I'd set off a gun behind her. Her eyes found mine, and she relaxed. "Grant. Hi."

"You okay?"

"Sure," she said. "Just a long day. You know how it is. Did you need something for tomorrow?"

My instincts were *screaming*. She was lying. Something

was bothering her, and she was scared of it. I walked down the porch steps and made sure that I didn't look threatening in the slightest. That wasn't what she needed. I wanted to be a place that she felt safe, no matter what.

"We've lived next door to each other for years, and I've never seen you look like this," I said softly.

"Like what?" She didn't meet my eyes.

I took a step closer. "Pale. Terrified. When I said your name, you jumped like you were starting the hundred-meter dash."

Cori swallowed. "I must be more tired than I thought. I'm always jumpier when I'm tired. But don't worry, I'll be all set for the wedding."

She still wasn't looking at me. And her fingers hadn't stopped moving, fiddling with her keys. "Cori?"

No response. Not a verbal one, at least. She shook her head a little. The only time I'd seen her even come close to this was the other night with *him*. I cooled the immediate anger that came with thoughts of her ex and put it aside. "Was it Joel?"

The reaction was immediate and visceral. No words, but she turned from me, heaving nothing up onto the grass. Her body shook like a leaf, and pure terror combined with rage swam through my veins. What did he do to her?

"Cori?" I leaned down and touched my hand to her back.

Shoving herself upward, she turned to me. "I'm fine. I'm okay, I promise."

"Forgive me, but that doesn't look true."

"I'll be okay." The words were so quiet they made me ache. I wanted to touch her. Hold her. Make sure she was completely fine before ever letting her go again.

I could see red marks on her arms that didn't look like

something she could have done herself. They looked like rope marks. Some scratches that could be defensive wounds. Jesus.

"Cori, do I need to take you to the hospital?"

She shook her head, voice still painfully quiet. "No. Thankfully."

"The police?"

"No."

I slipped my hands into my pockets to keep myself from reaching for her. "I don't know what happened," I said, though I could guess enough. "But I want to help. If Joel is being a problem, then it's easy enough to get a restraining order. Charlie knows you, and he knows that you wouldn't lie."

Cori laughed. "I'm sure he would give me one. But I'm not sure what good it would do."

"Why?"

Her eyes were suddenly full of fire. "Because a piece of paper isn't going to stop him from doing shit. And because by the time I called the police, it would already be over. And besides, how is it going to help when I literally have to go to his house to take care of the animals? There's no other vet close enough to take over and…" Cori's face crumpled, but she caught herself before she started to cry. "No. A restraining order doesn't matter. I'll just have to deal with it, I guess."

"We can get someone to come out, Cori. You don't have to do that."

"Yes, I do," she said quickly. "It's not like I want to be out there or anything. There's just this horse… I don't want to talk about it right now, but there's a case I'm invested in, and I don't trust another vet with it at the moment. I know it sounds stupid."

"It doesn't." I shook my head. "It absolutely does not

sound stupid. You care about your patients. That's the mark of a good vet. And a good person," I added quietly.

"Thanks."

"I don't know if this is an overstep, but I could come with you if you like. Whenever you have to go out there, if you don't want to be alone, call me. I'll go with you."

Cori's shoulders melted in relief. "Really?"

"Of course. You shouldn't have to feel scared or nervous when you're doing your job."

"I'd like that," she said, wrapping her arms around herself. "Really."

"When are you supposed to go next?"

"In a few days. I'll deal with it after the wedding."

I nodded. It wasn't my goal to push her or attach myself to her side, but anything that let me spend more time with her wasn't something I was angry about. And my responsibilities at Resting Warrior were flexible enough that no one would mind.

But that didn't solve the problem of right now. Cori still looked as if she might fall over at any second. She hadn't thrown anything up, but that didn't mean she wouldn't. Or if she'd already thrown up elsewhere, she would need fluids. Crackers. Something to bring color back to her skin without triggering more illness.

We were taking it slow. I knew I shouldn't ask, but the words were already in the process of coming out of my mouth. "Do you want to stay over at my place tonight? Or if you'd rather sleep in your own bed, I'll sleep on your couch. If you want."

The way she looked at me was full of shock. "You'd do that?"

"Of course. If it will make you feel better. But given that this is a problem with Joel, if being that close to a man will make you feel worse—"

"No." Cori cut me off. "I can't imagine you ever making me feel worse."

A swell of primal pride and pleasure filled me, and I pushed it aside. The last thing Cori needed right now was my fucking bravado.

"If…" She swallowed again. "If you'd be willing to sleep on the couch, that would be good."

"Of course."

She turned, and I followed her up the steps to her porch, at a distance where I wasn't crowding her. I didn't want to make her jump again.

But her hands were still shaking. Enough that she was having trouble getting her keys into the lock. She huffed out a sigh of frustration. "Can I help you?"

"Yeah. I feel silly."

I took the keys and opened the door to her house. Held it open for her. This was actually the first time I'd been inside her house, and though I hadn't known what to expect, the house was entirely *her*.

A mixture of colored walls and comfortable furnishings, it fit her personality. Quirky and fun, just like I'd always known her to be. "I'll be honest, just looking at that couch, I'm pretty sure it's more comfortable than mine," I said as she passed me.

Cori laughed, but her heart wasn't in it.

I locked the door behind us, and she watched me do it. So she could see it was secure, I tested the door handle.

She looked lost in her own home, and that hurt. Maybe it was because they'd fought here, or maybe it was just everything all packed together. "Do you need anything?" I asked. "You almost threw up. Water? Or I can run to Arrowhead and grab you some saltines and juice with electrolytes."

"Please don't leave." Cori turned so fast that she almost tripped, and she grabbed my arm. "Please."

Slowly, I covered her hand with mine. "I'm not."

She nodded. "I'll get some water. I think that's all I can stomach for now."

"Fair enough."

Following her to the kitchen, I watched her fill a glass with water and drain it. Then fill it again. The kitchen was a bright shade of yellow that I imagined was brimming with energy in the morning when the room would be filled with sunlight. "I like your house."

"Really?"

There was a trap here. I saw the caution in her eyes. Something about that statement was a land mine that I had to be careful of. But I wasn't lying. "Yeah. It really suits you. Fun. Colorful. Comfortable. You've made it your own. My house is boring in comparison."

Cori smiled, and it was the first genuine one I'd seen today. It even reached her eyes, though I knew her real joy was so much brighter. "Thank you. Joel always hated it. Complained whenever he came over. I think he felt like he was slumming it."

Ah. That was the trap. "No," I said. "I really do like it. You should help me decorate my house. I have a bad habit of function over form. Old SEAL habits die hard, I guess."

"It can't be that bad."

I grinned. "Want to bet?"

She finished the glass of water in front of her. "I…I know that it's not really late enough for bed, but all I want to do is sleep. Please make yourself at home. Watch TV, eat whatever you want. I'm just grateful that you're staying."

"I'm happy to, Cori."

She blushed and looked away.

The attraction that always seemed to sing between us rose, but there was no way in hell I was going to push that right now. Especially when she still looked pale and drained. If I ever got a hold of Joel again, he wouldn't walk away unscathed.

Cori stood and put her glass in the sink. To get to the stairs, she had to pass me, and she paused. Breathless tension simmered in the small space between our bodies. Nothing was going to happen tonight, no matter how much I wanted to carry her upstairs and explore the depths of that tension.

But she needed more than just this. I knew it so deep that I'd bet my life on it. There wasn't anything to say that would make her feel better, so I opened my arms. She stepped into them and let out a sigh of relief and contentment that had my blood flowing south.

I wrapped her in my arms. This was so much closer than we'd been in that little shack, and it was so much better. The tension that was left in her melted, and the way she fit against me…it was more perfect than I'd imagined. And I *had* imagined it.

We stayed there for long minutes. I didn't want to let her go. If she didn't, I'd hold her all night to make sure she knew she was safe. I would make sure she was safe as long as she wanted me to. That was the end of it.

Just like in the shack, I lifted my hand. Cradled her face. I kissed her temple. It was the only safe move I had besides taking it way too far. Cori shuddered and leaned closer before pulling away.

"Sleep well," I said quietly.

"You too." She looked up at me, about a thousand unspoken words in her eyes. "And thank you."

I smiled. "I'll see you tomorrow."

Cori looked back at me before she climbed the stairs, as

if she was checking to make sure that I was real. I was very real. And like hell was I going anywhere.

Pulling off my boots, I made myself comfortable on her couch, making sure I could see both the stairs and the door. She was safe. For tonight, that was good enough for me.

Chapter 11

Cori

I felt better in the morning. Shaken? Yes. But better. The sight of Grant sleeping on the couch when I came down the next day was a big part of that. Because he was still there. He stayed just like he said he would, and I didn't think he'd ever truly know how much that meant.

If I hadn't known that he was in the living room, I would have been in a panic, listening for the door downstairs and the moment when Joel broke through it. No matter how unrealistic that possibility was.

Grant simply smiled and left when he woke, waving off my offer of coffee. We were meeting soon to drive over to the wedding, and I was nervous. Not just because of yesterday and what Joel had threatened, but because of that hug last night.

Though calling that a hug was like calling a tsunami a wave. It felt like *everything*. Grant hadn't fully held me during the hailstorm. And feeling the way I fit into his arms made me realize yet again how much I'd been missing. And if I felt that much with only that minimal amount of contact? I wasn't fully prepared for what I would feel when we went further.

As far as I was concerned, it was when and not if.

I canceled the few appointments I had at the clinic. I wasn't up to it. I was already going to have so much on my plate for the wedding; I didn't want to deal with anything else. Instead, I stayed in bed most of the day and read a book until it was time to get ready.

Now I was putting the final touches on my makeup and hair. Thankfully it wasn't cold today. Like summer had decided to make one last hurrah just for Grace and Harlan.

The dress I chose—and which had been approved by Lena—was a deep teal that matched the streaks in my hair. It slipped off one shoulder, and the skirt gathered in a high waist before dropping all the way to the floor. I felt beautiful and graceful in it. And after Grant had looked at me like that in Deja Brew, I wanted to see the way he would react to the dress.

My hair fell in curls around my shoulders, and my makeup wasn't quite as dramatic as what Lena had done on me. But it was certainly more than I wore every day.

On the bathroom counter, my phone chimed. It was time. I didn't want to wait until Grant knocked on the door. That was a little too prom for me, so I grabbed my clutch and my jacket for later in the evening and headed downstairs. And I made very sure that the door was locked behind me.

The sound of a door shutting across the way drew my attention, and all the breath I had left my chest. Grant hadn't seen me yet, but I could see him. And…oh my God.

He was wearing a tuxedo. There was a reason they

were called porn for women. It was an outfit almost universally associated with strength and power—a good tuxedo could charm the clothes right off someone.

I wasn't ashamed to say that I was one of those people.

And this tuxedo wasn't one that was rented or off the rack. No, this one was tailored to fit Grant exactly. Slim hips and broader shoulders. It showed off the solid build I already knew he had in a way that I hadn't been prepared for. He looked like someone from my past life. Like a man I might encounter at one of my parents' parties.

But it was knowing he wasn't anything like those men that made all the difference.

Grant turned and saw me on my porch, and his face went slack with shock. I recognized that stunned look from the other day in Deja Brew, and if he were closer, I could imagine the kind of heat that I would find in that gaze. The storm of butterflies was back in my stomach, and the terror and sickness of last night washed away as he came down the steps and across our yards to me.

I was glad that I was going with him. Happy that he'd asked me. Desperately sad that I hadn't noticed this man in the way he deserved to be before now.

His eyes didn't stop exploring me, from my toes to my hair to the exposed skin of my collarbone. In an impulsive move, I'd brushed on the lightest shimmer across my shoulders, hoping it would look pretty under the lights at the reception. There weren't a whole lot of occasions to get dressed up in Garnet Bend if you didn't count church, and that wasn't the same.

When I'd stepped out of my room, I'd felt pretty. The way Grant was looking at me? It made me feel beautiful.

"Cori, you look unbelievable."

"Thank you," I said, not fighting the blush that I could

feel rise to my cheeks. "I can say the same thing about you. It's a shame you don't get to wear that more often."

He smiled. "Well, at least once more when Evelyn and Lucas finally get to the altar."

"I'll look forward to seeing it again."

For a moment, we just stood there, taking each other in, until we both laughed. "I guess we should go," I said. "You're in the wedding. We can't be late."

We were going a little early so that Grant could be with the groomsmen. And even though I wasn't in the wedding, Lena had invited me back to the bridal suite so I didn't have to sit in the church alone. Waiting.

Today, I was glad for that more than ever. Alone was the last thing I wanted to be.

"Yeah. Shall we?" Grant turned and offered me his arm, and my stomach did a little flip. I knew that I shouldn't be comparing behavior, because on the most basic and fundamental level, there was absolutely nothing worth comparing between Grant and Joel. But I couldn't help but think about the last time I'd been dragged into going to a big family function.

Not once had my ex offered me his arm or opened a door for me. He'd spent most of the night on his phone and talking with my family—ignoring me.

Grant had already shown me more courtesy before we got into his truck than Joel had that entire night.

Grant walked me around his truck and opened the passenger door. He helped me step up into the cab and then made sure that my skirt—which was slightly too long—didn't get caught. I had a moment where I felt like a heroine in a Jane Austen novel.

He lifted my skirt out of the way, and it slipped up, revealing my shoe and ankle. For the smallest second, he froze, and I never realized a moment like that could be so…charged. Erotic. Now I understood the scandal of revealing mostly innocent skin.

The moment was lost as he left to walk around to the driver's side, and I thought I saw Joel's truck drive slowly by. No, that couldn't be right. I shook off that bad feeling.

"Everything okay?" Grant asked as he climbed in.

I forced myself to relax. "Yeah, everything's great."

With a breathtaking smile, he started the truck and headed toward Grace and Harlan's ranch.

This wedding was a mixture of Grace's practicality and Lena's whimsy. Now that Ruby Round Ranch wasn't a functioning ranch, it was actually the perfect place to hold the wedding and was big enough to have a separate ceremony space and a tent for the reception. The wedding would take place right at sunset, and then we would all party into the night. Or at least that was what Lena told me was going to happen.

"On a scale of one to ten," I said, "how much do you think Lena is freaking out right now?"

Grant laughed, and my stomach did another flip. I hadn't fully noticed the richness of his laugh before and the way it could simply draw you in. "Is there an eleven or twelve on that scale? Because she's either got it completely under control, or she'll be as jumpy as a barn cat."

"Guess we'll find out soon. I'm hoping that she's got everything under control."

"Me too," he said. "But knowing Lena, she's got everything under control and is still freaking out anyway."

I smiled. "You're not wrong."

The silence was easy between us, but I still wanted to tell him before we made it to the ranch and other people were around. "Thank you again, Grant. For last night. And for asking me to the wedding."

He looked over, and I caught the seriousness in his eyes

before they returned to the road. "You're welcome. But neither of those are things that you need to thank me for."

"I wanted to."

A small smile appeared on his lips. "It was and will be my pleasure."

Something about the way he said the word pleasure had delightful little chills running down my spine. I hoped it would be his pleasure in a much more literal way sooner than later, but I shoved the thought from my head. After last night and the possibility that I'd seen Joel snooping around earlier today—

No. I wasn't going to think about it. Today was about my friends getting married. Nothing more. I wasn't going to think about Joel at all and would focus on this simmering tension between Grant and me later. Sometime more appropriate. It wasn't like I was never going to see him when we lived next door to each other.

We pulled into the Ruby Round driveway. It was full of commotion as people unloaded last-minute things from a couple of vans and trucks. But there weren't too many cars yet. Grant put the truck in park, and I reached for the handle of the door. "Wait."

He jumped down from the cab and circled the truck before opening the door for me. I grinned at him. "I am actually capable of opening my own door. In case you didn't know."

Grant's hands landed on my hips, and he helped me down from the cab. He lowered me to the ground slower than he strictly had to. Our bodies brushed together, and I was incredibly aware of his strength. Of the way he could easily overpower me, and the fact that I knew he never would. "I think there's very little you're not capable of, Cori. But just because you *can* do something doesn't mean you need to. Call me old-fashioned for it. But when a woman rides with me, I make sure she's taken care of."

A fiery blush crawled up my cheeks and neck. Of course, he was talking about opening the door. But it was easy to believe that he was talking about something else. And the sparkle in his eyes told me that he was well aware of the double meaning of his words.

He offered me his arm again. "Shall we?"

The house was a cozy bustle of activity, and Lena happened to be passing by. "Cori! Perfect timing. Come with me." She grabbed my hand and yanked me toward the stairs. I looked back at Grant and waved. He just smiled and shook his head. Neither of us expected anything less from Lena.

"I'm glad you're here."

"You know I'm not technically supposed to be, right?"

"Whatever." I heard the eye roll. She ushered me into one of the guest rooms, where Grace was sitting at a table and being made up in the exact makeup I'd had on the other day. Her dress hung against one of the windows, and a nearby table was filled with champagne flutes and cookies. A photographer lurked, taking photos.

Grace spotted me. "Hey, Cori."

"Hi. Thanks for letting me come back."

Grace waved a hand. "You're a part of this too. If we weren't keeping the wedding as small as possible, you would have been in one of the bridesmaid dresses." She glanced at Lena. "It's already bigger than we expected."

"Oh hush," her friend said with a grin. "You know you love it."

Grace smiled.

Lena turned on me. "First, you look fabulous. Holy hell. And second, Grant? That man is *fine* in a tuxedo."

"Don't let Jude hear you say that," I teased.

She snorted. "Odds are he'd agree with me. I don't think there's any sane person who would say that man isn't smoking hot barbecue right now."

"Barbecue?"

"Good enough to eat," Lena clarified.

I burst out into a laugh and sat down. This was good. Nice. I was glad I didn't have to be alone. The bridesmaids' dresses were a cool purple. Lovely for the time of year, and they'd done that thing where everyone had the same color dress, but they each had a style that suited them. It looked great.

"Okay, Cori," Evelyn said, sitting down next to me and handing me a glass of champagne. "Don't kill me."

"I can't think of a single reason that I would have to kill you."

She smirked. "I was running a couple last-minute errands this morning for the wedding, and I drove by your house."

"Okay?"

Sipping her own glass, she drew out the drama. "As I was driving by, Grant came out your front door."

The whole room went silent, and everyone turned to look at me. My whole body went pink, and I took a much-needed sip of my drink. "It's not what it looks like."

"Honey," Lena said. "Did we mention the barbecue? None of us would judge you if it was *exactly* what it looks like."

I laughed. "No, he slept on my couch."

Evelyn looked at me, and she suddenly went serious. "Are you okay?"

"Yeah," I said, smiling too brightly. "Not something to talk about on a happy day like this."

She searched my face and nodded once. But she

reached out and touched my hand. "If you want to talk about it, let me know."

"How did you know?" I lowered my voice.

"Lucas stayed on my couch when I didn't feel safe. It was one of the things that got me to truly trust him. And the Resting Warrior guys, they're always like that. Grant has a perfectly good bed next door. So, if he was sleeping on your couch and not in his bed? There's a reason."

I swallowed. "Maybe later."

"Okay."

"Time for the dress!" Lena called. The photographer clicked away while we all helped lower the dress over Grace's head to avoid wrinkles. It was gorgeous. More delicate and feminine than I thought Grace would choose, but since everything had happened and she'd been with Harlan, she'd unlocked that side of herself more.

The dress was strapless, the skirt a gentle swoop of a ball-gown style. The fabric glimmered. In the sun, it would sparkle like crazy.

Lena teared up and turned to dab her tears. "It's perfect."

"It is," I said. "Time for photos?"

The photographer took one more picture. "Yeah, time for the first look."

Everyone who wasn't Grace filed out of the room and down the stairs. The men had congregated in the living room below. "I just need the groom. Everyone else, please wait outside. We'll call you for photos soon."

I saw Grant walk out, and I followed in the cloud of bridesmaids. Looking back, I saw Grace come out of the room and look down at Harlan. And the way he looked at her…

My heart ached. I wanted that. He was looking at her like she was the most stunning, perfect woman in the world. Like nothing would ever change the way he felt about her.

That look was the dream.

Pictures were a whirlwind. I wasn't in most of them, though Grace made me jump into a couple. The photographer captured every combination of people possible. Groomsmen, bridesmaids, the couple themselves. The Resting Warrior crew. Neither Harlan nor Grace had any family. *This* was their family.

Soon, the sun was setting, and people had filled the area where the ceremony was meant to take place. Since I was friends with both the bride and the groom, it didn't really matter where I sat, but I found a seat near the front on Grace's side and sat.

Lena did an incredible job. The white tent blew gently in the breeze off the mountains, the actual ceremony space decorated with twinkling lights, fabric, and white flowers that made it both subtle and beautiful. Everything was shades of white with that cool purple sprinkled through.

If I ever got married, I needed to hire her. Hell, she might have launched an entirely new business for herself with this wedding.

The music, which had been soft and unobtrusive, changed. There was something nice about this wedding being so simple. It didn't need much. Grace and Harlan had a hell of a story, and they'd waited years for this. They didn't need extra complications.

Lucas walked down the aisle with Evelyn. Jude walked down with Lena, and she was so stiff next to him that I wanted to reach out and smack her. But of course it would make her nervous. The two of them danced around each other like nothing else.

Grant was escorting one of Grace's friends that I didn't

know. As he passed where I sat, he winked at me, and I felt that wink all the way down to my toes. Holy shit.

Music changing again, Harlan turned and looked down the aisle at Grace. There was that look again. That awe and love that were so bright and so deep, it almost hurt to look at. And under Grace's veil, she had tears. Seeing how happy they were brought tears to my own eyes. They deserved this. Finally.

I was listening as the ceremony began, and yet I wasn't. Because suddenly, I felt a sadness in my chest that this wasn't me. It wasn't my wedding. That wasn't a rational thought, but I still felt that ache.

Before everything happened, I'd thought that Joel and I were on a marriage path. Clearly, that would have been awful. A disaster. And I was grateful I'd avoided the hell a marriage like that would have been. Still, I wanted this.

Not the wedding, but…a partner. Someone who looked at me the way Harlan looked at Grace. The marriage. Not having to shoulder everything in life by myself. Someone who would be able to help sort through the stuff with my family and not judge me for it. Someone I could laugh with and cuddle with and look forward to seeing at the end of the day.

I would find someone else.

Grant came to the forefront of my mind and how good he looked. How all the girls said he was practically edible. With him standing up there with the rest of the groomsmen, I didn't disagree.

Down, girl.

No matter what had already happened between us, this was barely a date. After last night, he knew that something had gone down with Joel. Grant probably didn't want to touch me now. Might even be scared of touching me so he didn't hurt me or trigger me.

Then again, Grant Carter didn't strike me as a man who was scared of anything.

As if he knew I was thinking about him, he looked up at me. Our eyes locked, and the air charged between us. I needed to not get caught up in this so fast. I needed to respect his wishes to take things slowly.

But that didn't stop all the many possibilities from blooming in my mind.

Chapter 12

Grant

I wasn't expecting the emotions that hit me during the ceremony. Watching Grace and Harlan make their vows to each other filled me with longing and other things that I had a hard time naming.

Equally emotional was seeing Cori in the audience, tears misting her eyes. Her gaze—her expression—was full of the same longing. And given everything she'd been through in the last week, seeing this must have been harder for her.

I felt her gaze on me at the end of the ceremony, and I looked. Locked eyes with her. If I were a scientist, I would have tested the air surrounding us, because I swore that it changed.

Something passed between us. Something deep and electric that didn't have a name. I had no way to put it into words, but all I knew was that when I was around Cori, I felt better. There was less pain, or I noticed it less. She brought me out of my head. And I intended to enjoy tonight. Thoroughly. No matter how slow we needed to go.

Seeing her standing on her porch… I felt stupid for not expecting how incredible she looked. The dress and the hair. It took all my control not to kiss her right there. The one concession I made was lifting her down from the cab.

If I weren't careful, I wouldn't be able to take it slow. As it was, I already felt like I was hurtling toward her at full speed with no regard for the safety rails.

We were still staring at each other, and the eruption of applause startled me back into the moment. I looked over to find Grace wrapped around Harlan as he dipped her back and kissed her thoroughly. I'd never seen either of them look so happy.

I couldn't help but look back at Cori and notice the way her eyes were shining. Or the way that now she wouldn't meet my eyes.

The bride and groom made their way out of the tent, and the rest of us followed. The transition to the reception was smooth and easy, with the bridal party retreating to the house before we were announced.

Technically, Grace and Harlan were already married, and this was merely a celebration of what they'd done out of desperation and necessity—what should have happened years ago.

"Is everyone ready?" Lena asked. "The MC is ready for us."

She arranged us in a line outside the reception tent and stopped by me and the bridesmaid on my arm. She was nice enough, and pretty, but my thoughts were occupied by someone with turquoise streaks in her hair. "Meredith," Lena said. "When you get to the head table, your seat is on the end, okay? You'll see your place card."

"Okay," Meredith said.

Lena just winked at me before she swept away to be announced with Jude. That was odd…

The party was announced, and we all took our seats at the head table, waiting for the happy couple. The seat next to me was empty, and the small place card read *Cori Jackson* in delicate script.

Jude was seated next to me, but Lena was on his other side. "You did this?"

"You didn't honestly think I'd let you sit without your date, did you?"

Grinning, I inclined my head. "Thanks."

The announcer spoke into the mic. "And finally, without any further waiting, let me introduce to you, Mr. and Mrs. Young!"

They came through the door to the tent with beaming smiles on their faces. On the way to the table, they gave the crowd what they wanted. Harlan dipped her back in another kiss. That was probably going to happen a lot more. Glasses were already clinking in order to get them to do it again.

Lena leaned forward and stared at me. "Well? Go get her."

I scanned the room and found Cori on the far side of it, standing against the wall of the tent. She looked anxious and out of place. Not what I wanted her to be feeling. I was out of my chair and moving to her before I'd fully formed the thought.

She looked relieved when I approached. "I can't find my seat. I think they forgot about me."

"They didn't forget about you," I said. "They put you next to me."

"At the head table?" Cori paled a little. "That can't be right."

"Why not?"

"Because I'm not in the bridal party! I don't match. It will look weird if I'm up there."

I extended my hand. "Lena made it very clear that's where she wants you. And she said there was no way in hell she was going to make me sit without my date."

"She really said that?"

"In so many words."

Her color returned in the form of pink cheeks. "All right." Setting her hand in mine, she let me guide her up to the head table, and I pulled out her chair for her.

"There you are!" Lena said with a smile.

"Lena, are you sure I should be here?"

She made a face. "Yes. Obviously."

"Okay."

In her lap, Cori's hands fidgeted. She was still nervous. "I won't force you to sit here if you don't want to," I said, lowering myself into my own chair. "I'm sure we can find somewhere else."

"No," she said quickly. "No, it's okay. I just feel weird."

"Don't feel weird." Lena leaned forward so she could peek past Jude's massive frame. "There's no reason you should feel weird. We all want you here."

Cori blushed again and looked down. But I spotted her hidden smile. She was happy to be wanted. However, I understood her hesitation. Definitely in our community, but sometimes on the edge of it. She didn't want to overstep. Hopefully, this would help her learn that she never would.

"Can I get you a drink?" I asked quietly.

"White wine would be lovely."

I brushed her bare shoulder with my fingers as I stood and made my way to the bar. One touch shouldn't affect me this much, but it felt like pure electricity. I only looked back once I reached the bar. The sun was underneath the mountains now, the artificial lights of the tent taking over instead of the sun.

Was it my imagination? From here, it looked as if Cori's skin was actually shimmering. As if she glowed from within. It had to be my imagination, and yet I couldn't seem to drag my eyes away from her. The bartender had to tap me on the arm to get my attention.

One drink. That's all I was having tonight. I needed to drive us home later, and I didn't want to be muddled at all. One white wine and one whiskey in hand, I returned to the table.

"Thank you," she said. I was distracted by her lips on the rim of the glass and took a sip of my own drink to concentrate.

"Maybe the wedding isn't the time," I said with a laugh. "But I was wondering about the patient you had. The one where I'm going to go with you."

Cori frowned. "Yeah. It's kind of a mystery that I can't seem to figure out. On the surface, the horse—Sunrise—is fine. There's nothing wrong with her. No injuries, no symptoms of illness or stress. But when I saw her yesterday—" she glanced at me quickly "—before anything else happened, she was struggling to breathe. I need to get her into the clinic for testing, but Mr. Pearson won't let me."

"Did he say why?"

She shook her head. "I called him, and he just wasn't interested. The first time I examined her, he said no too. There's clearly *something* wrong with her, but I need to be able to run more tests than I can in a stable. I gave her a steroid shot, and I hope I can convince him to let me bring her next time I—we—go out there."

"That does seem odd." I wasn't a vet, but I took care of enough horses that it was strange.

"Yeah." She looked at me, passion coming from every

inch of her. "I can't imagine what would possess an owner to ignore what's clearly a sick animal."

I smiled. "You'll figure it out."

"I hope so. I don't like unsolved puzzles. The only things I like less than those are sick animals."

"Well," I said. "If I can help in other ways besides just making sure you're safe while you're there, let me know."

"I will."

We'd never really talked about this before. "Do you have any favorite clients?"

Cori grinned. "Animal or human?"

"Either."

"Hmm." Her body was so much more at ease now. This was her comfort zone. Her work. "Human? Probably Jerry. A rancher who *loves* his animals. I delivered a calf for him a little over a week ago. He trusts me, and he's never fought me on treatment or thought he knew better, like some people."

I fought a smile and failed. "Always a good thing."

"Animal clients, I have a few. Banana is a good one."

"*Banana*?"

She laughed, and I absorbed the sound like a plant soaking up the sun. "Banana is a sassy orange cat. He's hilarious. A ball of energy and mischief. It's always an interesting day in the office when he has an appointment.

"Oh, and Geo. She's a sweet old golden retriever. The kind of dog that will just erase any worries you've ever had. No matter how bad the day has been, even if it's been a great day, Geo makes it better."

I took a small sip of my drink, and it felt like the most natural thing in the world to put my arm over the back of her chair. She noticed, and she didn't move away. If anything, she moved closer. "How come you don't have any pets of your own?"

Cori looked away and finished her glass of wine. "It always seemed self-indulgent, when I could help other animals. I don't need to have my own."

My instincts didn't buy that for a second. "What's the real reason, Cori?"

She huffed out a breath. "Nothing gets by you Resting Warrior guys, does it?"

"No, not really." I grinned. "But it's good, in a way. It means that you don't ever have to worry about lying because we'll already know."

"None of you are human lie detectors, even if you think you are."

"I don't know," I said. "Jude is pretty close."

"What?" From my other side, he looked over. "What about me?"

Lifting my drink in a cheer, I winked. "Just telling Cori that you're as close to a human lie detector as we have at Resting Warrior."

The big man chuckled. "Lie detector, huh? Maybe."

Cori's eyebrows rose into her hairline. "Okay."

"Seriously," I said. "You should try it sometime. Say three things in the same tone of voice, and he'll always be able to tell which one is the lie. He hasn't lost yet. Not from what I've tried."

"Don't scare her, Grant."

"I'm not scared," Cori said quickly. "But maybe I'll try that another time. Right now, I'm going to get myself another glass of wine."

"I can get it."

"That's okay. I want to."

I stood anyway and pulled back her chair.

"Opening doors and helping with chairs? I didn't realize you were such a gentleman."

She turned and walked away before I could answer, and Jude nudged me with an elbow. "Gentleman?"

"Shut up," I said. "I am."

"To a point," he said under his breath.

Jude was one of the only people who knew that my activities in the bedroom weren't always strictly vanilla. Because neither were his. Though it had been years since he'd played. "I will be a gentleman until the moment she asks me not to be," I said. "But we're taking it slow."

"Nothing about the chemistry between you says slow."

Looking over, I intentionally let my gaze drift to Lena and back. "You were saying?"

"It's not the same, and you know it."

I sighed. "Look, Jude. I don't know where this is going with Cori. I like her. You know that—everyone knows that. And I want to explore it as far as we can take it. But neither Cori nor I are the only ones who deserve to be happy. You deserve that, too. So does Lena." I added in a whisper.

"I don't want to hurt her," Jude said.

"Not a chance in hell you'll hurt that woman." Speaking of his lie detector abilities, he could tell that I wasn't lying. "Just think about it," I said. "Because trust me, she is. And so is the entire town."

Cori was crossing the room back to the table, and the first notes of one of my favorite songs came over the speakers. *Perfect.* Another sip of whiskey and I stood, moving and meeting Cori at the front of the table. I took her glass of wine and set it at her place. "Dance with me?"

She froze for a second. Then her face broke into a smile that I could live on more than oxygen, and she took my outstretched hand.

Chapter 13

Cori

My whole body was swarmed with butterflies. I slipped my hand into Grant's, and he swept me out onto the dance floor.

The wine he'd gotten for me was swimming warmly in my veins, plus the sip I'd taken of the second glass. I didn't drink much, and I hadn't really eaten, so I could already feel it. Not yet to where I would call myself drunk, but enough to call myself tipsy.

This was my favorite feeling when it came to alcohol. I loved the feeling of everything unimportant falling away and just being in the moment.

A slow, jazzy number played over the speakers, and as Grant put his hand around my waist, he smiled. "I love this song."

"Is that why you asked me to dance?"

"No," he said. "I was going to ask you either way. But it

would have been a little later in the evening. After the food, at least."

I smiled back. The bad thing about being a little tipsy was that all the things I was feeling about Grant—I couldn't filter them. I couldn't convince myself that they didn't mean anything and that he was just being polite. I couldn't explain away the delicious tension I felt when he smiled directly at me.

Dancing like this, I was allowed to look at him. Even when we were trapped in that tiny shed in the field, my gaze had been hesitant. Now if I wasn't looking at him, anyone who saw us might question, so I looked at him. Drank him in would be a more accurate description.

Dark hair that was nearly black. Nearly because I'd seen it in the sun, and I knew there were shades of red in it, and that it was really the deepest of browns. Green eyes that were pure as a pine tree on fallen snow. My own hazel ones were muddy in comparison. His were…

My tipsy mind wanted to say *perfect*, but that didn't seem descriptive enough. How did you describe someone's eyes when you just wanted to stare into them forever?

Wow, Cori. Calm down. Tipsy brain might be moving too fast.

"What was that?" he asked.

"What do you mean?"

His smile had faded into an intensity that I didn't hate. Not anger or sadness, but something else entirely. Like Grant Carter could see through me.

"I mean that you were looking at me, and then everything in your face changed."

I blinked. "You're very observant."

"I am," he said. "When it comes to you."

My stomach fluttered, and I had to look away. Because

there was no way I could meet his eyes while he was making me blush. That was simply impossible.

He laughed quietly. "I swear it's less creepy than I made it sound."

That made me look back at him. "Creepy wasn't the thing that came to mind."

His eyebrows rose. "Oh?"

"Nope." I bit my lip and shook my head. "I don't want to talk about Joel, but every single thing you do makes me realize how dead that relationship already was, even if I didn't see it. So no, you noticing things about me doesn't make me uncomfortable. Or nervous. It's nice to have someone notice things about me."

The look in his eyes changed. A simmering anger that I knew wasn't directed at me, and at the same time, a longing I didn't know if I was meant to see.

"And I'm also realizing that wine makes me talk. I'm not drunk, I swear."

There was that smile again. "I know that. And I want you to know that I'm not the kind of man who will care if you talk about your past. Expecting you to ignore years of your life isn't okay—both the good and the bad."

I was warm enough and brave enough that I stepped closer in our dance. Grant didn't miss a beat, tightening his arm so he was now holding me closer. He smelled like pine and that crisp, clean air that came with snow. Maybe that was where I'd pulled the image of his eyes.

This man was wilderness that was tamed and bound into a body. I had a feeling there was so much more to Grant that he kept locked under the surface. I wanted to see all of it. All the parts of him that he kept hidden for whatever reason. There was a force inside him, and not just the lethal SEAL training that every one of the Resting Warrior men had had. Something more…a feeling that once he set his mind on something, there wasn't anything in the world that would hold him back.

My stomach dropped at the next thought and then pushed it aside. Because the way he was looking at me, I wondered if the thing he'd set his mind on was *me*. And the idea was tantalizing. I wanted it so much that I was almost afraid of it.

I nearly forgot what he'd said. "Okay. Thank you. But I also don't want to only talk about him. Not ever, really. But I don't think that will be possible for a while."

Grant leaned a fraction closer, eyes darkening. "I can think of ways to distract you."

My mouth opened to ask how, and I let out a small cry of surprise as he dipped me back so I was leaning solely on his strength. I came back up dizzy. "That's very distracting."

His eyes focused on something past my shoulder, and he grinned. "Don't look now," he said. "But there is a move being made."

"What?"

Casually, he spun us so I could see in that direction, and I tried not to stare. Jude was escorting Lena to the dance floor, and everyone in the tent was desperately pretending they were not aware of it, though we all were.

Jude was a giant of a man, and Lena was shorter than I was. They were almost comically mismatched in height, but that didn't matter to them. The care with which he held her was something no one would miss. And she was looking up at him in wonder, the first time today I hadn't seen any stress or worry on her face.

"I hope they admit it," I said.

"Me too."

Next to them, another couple caught my eye. Evelyn and Lucas, dancing slower than the rest. They weren't even bothering to pretend they were really dancing. Evelyn was pressed against his chest, eyes closed. Peaceful. Even from here, I saw the way Lucas held on to her.

I didn't know if there would ever be a time when they wouldn't be aware of how close they'd come to losing each other. Something like that made everything else seem…insignificant.

Evelyn was also wearing a dress that had no sleeves. Her scars were on full display, and she was beautiful. No one that I'd seen had even given her a second glance. Almost everyone in town knew her story now, and though not everyone in Garnet Bend was a person I wanted to spend time with, for the most part, they were kind.

The song ended, and neither of us made a move to separate. "One more song?" Grant asked.

"One more."

Dancing with him was a dream I didn't want to end. An image floated into my mind, of us just that much closer, Grant holding me the way Lucas did Evelyn. *That* was what I wanted. A love so desperate and deep that you would never let go.

The fact that I thought Joel had ever been that person made me feel stupid.

"Wherever you just went," Grant said quietly, "come back."

"I'm never going to be able to get away with anything with you," I said with a grin.

His answering one was playful. "No. You won't. But then again, if you feel with anyone that you have to get away with things, then they're not the person for you."

"Ouch," I said. "Direct hit. You have sunk the battleship."

"Battleship? Really?"

"Come on," I said. "You're a military man. A *Navy*

SEAL. You can't tell me that you've never played Battleship."

He laughed, and it rang out across the dance floor. "No, I think the problem is that I've played too much Battleship."

"So you're saying you could beat me?"

"Definitely."

"I'm not sure about that," I said. "I've played my share. I loved it as a kid, and it was one of the only games I could get my sister to play with me."

The music came to an end, and Grant guided me back toward the head table, where food was being served. "We'll have to test it. A childhood prodigy versus years of that being the only game in our lounges."

"There's no way," I said. "You can't convince me that you guys didn't have access to some kind of shoot 'em up video game that you played when you were bored."

Grant grinned. "Guilty as charged. But that doesn't mean I can't absolutely *crush* you at a children's board game."

"We'll see." I retrieved my glass of wine and took a sip. This was my final drink for the night. I didn't want to get too drunk and too sloppy. I didn't know what was going to happen between Grant and me, but I knew I didn't want alcohol to be a reason that it couldn't.

The food was delicious, and the conversation was easy and hilarious. Especially when the entire head table was involved in an all-out argument—in fun—about which flavor of cake was the best.

Of course, the bride won. Red velvet cake, which Lena had made and was decorated in the same shades of white and lavender. It was beautiful. Harlan and Grace cut a piece, and much to every woman's relief and every man's disappointment, there was no smashing of the cake into the couple's faces.

"Harlan is a smart man," Grant said from where he stood behind me. He was so close that I could feel the heat coming off him.

"Yes, he is. If the bride doesn't want cake smashed in her face, and the groom does it anyway? That's a big red flag."

We were standing in the crowd of people that were clapping and watching the bride and groom eat cake. And suddenly, his hand wrapped around my waist, pulling me back against his body. No one was watching us or judging us, with all eyes on the bride and groom. Grant's breath tickled my ear. "Thank you for coming with me, Cori."

I couldn't *breathe*. It was all I could do not to melt into him entirely. "Thank you for asking me."

"Okay, folks," the MC said over the speakers. "It's time for us to wish the happy couple good night if they want to catch their plane. But don't worry, the party will still be going long after they're getting their happy ending."

Scattered laughter erupted, but we filed out of the tent together, lighting the sparklers Lena had supplied for this. The photographer snapped photos, and we cheered as Grace and Harlan ran through the tunnel of sparks to the truck that was decked out in ribbons and streamers.

"Where's the honeymoon?"

Grant took my sparkler, since it was almost dead, and snuffed it before tossing it into the nearby can. "Europe. Grace always wanted to go, and she was never able to."

"That's nice."

"Where would you go?" he asked. "If you could go anywhere."

Having a wealthy family, I'd gotten to go to plenty of places. Europe and Asia and the beach locations. All on vacation. But those memories included *he who shall not be named*, and I didn't want to go back there. Not now, at least.

"Ireland," I said finally. "My family was never interested in going, but I've always wanted to."

"Why there?" Grant only looked curious, and another comparison popped into my mind, though I didn't want it to.

I'd asked *him* if he wanted to plan a trip to Ireland with me, and he'd made a face and asked what there was to do in a country that was only grass.

"Every picture I see is beautiful," I said. "Feels peaceful. And maybe it's not. But I just…" I shrugged. "I've always wanted to see it, you know? So I could see if what I felt in the pictures is the way it really is."

He nodded. "That makes sense."

"You don't think it's stupid?"

"Why would I think that's stupid?" he asked, frowning.

"I—"

Grant stepped into my space, looking down at me. Inside the tent, the music was playing again, and the sounds of merriment filtered out to us. The moon was bright, and the temperature was dropping. I could see our combined breath, and I knew down in my gut that I would always remember this moment.

"Nothing you could ever want…" he said quietly, then smiled. "Well, nothing outside of maybe murder, would ever make me think you were stupid, Cori. And it makes me angry that anyone—even if it wasn't him—made you feel differently. You are *allowed* to want the things that you want, without having to feel lesser or embarrassed."

I was suddenly very glad that it was dark out here. He hadn't heard what I'd asked Joel for. I knew that for sure. And yet, it felt as if he were speaking about exactly that.

His sentiment echoed what Lena and Evelyn had said

too. That I was in the right, and there was nothing wrong with curiosity. No matter what, I needed to remember that. "Thank you."

"Would you like to go back in?"

Glancing past him to the tent, I saw people dancing and laughing, and it was beautiful. But it was all still catching up with me. Last night, and the overwhelming feelings of tonight. I wanted to be home. Either alone…or with Grant.

"No," I said. "Do you?"

A half smile. "Not really."

"I did leave my jacket, though."

He intercepted me. "I'll grab it."

I watched him weave his way through the dancers and retrieve the light jacket from the back of my chair. He shook hands with Jude, and they shared a few words. Then he came straight for me. Not even a hint of really wanting to stay or talk with other people. Just to me, where he spun me around and helped me into my jacket. "Thanks."

We were quiet as we made our way to his truck. There was a tension in the air. Not a bad one, but I could feel the space between us as if it was a physical thing. A question that was being asked and neither of us knew how we were going to answer yet.

"That was great," I said. "As far as weddings go."

"Definitely been to worse," he said. "You have any stories that are really bad?"

"Oh my God," I said. "*Yes*. So there were these two people my parents knew. Other rich families and their kids. This was basically an arranged marriage. I think they *are* actually happy now, but I don't think that getting married was what they wanted at the time.

"I'm not joking. When they kissed, they banged teeth so hard, the entire church heard."

"No," Grant said.

I laughed. "Oh, yes. I'm not even sure they'd ever kissed before that. But it was awful. I felt so bad for them. What about you?"

"Well…" He rubbed a hand over his face with a laugh. "I was at one of those weddings that I thought were only in movies."

"How so?"

He glanced over at me and grinned. "The officiant asked if anyone wanted to object, and some guy came running in, declaring his love for the bride and that he wanted her back."

"Oh my God."

"Yup." He was laughing through his words now. "And the bride was *not* having it. She had all the groomsmen throw the guy out on his ass. Whole place clapped when he was gone."

I shook my head. "Not that I would ever be in that position, but I don't know what I would have done."

"You would pick who you really wanted," he said with a shrug. "That's what she did."

"Yeah, I guess so."

We were pulling up to our houses now. Grant had helped me into the truck and shut the door. This time, I waited for him to come around, because I knew that he would. But as soon as he did, the air sizzled like a hot frying pan between us.

I wanted to invite him in, but I wasn't sure that he'd say yes after last night. After telling me that he wanted to take it slow.

He helped me down from the truck and placed a hand on the small of my back, guiding me toward my house. "Walking me to the door? What a gentleman."

I cringed internally. The nervousness was apparent in

my voice. We made it all the way to the porch, and I turned to him.

Grant spoke before I could. "When I invited you to the wedding as neighbors so it would be less awkward…" His voice was quiet. "I meant it."

"I know."

In the dim darkness of the porch, he was in silhouette. The rest of his house, our trucks, were drenched in moonlight. He slipped his hands into his pockets. "When I told you that I want to kiss you, I meant that too."

"God, I hope so."

I felt more than saw his smile. "But I need you to know a couple of things."

Breath was shallow in my chest. My entire body was frozen, because I was afraid if I moved, he'd walk away. That was the last thing I wanted.

"Joel has nothing to do with me wanting you. Not any of his actions. I'm not doing this for you to feel better or for pity. I've liked you for a long time, Cori."

The breath that had been shallow was now entirely gone. "You have?"

"Yes." He took a step closer. "And I like you too much for this to be a rebound. If I kiss you, I don't want to stop."

My stomach dropped in that way you felt it on a roller coaster. Pure anticipation.

"The breakup may have just happened," I said. "But I've been realizing how long it was really over. And there's nothing about you that I want to be a rebound. I know we said we'd take it slow, but—"

Grant leaned down and captured my lips with his. Warmth and the barest taste of whiskey. Everything froze, and then it thawed and we were moving toward each other.

I felt his kiss in every part of my body. It was slow and

determined, but not shy. Grant pulled me firmly against him and tilted my head so he could kiss me that much deeper.

One single kiss and I was more turned on than I had been in years. Not only because Grant had become the star of my fantasies, but because the man could *kiss*. More. I needed more.

Breaking away, I looked up at him. "Come inside?"

His smile rested against my temple. "Inside isn't slow."

"No," I said. "It's not."

Unlocking the door, I went inside, and Grant was only a step behind me.

Chapter 14

Cori

As soon as we were inside, every pretense fell away. Grant caught me and pushed me back against the door, claiming my mouth again. Deeper. Harder. Tracing his tongue along my lips until I opened them and we danced together.

We didn't ask any questions about what we should be doing or how fast. Where we should be doing it. Nothing. Grant had me pinned to the door with his body—firmly enough that I knew that I wasn't going anywhere, and gently enough that I knew I could push him away if I needed to.

The comparison to the stable came to mind, and I violently shoved it out of my mind. Tonight was not about *him*. Tonight was about me and this man who seemed to know exactly what I needed without ever having to ask.

He broke away, lips kissing along my jaw. "How much did you have to drink?" A soft laugh. "Just want to make sure I'm not crossing any lines."

"Just the two glasses," I said. "I'm not so drunk that I can't say yes. I am saying *yes.*"

"Thank fuck," he murmured before slanting his mouth over mine again. Just those words sent heat streaking through me. Nothing to do with anyone else. I just didn't think I'd ever been this *wanted.* By anyone.

Until now.

"Your house," he said quietly. "You decide where we do this."

"Oh, so we're doing this?" I said with a grin. "What is it that you have planned?"

"As much or as little as you want, Cori. If you want to make out on your couch like teenagers, I'll make sure it's something you never forget. If you want me to lay you out on your kitchen table and eat you until you're screaming, that's a good option. If you want me to fuck you until you don't know your own name, then we'll do it. Tonight is all about what you want."

I liked the implication that there would be other nights, and that some of those would be about what *he* wanted. The shiver that ran down my spine had nothing to do with temperature. "What if I want all of those things?"

"Then maybe later tonight, we'll need some coffee. But right now, we go upstairs." Leaning down, he brushed his lips over my neck, the barest touch. "Because I don't want our first time to be up against a door."

I ducked under his arm and caught his hand, pulling him up the stairs. "Okay," I said. "But at some point, I'd like to try the door thing. Or a wall. Really. Anything like that would be good."

At the top of the stairs, his arms came around my waist like they had at the wedding, and his words were hot in my ear. "Believe me, Cori, taking you on any and every available surface will not be a hardship."

"Fuck." I let out the curse unintentionally. This Grant, the Grant that was just this side of polite, but telling and showing me exactly what he wanted? I loved this Grant. And it was more than I ever imagined.

He laughed as we walked forward again, and I paused in the door to my bedroom. "Umm…it's not much. And I'm sorry I've got some clothes around. I was getting ready for the wedding."

Grant walked past me into the room and flipped on one of the lamps by the bed so there was a warm glow in the room that didn't break the atmosphere.

Back in front of me, he slipped a hand behind my neck and tilted my head back so that I was looking only at him. "I'm sorry that there was ever any man who walked into a room with you and decided there was anything else worth noticing."

My heart skipped a beat. That was what that was, right? The shock was so sudden and so arresting that I blinked. I hadn't said that was what happened, but it had.

He kissed me again, soft and slow. New warmth unfurled inside me. Grant would never really know the impact of those words on me, or how they were the ones that made that last tiny piece of me know that I was safe with him.

I pushed my hands under his jacket so I could get it off his shoulders, and he pulled away with a devious grin. "No."

"No?"

Grant looked me up and down as if he couldn't decide where to start, and a blush rolled across my whole body. He shook his head. "No, you're going to come before a single article of my clothing comes off."

My mouth popped open. "What?"

Slowly, he spun me so my back was nearly against his

body and shifted my hair over one shoulder. Kissed the back of my neck. "May I undress you?"

I was dizzy with all this. The declaration of pleasure and then asking. It was all…I didn't know. But I knew that I wanted his hands on me with as little between us as possible. "Yes."

This dress had a zipper along one side, and he drew that down with such excruciating slowness that I thought I was going to die if he didn't speed up. All of reality had narrowed to that single point. That zipper that had seemed insignificant just minutes ago.

The single shoulder of my dress slipped down, and the rest of it followed, falling in a puddle around my feet. I went to step out of my heels, and he stopped me again, hands on my arms. "Not yet."

No explanation, no hesitation, just quiet command.

Shit. Everything about this was what I wanted, and I had no way of telling him that he was ticking every box I'd ever dreamed of. And just this small taste was enough to tell me that the fantasies I'd had were spot-on.

I wanted more.

Grant unhooked the strapless bra I'd worn and let it fall. Fingers brushed my hips and up my stomach before he finally touched me. *Really* touched me. Held my breasts in the palms of his hands and teased the nipples. "You are so beautiful."

"You can't even—"

He lifted my chin, and in the heat of his attention, I'd forgotten about the mirror. Right across from us. Reflecting back the image of me nearly naked and Grant casually exploring me with his hands. Even from here, I could see that his eyes were dark. Hungry. A kiss on my shoulder, and the reflection…

Oh my God, I was wet. Aroused. More than I'd ever

been in my life. I wanted everything from him. With him. It was all I could do not to turn around and wrap myself fully into his arms. The only thing that held me back was the curiosity about his plan and what he was about to do.

But I couldn't resist it. I turned around to face him and got caught in his stare. Grant guided me back to the bed and sat me down before kneeling. Something about watching him kneel made my heart tumble into my stomach. "What are you doing?"

He smiled. "Taking your shoes off."

"I—" The words died in my throat. He pinned me with a stare, eyes never leaving mine as he extended one leg and pulled off the shoe.

I had no idea that someone taking off a shoe could do what it did to me. Could be that intense and arousing. And I was also incredibly glad that I'd shaved my legs because the feel of his hands on my skin was incredible.

Grant dragged his eyes over the rest of me. I was nearly naked now, and it didn't feel strange. I felt none of that hesitation or questioning that sometimes came from the first time with someone. It felt natural—so natural that it was nearly terrifying.

"Still with me?" Grant asked.

I nodded.

"Words, please."

"I'm with you."

He rose up on his knees, taking my face in my hands. "I don't ever want to get the signals crossed. Especially not so close to what happened. So, if you need to stop, you tell me."

"Only yes from me right now."

Grant's smile turned wicked. "Then lie back and close your eyes."

I did, my heart pounding, adrenaline rushing through

my blood. With my eyes closed, everything was *more*. Like the rough surface of his fingertips on the tops of my legs, sweeping down to my thighs and pressing them open.

Another blush. This time, I was sure even the parts of me he was looking at turned a deeper shade of pink. There was no chance he wouldn't see how aroused I was, and part of me was embarrassed. Another part of me loved that he did that and now was going to see the results.

Taste the results.

Nothing was left on my body but a lacy thong. I expected him to shift the fabric over my hips and strip me. I didn't expect to feel his tongue through that lace, dragging over it and teasing me with all those sensations at once.

I gasped, my hips moving on their own. "Oh shit."

"If that's the response I get from one taste…" Grant kissed the inside of my thigh, but he was smiling.

There was nothing I could say. Every word had drained out of my head with that brush of his tongue. I had no chance to form words either as he stretched the lace over my clit and licked me again. Harder.

That little bit of texture added just enough friction. Perfect. And I still wanted more. I was going to come too fast, but I wanted all of it.

"Are you particularly attached to these panties?"

"No," I managed to say. "Why?"

He made a humming sound as he sealed his mouth over my clit and dragged it deep. "I was thinking about tearing them off you."

"Oh my God."

"Bad?"

"Hell no. Good. Very good."

Grant chuckled, and I opened my eyes and sat up just

in time to see him fist the lace and pull it apart as if it was made of cotton candy.

Tossing the lace aside, he buried his face between my legs, and I could see his tongue moving over me, flicking and tasting and teasing. It was the hottest thing I'd ever seen. And probably the best thing I'd ever felt.

The slick combination of lips and tongue, suction that pulled at the very center of me, the way Grant's hands pushed my thighs apart so he could feast on me. I couldn't breathe.

When was the last time I'd had this?

Never. That was the answer. I'd never had a man who did this as anything more than a courtesy. A few minutes to say that he'd done it, and that was it.

Grant covered me with his mouth and pushed his tongue deep inside me, taking that intimate pleasure to the next level. I fell back onto the bed, closing my eyes just like he'd told me to, and I collapsed into pleasure.

The orgasm came from nowhere. It was all white light and shock, and then it was more than pleasure, crashing over me in a warm wave. Golden and perfumed and perfect. It drew out my voice so it echoed off the walls, moved my hips so I was begging for more even as I was savoring the sharp edge of that bliss.

So much for being a quiet lover. Maybe I'd just hadn't had a lover that made me want to use my voice.

Grant had done exactly what he said he would do. There was something inexplicably hot about a man still in a full tuxedo with his mouth between your legs.

I watched him slip the jacket off his shoulders and drape it over the chair in the corner. His shoes and socks were next. Every movement methodical and efficient. As opposed to me, wantonly spread across the bed, watching him.

Now I felt more drunk on pleasure and my orgasm than the wine. All the same, it was luxurious and glorious to watch Grant undress. I'd heard Lena and Evelyn talk about seeing the Resting Warrior men shirtless, but I never had. Until now.

Grant's eyes were on me as he unbuttoned the cuffs of his shirt and then the shirt itself. Holy. Shit. The view was worth the wait. Knowing that his body was probably perfect beneath his clothes and seeing that perfect body beneath the clothes were two entirely different things. Muscles that drew my eyes from one place to the next, from his neck down his arms and back to his chest and flat, defined stomach.

His mouth turned up in a half smile at my observation. "Meet your approval?"

Too tongue-tied to actually speak, I nodded quickly.

He turned to put his shirt with the jacket, and I gasped. Grant's whole body stiffened, and I wished I could take it back, but I'd had no idea. His back was covered in scars. Long lines that looked like something had been dragged across it. His lower back too, scarred though I couldn't tell from what.

I climbed off the bed and went to him. His whole body was still tensed. This was something he was nervous about. "Can I touch you?"

"Yes."

The scarred skin was rough under my hands. Well healed. These were old. "What happened?"

Grant turned to me, and suddenly it felt like we were almost too close, his dark eyes locked on mine. There wasn't anger there. Just sadness. "IED. Roadside bomb. Lots of shrapnel. And years of physical therapy."

"I had no idea."

A flicker of a smile. "I try very hard to make sure that no one knows, even on days when the pain is bad."

"You're in pain?"

"Not right now. But there's a piece of shrapnel pushing on the base of my spine. Some days it's bad. Tonight, though…" He leaned down and brushed his mouth over mine. "Tonight is nothing but pleasure."

As he pulled me into the kiss, I decided right then that nothing was as decadent as being skin to skin with him. Grant explored with his hands, and I did the same. Every ridge of muscle and healed scar. I didn't care—I just wanted to feel all of him.

"Mmm," I moaned into his mouth when his hands reached my ass.

He chuckled. "I could get used to hearing that sound."

"Keep touching me like this, and you'll get your wish."

"Oh, I plan to. Maybe all night."

I managed to keep my instinctual shock off my face. Mostly. Or maybe I didn't, because Grant's eyes narrowed, and he searched my face. "Why does that surprise you?"

I blushed pink. "Sex…usually doesn't even take this long."

One eyebrow slowly rose. "I'm not bringing anyone else into this bedroom with us, but later I would like to make it clear how I feel about that."

"I think you're already making it clear," I said, pressing myself harder into his body. He was hard—it was impossible not to feel it through his tuxedo trousers.

"Still with me?" he asked, voice lower. Raw and hungry.

"I'm with you."

When he bent to kiss my shoulder, the touch lit me up like a firework, the sensation racing south to wake up my nerves all over again. Make me wet all over again. "I tried not to think of you," he said quietly, moving his mouth over my collarbone to my neck. "Because you weren't mine. But there were times I couldn't help myself."

A shudder went through me, followed by heat. I probably shouldn't find that as hot as I did, but right now, I didn't care about anything other than the fact that I was in his fantasies. Just like he'd been in mine. "What did you think about?"

"It would take more time to tell you that than I'll be able to hold myself back," he said. "Everything. I thought of everything."

"Like…that?" I inclined my head toward the bed.

"Yes." No joking smile or anything to reduce the intensity of that statement. "I imagined tasting you just as much as I imagined you on your knees. And you underneath me. *Everything*, Cori."

On your knees.

I suddenly wanted that. To give him exactly what he'd just given me. "Like this?" I sank to the floor, and his eyes followed.

Grant didn't protest or tell me that I didn't have to. His eyes merely darkened, and he took all of me in. "Yes. Exactly like that. Stay there."

He turned away, and I was glad. If he hadn't looked away, he would have seen the way that command brought everything in my body to attention. I knew deep down that even if I asked Grant for the same things, he wouldn't react as Joel had. But I still wasn't ready. In case he said no.

There were no more thoughts of that, because Grant was now naked, and I was treated to the sight of one of the most perfect asses in existence. I would never have said that I was an ass woman until exactly that second, but his ass was the kind of ass that could get framed on a wall in black-and-white and be called art.

And that was before he turned around.

Wow.

He laughed. I'd said that out loud without realizing it. "But seriously, wow."

Every inch of him was hard, and from the perfect view I had right now, there were quite a few inches. I'd never been with anyone that big, and I'd definitely never attempted to fit something that large in my mouth.

But I was certainly going to try.

I wrapped my lips around the tip of him, taking him deep and fast, overwhelmed by the rich taste of his skin before he wove his fingers through my hair and gently pulled me back. "Slowly."

He guided me and drew my mouth to the base of his shaft. "Start here."

There was no power in the grip he had on me—not yet, at least. Just the knowledge that the strength was there and dormant was enough to send another rush of need spiraling through me. My nipples hardened into peaks, and I was wet enough to be considered my own river.

I obeyed. Slowly, I kissed the lines on his hips that pointed like arrows to the hard length of him. Dragged my lips up his shaft and flicking out with my tongue before finally reaching the tip again. This time when I sealed my mouth over him, Grant's groan was enough to make me shiver.

That sound was so full of lust and power, I was shifting, pressing my legs together at the same time. Now, his fingers tightened in my hair, and he absolutely controlled the speed I took him. I loved that.

"I imagined this," he said, guiding me deeper. "Watching you wrap your lips around my cock and seeing them stretch around my shaft. Leaving lipstick marks on my skin. Helping you take me as far as you possibly can down your throat."

Grant's words stuck me right in the chest, and the sound I made, muffled by him, only made his fingers tighten.

He pulled me back and helped me stand, but his hand was still in my hair, angling my face gently. "Cori Jackson likes dirty talk," he said with a smile. "Good to know."

"We weren't finished."

Lifting me off my feet as if I weighed nothing, he placed his lips at my ear. "Your mouth is so fucking perfect, but I want to be inside you more."

I could stay like this and be happy just in his arms if I didn't suspect that what was coming would be that much better.

We tumbled onto the bed together, and I laughed. I liked this. The seriousness and the playfulness together. Grant kissed me, stilling me underneath him. How did this feel so natural? So easy? Even with Joel—whom I'd known for *years*—it had felt weird and strange the first few times.

Then again, given who he was, maybe that was just my mind telling me to run the hell away and me steadfastly ignoring it.

"What's your favorite?"

"Favorite what?" I was distracted by the way his hand was tracing over my hip.

Grant dipped his head and covered one nipple with his lips. Teeth grazed my skin, and I arched into him, chills running all the way down my skin. He barely let go of me to speak. "Position."

"Favorite position," I repeated, gasping as he moved to my other breast and swirled his tongue around that taut peak as well. "I'm boring," I managed. "Missionary for me. Or, at least, that's what I'm used to."

"Mmm." Grant lifted his head with a grin. "Believe me, missionary doesn't have to be boring, fast, or without thrill."

That was exactly what it had been with Joel.

Grant drew a line along my collarbone with his lips. "I *love* missionary position." My pulse sped up as he raised his head to look at me. He was over me like a predator—a mountain lion stalking very willing prey. I was in his sights, and I desperately wanted him to catch me. "Want to know why?"

"Yes," I breathed.

"Because I get to watch." He reached between us, stroking his shaft slowly. Intentionally. "I get to look down and see the way your body is taking mine. How we're both slick with pleasure. Then I get to see your face when that pleasure overtakes you completely."

That definitely sounded like the missionary I wanted.

Arousal was a cloud in my mind. So thick and hazy that I felt high. Was that possible? Could you be high on another person like this? I wasn't sure. But if it was possible, then that's what was happening right now.

"Condoms?" he asked.

"Drawer."

It was on in seconds, and then he was looking me in the eyes. "Still with me?"

"Yes. Please."

The first touch of his cock was like an electric shock to my system. Something that I'd been waiting for but didn't *know* that I'd been waiting for. One slow, hard slide into me. Deep and deeper.

Grant was bigger than anyone I'd been with, every inch of me feeling the difference in that friction. The way he filled me then held himself there. "Jesus," he muttered. "You feel fucking incredible."

"Like you imagined?"

"This is not even close to what I imagined, Cori. I'm going to embarrass myself and not last."

I wrapped my arms around his shoulders and my legs around his hips. "I don't care. I just want you."

"You have me."

We moved together, pleasure bursting outward. I wasn't going to last either. Already, my orgasm was gathering. Deepening in that intangible, out-of-reach place where it distilled until it exploded like a firework.

Grant angled his hips, moving in circles until the next thrust made me cry out. Again. Sparks of pleasure and bliss every time he slammed into that spot. "Oh my God."

"That's right," he said in my ear. "You're going to come again for me."

He rolled his hips with his next thrust, the movement grinding down on my clit and making it completely impossible to hold anything back.

"When I'm done with you, you're not going to remember your name. The only name you're going to remember is mine, and the fact that you love being filled up with my cock."

I shuddered at his words. He was choosing them on purpose because he saw what they did to me and the fact that I got wetter when he said them, letting him slam into me even harder.

"Look," he said, the word a low command. "Look at how I'm fucking you."

He lifted his body enough that I could see the way we crashed together over and over again. That was all I needed. A nova of pleasure ruptured, and I let everything go. Threw my head back and let myself make whatever sound came out. Relished the feeling of him still thrusting, driving me deeper into my own pleasure. Savored the feeling of his lips on my skin, tasting me just like he had between my legs.

Falling through whatever I'd imagined this would be like, and so much more.

Grant groaned into my neck, thrusting hard and deep as he came, shuddering, finding my lips with his once more.

Together, we came to stillness and found our way back to the present in pieces.

I was still breathless, still blown away by all of that. I had let myself imagine a lot. But that was so much more than I'd ever dreamed of.

He pulled back to look at me, now a mixture of the kind, steady Grant I knew and this new man who knew how to drive my body *wild*.

"Hi," I said.

Grant chuckled. "Hello." One more soft kiss on the lips, and he pulled away, leaving me and ducking into the bathroom to clean up. I did the same with wipes I kept in the drawer. The only way I could get Joel to stay with me after was to clean up fast.

Stepping back into the room, he was gorgeous in the warm light of the lamp. Completely unbothered and unashamed about being naked. And I was completely unashamed to be looking at him. He was *gorgeous*, and at least for tonight, he was mine.

He leaned down, bracing his hands on the bed so our faces were close. "I'll do whatever you're most comfortable with, Cori. But if you are comfortable, then I'd like to stay."

My lips parted. It hadn't occurred to me that he might leave. I desperately wanted him to stay. Grant must have seen it in my eyes, because he leaned forward and kissed me. "Verbal answer, Cori."

"Please don't go. You don't have to hold me or cuddle anything if you don't want, I just don't want to be alone."

Slowly and deliberately, Grant pulled back the blankets and helped me underneath them. Then he slipped in with me, and all I felt was warmth. He folded himself around my body, molding my back to his chest and almost lazily exploring my skin. I wasn't used to that kind of casual touch, and I loved it.

"The only way that I wouldn't hold you is if you told me not to."

The words hit me in the gut. I didn't answer, because if I did, there would be too much emotion. Too much desperation. So I closed my eyes and savored the feeling of being held before I fell asleep.

Chapter 15

Grant

I woke with the sun.

That was a habit I'd never quite shaken from my military days, and now working on a ranch, it was a good habit to have. Right now, it was perfect, because I was able to watch Cori sleep.

She was so fucking beautiful up close, and the longer I stared, the more details I found that were fascinating. Her face had freckles. Light ones, but they were there. You couldn't see them until you were up close. She had long eyelashes that caught the morning light.

There was a tattoo on the center of her spine, a delicate moon in a twisting, nearly Celtic style. It was at once stark and beautiful, and not at all what I would have expected. Then again, there was almost nothing about Cori that was truly expected.

Her breath was slow and even. She still relaxed into me effortlessly, and I didn't think there was any sign of trust greater than the fact that she let me into her home, her bed, and her body, after what had happened with that asshole.

It was everything I'd ever thought about and more. She *bloomed* under me. Responded to the shade of dominance I'd shown her. Made me want to wake her up with a kiss and start last night all over again.

As much as I wanted to do that, I shouldn't.

I couldn't believe I'd actually done that last night. Not a chance in hell that I regretted it, but this was probably too fast. I didn't want to mess this up, and we both knew that. So I wouldn't wake her up and give her the leisurely, thorough morning fuck that I was dying to.

That would have to come later.

Slowly and quietly, I slipped from the bed, making sure that Cori was still fully ensconced in the blankets and that I didn't wake her. I needed a shower and a change of clothes that wasn't my tuxedo, and I would be back.

I grabbed the spare key by the door to lock it behind me. The chance that something would happen in the twenty minutes it would take for me to shower and change was incredibly slim, but I wasn't going to take any chances. Not with her.

It didn't take long for me to shower and dress in clothes for the ranch. The wedding last night had not been a weekend, something insisted on by Grace in an attempt to keep the wedding smaller—not that it had worked in the slightest. But all of us now had to return to work.

Cori would have patients to get to, and I had my own work to do at the ranch. I felt a little twinge in my back today, probably from our very…vigorous activities last night. If that was the price to pay, then I would pay it gladly. And do it all over again.

Grabbing everything I needed, I headed back across

the yard to her house. Based on the silence inside, Cori was still sleeping. Good. She deserved it.

Just like I thought, the kitchen in the morning light was bright, cheery, and was basically an adrenaline injection straight into my veins. I felt more awake just by standing in the room. But nothing would replace coffee.

Searching the kitchen for mugs, I pulled out two and started the coffee in the coffeemaker. When she woke, Cori needed to tell me how she took her coffee. If I were going to guess, I would say a lot of cream and a little bit of sugar, but I wasn't going to presume. Especially when I was in her space.

I heard the soft sound of her footsteps on the stairs. She appeared in shorts and a T-shirt, bleary eyes and messy hair. She looked adorable and sleepy. Not to mention that I was distracted by what was under her shirt.

"Good morning."

She blushed a beautiful shade of pink. "Good morning."

"Sleep okay?"

"Yeah." She pressed her lips together, and her cheeks turned a deeper pink. Adorably embarrassed, though there was nothing I could think of to be embarrassed about. "Best sleep in a long time, actually."

I reached a hand toward her, and she came over to me like it was subconscious. The very male, instinctual part of me loved that it was her natural reaction to drift in my direction. Like I made her feel safe.

As soon as she was within arm's reach, I pulled her to me. Not even an hour away from her and I'd missed the feeling of her curves, and more, the way she fit against me. Comfortable. Natural. Tilting her face up to mine, I brushed my mouth across hers and savored her tiny gasp.

"I thought you were gone," she whispered.

"I went home to take a shower. And to grab non-wedding clothes."

This time, she kissed me. She was still nervous. The way her fingers held tight to my arms told me that. But I liked that her confidence was growing enough that she actually would kiss me.

"You still with me?" I asked her quietly.

"Yes. Absolutely."

I smiled. "No regrets, even though that was kind of throwing slow out the window?"

"Sometimes slow is overrated. No regrets."

"In that case," I said. "How do you take your coffee? I was already making it when I realized that's something I don't know about you."

"You don't have to do that." I noticed her hands twist together, fidgeting. "I can."

I laughed lightly. "I know you can. Because you're an incredibly intelligent and capable woman. But I'd still like to make it for you."

She was looking at me like she was waiting for it to be a joke. It wasn't. Leaning against the counter as I was, I tightened my hands on the edge, squeezing out the anger I was feeling toward her ex. Other than two nights ago, I hadn't seen any abuse. But abuse was more than just physical, and it was an easy slope to slide down.

How had he really treated her if the idea of me making coffee for her was truly that groundbreaking?

"Or," I said, "should I take a guess and see how close I get?"

That snapped her out of the stare, and she smiled. "Think you have me pinned that well after one night? I don't know, Grant. A woman's coffee order is the key to her soul."

"Then I better not get it wrong. Sit."

She sat, but not before I noticed more fidgeting. She was used to being the one who did things. That was fine. Doing things was great in an equal partnership. But she didn't need to be the *only* one who did things.

In her fridge, I found creamer—a large bottle—and I spotted a small jar of sugar right near the coffeemaker. So far, my suspicions about how much of each she liked seemed right on.

I turned so she couldn't see what I was doing, pouring the coffee and judging the color by how much cream. Then one spoon of sugar. "You should close your eyes," I told her. "So you can't guess how close I am just by looking at it."

"Okay," she said. "But if you poisoned it and this is your way of getting me to drink it, I will haunt your ass to kingdom come."

"If I'd planned on killing you—which is the furthest thing from my mind—I like to think I'd be more creative than poison in your coffee."

Eyes closed, she fought a smile and lost. "This is a weird conversation."

"You started it."

I set the cup down in front of her and took her hands. She jumped a little at my unexpected touch but relaxed immediately as I put her hands around the mug.

Watching her lips too closely had me reconsidering the option of taking her to bed this morning. And the sound she made when she tasted the coffee had me hardening in my pants. Cori's eyes flew open. "Grant, holy *shit*."

"I got it right?"

"Yeah, but it's not like I make it. Somehow, it's better."

I smirked. "Anything that someone else makes for you tastes better. Just a fact."

She took another sip. "Well, don't let Lena know that

you can make drinks like this. She'll drag you into Deja Brew and never let you leave."

"As long as she feeds me cookies," I said with a wink before putting together my own coffee.

Cori drank her coffee in silence for a moment, looking out one of the windows that faced the edge of town and the fields that rolled away from it.

I wanted to know what she was thinking about. And I really wanted to ask her the truth about what happened with Joel. Both the other night, and during the breakup. But I also didn't want to ruin this morning. Because this felt amazing.

"So," I said. "No regrets. But I still don't want to rush things with you, Cori. Last night wasn't a one-time thing. Not for me."

When she looked at me, I was struck by heat. "I said last night that my relationship with Joel had been dead for a long time, and I meant that. If you want to take things slowly, that's fine. I don't want to make you uncomfortable or do anything that would make this fall apart. But after last night—" a sip of coffee as she blushed "—I don't want to go back to a version of slow that doesn't include that."

"Agreed."

"Normally, when something ends, you have to grieve that thing. Fill the void somehow. That's how rebounds happen. I'm not grieving, Grant. I'm just relieved that it's over. You're not a rebound." She stood and came over to me, stopping just short of making our bodies touch. "So if that makes you reconsider your version of speed, I'm all for it."

"It took everything in me not to roll you over this morning and wake you up with my tongue. Now I wish that I had."

She swallowed. "Wow."

"Too much?" I grinned.

"Nope." Cori retreated and downed what was left of the coffee. But I saw that she was fighting the instinct to tell me to do that right now. "Nothing about last night was too much."

I crossed the space and pulled her against me, pinning her back to my chest. The clothes she wore were thin enough that I could feel every curve of her. "So when I whispered dirty things in your ear, that wasn't overwhelming?"

"It was. In a good way."

"Mmm." I bent my head so I could kiss the place where her neck met her shoulder. "So when I tell you that if both of us didn't have to go to work, I'd do what I said last night, lay you out on this table and feast on you for breakfast?"

The only response was the tightening of her fingers on my arms where she'd grabbed them and the shake of her breath that told me she was unsteady.

I slid my hand down her stomach low on her T-shirt, not crossing any lines but indicating exactly where I wanted to go.

"I'm going over my schedule in my head and wondering if I can cancel any appointments."

"Maybe slow is the wrong word." I gently turned her around and loosened my hold. "Deliberate. I want to be deliberate with you. Because I don't think I can go back either."

Who was I kidding? There was no chance I was going to be able to resist this woman in my bed. In her bed. Wherever she'd let me have her. After wanting her for so long and resisting, being able to touch her was like a dream.

"Thank God," she said with a smile.

I couldn't stop my own. "I need to get to the ranch, and I imagine you have to get to the clinic. But before I go —" I kissed her. Not the gentle good morning kiss that we'd shared. This was what I wanted her to be thinking about for the rest of the day.

Coaxing her lips open, I tangled my tongue with hers. I held her until she melted against my body, becoming even more of a delicious fucking temptation.

"Call me later," I said quietly. "And we'll do something deliberate."

Cori bit her bottom lip. "Okay."

It took a lot of effort to let her go and step back, and even more to make myself walk out the door. But I did, feeling her eyes on me until the front door closed behind me.

Chapter 16

Cori

The cold air felt amazing on my face, and the afternoon light seemed to glitter through the trees as I drove. Everything felt beautiful. And it had for the past few days.

I couldn't lie. I'd been floating on a cloud since the wedding, and everyone could tell. The owners of my patients commented on how happy I seemed. When I went to see Lena at the coffee shop, she and Evelyn could tell too. They tried desperately to pry details about Grant out of me, but I resisted.

It didn't matter, though. I couldn't keep the smile off my face, and that told them enough about what had happened between us.

The one person I hadn't actually seen or had to face again was Grant. I did call him, but a new horse at the ranch threw a wrench into any plans. That was fine. Good. Because already, I was completely wrapped up in him. I wanted to see him and have a repeat of the night of the wedding.

No matter how sure I was, I wondered if Grant was right about going slow. Or *deliberate*. Which was a far sexier word and reminded me of how deliberate he'd been with me.

I needed to not think about him like that while I was just out and about, because now I was warm enough to sweat. But I liked Grant. More than liked him. It was as if now that I'd *seen* him, I realized I'd been watching him all along.

Right now, I was driving back from Jerry's, checking on the calf I'd delivered. Both mom and baby were doing great. And I was close enough to the Pearson ranch that I wanted to check on Sunrise, but it was too far to go get Grant for him to come with me.

There were no vehicles in front of the ranch house. I could be in and out fast. Plus, this could be a good reason to call Grant.

I pressed his number and put it on speaker as I turned down the lane. "Hello?"

"Hi."

"Everything all right?" The alertness in his voice made me feel better. Constantly aware. Constantly making sure that I was okay.

"Yes," I said. "But I wanted to tell you that I'm at the Pearson ranch. I had another visit in this direction, and it's too far to come back to Resting Warrior first. But as far as I can tell, no one is here."

There was silence for a few moments. "Do me a favor and keep your phone close. Call me if you need me, and let me know when you leave. If you see him, just go."

"Yeah. I will. This won't take long."

He wasn't angry at me, but I felt his concern through the phone. Grant wasn't a person who would stop me, but even now when we were barely involved, he wanted to make sure that I was safe.

"Talk to you soon?"

"Count on it," he said before I ended the call.

My heart beat a little faster as I parked my truck closer to the stable. They weren't here, but Joel hadn't been here when I'd arrived last time either.

I grabbed my medical bag and did my best not to sprint through the stable. It seemed like *no one* was here, which was also strange. The stable felt like a ghost town. I wished that I wasn't scared, but now that I was here, I was. This was a bad idea, but I was already too far to turn back.

Sunrise was in her stall, once again lying down. Barely breathing. "Shit." I whispered the word. This horse was about to die. I'd taken blood samples from Jerry's cows, and I didn't have any more vials. Damn it.

I didn't see any injuries, but Sunrise was clearly in distress. She whinnied when I touched her side, breathing labored. The air in the stall smelled vaguely spicy. What was that?

Could she be poisoned?

Fuck. I needed to get out of here. Mr. Pearson had already been strange enough about this horse that I didn't want to get caught by him. Or Joel. But I needed to come back and get a blood sample.

I hated walking away from an animal in pain.

As soon as I was in the truck, I sent Grant a text that I was leaving and sped to the clinic. I needed answers. Though I worked with a lot of horses, I wasn't a horse specialist. But I knew people who were.

Why would someone poison their own horse? It was

beyond me. I didn't stop moving until I was fully in my office, my heart still racing. Why did it feel like I was still running from something?

I hadn't had time to fully research what could be wrong with Sunrise, but I did now. Nothing. I found nothing strictly medical indicating something that would just make a horse waste away without any other indicators. So then, that could indicate something not medical.

Sitting down at my computer, I drafted an email, laying out my suspicions and questions to three of my colleagues from vet school who worked with horses. And worked with horses *not* in Montana. There couldn't be any chance this would get back to Joel or his father. Not after he'd so specifically told me to leave the animal alone.

"Cori?"

I almost jumped out of my skin. "Oh my God."

"I'm so sorry," Jenna laughed from the doorway. "Didn't mean to scare you."

Hand on my chest, I caught my breath before looking back at her. Jenna was my vet tech and was my saving grace a lot of the time. "No, you're good. Sorry. Just a little jumpy."

"Okay," she smiled. "Just letting you know that I'm going to head home, okay?"

I looked at the clock. "Oh wow, I didn't even realize it was that late." It was now after five. I'd gotten lost in my research and then completely lost the thread of time.

"Yeah. See you tomorrow?"

"Sure thing." I waved to her. "Have a good night."

She shut the door behind her, and I looked back at the screen. The email was about as clear as I could make it, given the fact that I didn't have a lot of information. It wasn't enough, but at least it was a start.

I sat back in my chair and ran a hand over my face.

The adrenaline from earlier had drained out of me, leaving only exhaustion. But I wanted to know exactly what was going on with Sunrise, and I was fighting the temptation to drive out there right now to take a blood sample. I didn't even care if someone would be home. That horse was suffering, and it made me sick to think about it.

My phone chimed, and I glanced at the screen, hoping for Grant's name. But it wasn't. It was Joel.

I've been thinking about you, Cori. Just want you to know that. I think about you all the time and can't wait to see you again soon.

I dropped the phone on my desk like it burned me. *Shit.* I didn't know if this was run-of-the-mill stalker stuff or a warning that he'd seen me on his father's property today. Either way, I felt like I was going to vomit. Joel was unstable. I don't know why I'd let myself ignore that while we were dating.

My phone chimed again, and I jumped up from my chair, sending it flying back. I wanted to ignore it but forced myself to look.

This time, it was Grant. Thank God.

Can I call you?

I didn't give him the chance, pressing his number for the second time today and listening for his voice. It was smiling through the phone. "I thought I was going to call you."

"I figured I'd save us a step." My voice sounded hoarse.

"Fair enough. Is anything wrong? You sound a little…off."

I didn't want to bring up my ex-boyfriend in every conversation. Especially since there was nothing about that text that was directly threatening. I tried to force myself to be calm and normal. "I'm okay. Just a little stressed. What's up?"

"That's perfect, then. I was wondering if you wanted to come over tonight. I'd like to cook you a stress-reducing dinner."

I froze for a second. "You want to cook for me?"

"Yes. I do."

In my mind, I flashed back to one of the community nights at Resting Warrior when I'd teased him about cooking. He'd claimed that he was an excellent cook. Might as well find out now.

"I'd love that," I said. "Thank you."

"Are you still at the clinic?"

I nodded, even though he couldn't see me. "I am. But I'm just finishing up. I can be there soon. Do you need me to bring anything?"

"No, just you."

Warmth and calm spread through me. Grant was steady. Grant was safety, even though I wasn't in danger anymore. As I looked at the sent email, in addition to that text from Joel, the situation *felt* dangerous, and I wasn't sure why. "Then I'll be there soon."

"I can't wait."

I believed him.

At the very least, this was going to be a good part of the day. A new kind of nerves swam in my gut. The *good* kind of nerves. I locked the clinic and ran to my truck, giggling like a schoolgirl.

But halfway home, the bad nerves were back as I caught a glimpse of a truck that looked like Joel's. It turned behind me, staying just far enough back that I couldn't be sure if it was him or not. I gripped the steering wheel until my knuckles were white.

When the truck turned onto another road without ever getting closer, I let out a shaky laugh. Sneaking around on

Joel's property and getting that text from him had me all paranoid.

I still kept a close eye out the rest of the way home.

When I got there without incident, I told myself I was being silly. More importantly, I didn't want to think about Joel; I wanted to think about *Grant*. I wasn't going to let anything steal that from me.

I looked over at his house, tempted to go straight there, but I didn't want to see Grant wearing clothes that smelled like cow. I loved my patients, but even I knew that wasn't sexy.

I rushed inside, jumping in the shower, taking time to shave my legs. There was no telling what might happen tonight. After two days of not seeing him, I was ravenous for more than merely food.

I couldn't remember the last time I'd felt this kind of excitement and butterflies when getting ready for a date.

What did I wear?

It was rare that I got to dress up and feel pretty. The wedding was nice, but I didn't have that many opportunities day-to-day. Might as well.

I pulled out a silky shirt that matched the turquoise in my hair. On a trip down to Missoula, I'd seen it in a store and bought it on a whim, and I'd had never had the chance to wear it. That, a pair of jeans, and brushing my hair had me ready.

Before I left the house, I checked my phone one more time and my email. No creepy texts from Joel, thank God, but also no response yet from my colleagues. I didn't expect them, but I couldn't stop thinking about the situation. What the hell was going on at the Pearson ranch? And why was Mr. Pearson so resistant to saving a sick animal?

Shaking my head to clear it, I locked my door and walked across the yard to Grant's house. All the windows were lit with warm and happy light, spilling out over the grass. Low music, jazz, floated out from the house and immediately put a smile on my face.

What was I waiting for? I sprinted up the stairs and knocked.

Chapter 17

Cori

It was only seconds before Grant opened the door, and I was glad I'd put on nicer clothes.

Dark jeans, button-down shirt, and a day's worth of scruff greeted me with a smile. "Hey."

"Hey."

All that anxiety just melted away.

"Come on in." He held the door open, and I stepped into a waft of fragrance that had my mouth watering.

"It smells amazing."

Grant smiled. "Hope I can prove once and for all that I'm a good cook."

So he remembered that, too. I flushed bright red. A part of me had hoped he'd forgotten. But then again, he seemed to forget almost nothing when it came to me. So far.

"What is it?"

He shrugged. "Just chicken. But it's a chicken that's evolved with a lot of experimentation over time."

"I can't wait."

Grant's house was nearly the opposite of mine. Pure white walls and no clutter. A utilitarian space that definitely spoke of a military background. Dark furniture and masculine textures. It made sense, but at the same time, it didn't fit the image that I had of him. Grant was warm and funny, and the sparse space didn't suit him.

He tracked my gaze. "I should hire you to come over and make this place better. Of the things I'm good at, design isn't one of them."

"I wasn't judging it." Grant raised an eyebrow, and I laughed. "I wasn't. I was just thinking that it doesn't really suit you because you're…warmer than this."

Grant picked up a wineglass and poured white from a bottle. "Like I said, I need you to come fix it up. I don't have the instincts for it."

"I'll think about it and see what I can do." I took the glass of wine, jumping when our fingers brushed.

"Everything okay out at the Pearson place?"

Grant's eyes were sharp, and I sighed. "No, actually. I mean, I'm fine. I didn't see anyone, but that horse is dying. Almost dead. And I have no idea why. I sent an email to some colleagues and hopefully they'll have some insight, but it's strange all around."

I left out the part where I kept thinking I saw Joel and was getting weird texts from him.

"I'm just nervous because Mr. Pearson was so incredibly adamant about leaving the horse alone, but she was barely breathing when I was there this afternoon. Why would you not want to help an animal that's clearly suffering? Aside from the moral stuff, he only owns high-end horses. Racers and thoroughbreds. It's not like this is a farm horse that's expendable to him."

"Yeah." Grant frowned. "You have a suspicion?"

I looked at him and took a sip of wine. "You work with horses. Has any horse you've ever encountered smelled like cinnamon?"

"None that I can recall."

"Me either. Nothing comes up in my research as a symptom. I'd like to think it's nothing, but what if it's poison?"

Grant walked to a small bar in the corner and poured himself a glass of what looked like whiskey. "Poisons aren't my thing. I don't actually think any of the Resting Warrior guys have that as an expertise, but if you need me to reach out to some people and find someone who knows, I can."

"Thanks. I want to see what my colleagues say. If they don't come back with anything, then I'll be taking you up on that. For sure."

"But you're all right?" he asked. "Any more problems with Joel?"

"Yeah. I didn't realize how nervous I would actually be. My heart was pounding the whole time. But it was like a ghost town. I didn't even see any stable hands while I was there." I winced. I needed to tell Grant the rest of what was happening, even if it ended up only being in my own mind. "And I thought I saw Joel following me a couple times, but the truck was gone before I could confirm it was him. It may be only my overactive imagination."

I followed Grant into the kitchen, where he stirred the chicken and vegetables on the stove. He looked pensive. "I don't like any of it, and if your gut is telling you stuff is wrong, you shouldn't ignore that. I'm glad that I'll be going with you next time, because this whole thing feels off."

Hearing it confirmed made me shiver. "Yeah. It does."

He turned and stepped closer. "And if you do confirm Joel is following you, you let me know. I'll have a talk with him if it's needed."

I offered him a shaky smile. "Okay."

He smiled, then turned back to the stove top. "This is ready."

I watched him move around the kitchen with utter ease, plating the chicken alongside the vegetables. He was cooking for *me*. I tried not to let my head get too far ahead of itself, because I knew that he would have had to cook for himself anyway, but this was different.

Something about watching him utilize the kitchen made him that much more attractive than he already was to me. That was a dangerous thing. Because at least on the surface, it seemed like Grant Carter was everything I'd ever wanted. Those were the kinds of thoughts that could get me into trouble and end up breaking my heart.

"Here you go." He set the plate in front of me along with silverware, and I inhaled the scent of rich spices. It was practically mouthwatering. Then I tried it, and it was, in fact, mouthwateringly delicious.

I looked up to find him smirking. "Holy shit, Grant."

"Told you."

He had every right to be smug. This was one of the best chicken dishes I'd had in a long time. "You know, I always thought about that night and cringed. I felt like I totally missed the mark on that joke."

"You didn't. But I also wanted you to know that I wasn't just another guy who expected a woman to cook for him." A faint smile appeared. "I guess I was trying to impress you even then."

"I wish I'd been less…oblivious."

"Cori—"

I held up a hand. "I was. It was a 'comfortable' relationship. The number of things that I let slide because it was easier than getting up the courage to actually change something? I should have left him much earlier."

Grant sat back, slowly spinning his glass of whiskey on the table. "I want to ask you, and if you don't want to tell me, that's fine... I just want to make sure that you're okay."

My plate suddenly became very interesting as the sheer embarrassment from the night of the breakup and everything that followed came rushing back up.

"Even before this, Cori, I knew you well enough to know that you're not any of those things that he called you. And I can't imagine what you possibly could have said or asked him for that would get that reaction."

"You and me both," I muttered. "Looking back, I know that his reaction shouldn't have been the thing that was the wake-up call. But it was. I never anticipated that."

He looked at me, eyes flicking over my face, dropping to my lips before coming back to hold my gaze. "I would never judge you."

"I know."

I did know that. Grant was the polar opposite of Joel. And I already trusted him more than I had Joel in our entire relationship. Taking a sip of wine, I focused on the food in front of me and started to talk.

"That day, I got a letter from my family with an ultimatum. My family—" I blushed. "They're incredibly wealthy."

"You can't help where you come from," he said softly.

I cleared my throat. "Right. Well, everyone in my family is a surgeon. Literally everyone. It's practically a dynasty, the way they talk about it in the medical world. I never wanted it. So I became a vet. But that's not good enough for them.

"They're changing the terms of my trust—money I was hoping to use to keep the clinic afloat and maybe expand—so that I only get it if I go back to medical school for surgery."

He sat forward now. "Are things that bad at the clinic? Do you need help?"

A smile broke out on my face. Of course that was where his focus was. Taking care of me. "No, we're okay. But it would be nice to have that cushion, you know? I haven't even really thought about the stuff with my family because I've been avoiding it. I don't want to go back to medical school, and I hate surgery. Human surgery, at least. And I don't want to leave Garnet Bend for that long."

"So, don't."

"It feels that simple," I said. "But it's my family, so it's not. And I can't ignore the kind of good that money would do if I had it. Hiring a second vet, another technician. Everything about the practice would be better and more effective.

"Joel said I should suck it up and do it. Mostly because he hates my house and wanted me to move. We fought about it."

"I'm sorry," he said.

I shrugged. "It is what it is. But that day, I was just…so overwhelmed. With work, with what they wanted, all their expectations, every single thing. The only thing I could think about was that I wanted to let go and not think for a while. Not make any decisions and just *be*."

Daring to meet Grant's eyes, I saw that his whole being was focused on me like a laser. Every movement and every breath was something that he noted. This was the part where I was supposed to tell him. Just open my mouth and blurt it out. I didn't.

Instead, I ducked my head and finished the last few bites of my meal.

Grant waited, still focused on me. He wasn't going to prompt me or beg me. This was my choice. Curling up in the chair, I wrapped myself entirely around my glass of wine. "So with that in mind, along with some…thoughts I'd been having, I asked if Joel would maybe like to try some new stuff in the bedroom."

A quick peek at Grant's face showed that both of his eyebrows had risen into his hairline. Shock, but not judgment. Not yet, anyway.

"And you saw how he reacted. I didn't know that kind of request would do that, and I didn't think it was that big of a deal. Thankfully, Lena and Evelyn agreed with me that it wasn't. But you caught the tail end of the tantrum. Thank you, by the way."

He simply nodded, and I pushed forward.

"Then a couple days ago, Joel found me in the stable. He assumed that we would still go to the wedding together—this was after you asked me, and even if you hadn't, I wouldn't have gone with him. That wasn't the answer he was expecting, so he cornered me up against the ropes in the stable." I shuddered. "Claiming he'd come around to the idea of trying new things and being spontaneous."

I saw Grant's hand tighten on his glass, and his body was taut like a bowstring ready to snap.

"I got lucky. A stable hand walked in, and Joel made it look like I'd fallen down and had gotten tangled. Told me I'd better not do anything adventurous with anyone but him." I swallowed hard. "And then, of course, him texting me with vaguely stalkerish messages and me thinking I see him following me is not helping the situation."

Grant's eyes glittered like ice. "Would you be opposed

to my fist having a conversation with his face the next time I see him?"

I let out a breathy laugh. "I would definitely not be opposed to that. But it would only make everything worse for both of us. Joel's family is as rich as mine and with more reach. He gets what he wants. It's better if I just lie low until this blows over and he's not focused on me."

Grant pursed his lips. "Certainly you have a better grip on the situation than I do, but your ex sounds a little unstable."

I took another sip of my wine. "He is. It's obvious now, and honestly, I knew it before, but I ignored it." How many times had I deliberately not spoken my mind to him because I hadn't wanted him to lose his temper? People should be able to disagree without anyone throwing a tantrum. "There were rumors when we were in high school and college that his family paid off people Joel got violent with. I didn't want to believe it—he was never physically violent with me. Until what happened in the barn."

"It seems like his family is enabling him. Hiding the problem instead of helping find a solution. He could be bipolar with violent tendencies. That sort of thing can escalate."

And I'd been the one to stick my head in the sand and date him. I felt like an idiot.

Silence stretched out between us, and that horrible self-conscious embarrassment took hold of me again. "Anyway. That's what happened."

I stood and drained the last of my wine before grabbing our plates and taking them to the sink. There was no dishwasher. Hot water and soap were the things I focused on. Wash the dishes and get them clean. He'd cooked. It was the very least that I could do.

Hands lightly on my hips made me freeze. "Cori."

Slowly, I continued to wash the plates and forks. "Yeah."

"Why are you hiding from me?" His voice was soft.

It was easier to tell him the truth when he couldn't see my face. "Because I'm embarrassed."

Grant's hands came around me and turned off the water, gently lifting my hands from the dishes. "I can wash my dishes."

"You cooked—"

"And I will clean in the morning. I wanted to cook for you, not make you do the work."

He turned me so my back was against the counter and dried my wet hands with a dish towel.

"Why are you embarrassed?"

I knew why. Because even though I knew that it wasn't, and that everyone agreed with me about being in the right, there was still a part of me that felt Joel's reaction was valid. That these fantasies I had made me devious and dirty in some way. "I just am."

Grant's touch was light as a feather as he brushed his fingers down my arms. "You said you'd been wanting to try other things in bed. This was something you've thought about for a while?"

"Yeah." My throat was dry, and I tried to clear it. "Particularly being tied up. I don't even know if I'll like it. So it doesn't really matter."

One finger tilted my chin up so that I couldn't avoid looking into Grant's eyes. "Do you really believe that?"

My stomach fluttered. I didn't want to lie to him. He would be able to tell. I wrapped my arms around myself. "No."

"No matter what you asked him for, nothing would warrant the reaction that I saw. *Nothing*. Not liking or enjoying something is fine. Verbally attacking the person you're dating so she feels like she has to protect herself the way I saw you do? That's never okay. And then using it as ammunition to try to *physically* attack them? I'm trying to keep my caveman instincts in check when I think about that."

"Caveman instincts?"

"I want to beat the hell out of him. Track him down right this second and make sure he knows that he's never allowed to touch you again unless you explicitly ask him to. But I'm not going to do that because it's not what you need, and you're the only thing that matters here."

My heart skipped a beat. "Thank you."

"I have a question," he said. "And I don't want you to be embarrassed by it."

I bit my lip. "That sounds impossible, but I'll try."

He searched my face. I didn't know what he was looking for, but he found it. "Would you really like to try some of the things you mentioned to Joel, or was it hypothetical? Like, being tied up. Is that something you'd definitely like to try? Because if so, I'd love to do that with you."

My heart rocketed in my chest. Was he saying what I thought he was saying? My mind went entirely blank, and a veil of arousal descended over my body. Just the possibility had all of me tumbling into overdrive.

It was too good to be true. Any second, he was going to start laughing and tell me that he was kidding. That he would never stoop to that kind of level.

Grant slipped a hand behind my neck, brushing my cheek with his thumb. "Cori? Did I kill you?"

"Maybe."

He grinned. "Tell me what you're thinking."

"I'm thinking I'm dreaming. That's the only way that you just said that."

"What did I say?" His eyes were full of mischief, asking me to repeat it back.

My breath was shaky. "You said that you would tie me up if I wanted it."

"Is that what you want?"

I was so full of everything that I could barely think to get the words out. "Yes. Yes, I want that."

Grant pulled me into his arms, brushing my ear with his lips. "It's nothing to be ashamed of. Any fantasy you want to try, Cori, it would be my privilege to help you explore."

"So you…like the idea?"

One of his hands dropped down my spine, pressing my hips into his, so I felt exactly how hard he was. "That would be an understatement. I like every idea involving you, me, and a lack of clothing. But you tied up with nowhere to go but to let me drown you in pleasure? That's one of the hottest things I've ever heard in my life."

I was on fire. That's what this was. I was literally on fire. The tightness and heat that spoke of pleasure gathered in my gut. This was real, and it was happening, and oh my *God*, this had to be a dream.

One full beat passed, and then his lips were on mine. A possessive kiss that blew every other kiss out of the water. Into the dust. Forget every other kiss. *This* was the one. And given how good Grant was at kissing, that was saying something.

When he pulled back, we were both breathless, and he grinned. "Are you with me?"

I smiled back. "I'm with you."

Chapter 18

Grant

Cori was looking up at me with such trust, flushed and breathless. There was nothing I wanted more than to carry her upstairs and show her that she *could* trust me. And that what she wanted wasn't bad, crazy, or anything else that had been put in her head about it. But there were things we had to do first.

Because I did value her trust.

"You have your phone with you?" I asked.

"Yeah, why?"

I smiled. "I'd like you to call someone. Someone you trust. Maybe Lena or Evelyn. Tell them what you're doing, and that if they don't hear from you in three hours, they should call Jude to come beat my ass, or if they feel inclined, the police."

Cori's eyes went wide. "Why?"

"I'm glad you trust me," I said quietly. "I fucking love that. But you're still putting yourself in an incredibly vulnerable position by letting me tie you up. Alone. In my house. Especially for the first time. It's for your peace of mind."

"But...what about Lena?" she asked, indicating who she would call. "She'll know about you."

I shrugged. "Then she knows. I don't mind. There's nothing wrong or shameful about this. And you said that you already spoke to her about it."

"Yeah." She tugged on her bottom lip with her teeth. "Three hours?"

"I would say all night, but that seems selfish the first time." I smiled and watched her process the idea that this was the first time we would do this and not the only time.

I had every intention of continuing. She'd let me step into this role the other night without any effort, but this would be more intense. No part of me was interested in taking control away from her during day-to-day life. But in the bedroom? I would take whatever control she gave me gladly, with the intent of making the pleasure sharper for both of us.

Cori stepped back and pulled out her phone. She called whom I assumed was Lena and spoke quietly. She was still flushed, probably from embarrassment, but the odds of her telling her friends about this after the fact were high anyway. I'd rather she feel completely safe.

She hung up and looked at me, placing her phone on the table. "What now?"

I took her hand and pulled her into the living room with me. "Now we're going to talk for a minute." I sat on the couch and brought her with me, settling her so she was straddling my lap. The position she would have the most control in for the rest of the night.

"It feels like you've done this before," she said.

"Yes, I have. But not for a very long time." Curling my

fingers under the hem of her shirt, I lifted the fabric, and she helped me take it off. The color looked beautiful with her hair, but I wanted the feel of her skin. And for her to feel some vulnerability here. This wasn't as easy as she thought it would be.

"We need to talk about what's okay and what's over the line. Not everything has to happen now, and I don't want to do something that will make you panic." I dragged my hands up her ribs and felt her breath quicken.

"You can do anything," she said. "I trust you."

I tightened my hands. "Don't ever say that," I said firmly. "I don't even want to think about you doing this with someone else, but in case you do—what does 'anything' really mean? Could I poke you in the eye? Take a knife and slice you open? *Anything* covers more than you want."

She stared at me for a second. "I didn't think about that."

"That's why we're doing this."

Cori's hands fell on my shoulders. "But what if I don't know what I want yet?"

I stroked my hands down her spine this time. "I'll tell you what I'd like to do, and you tell me if anything is off-limits. And before I do that, I want to be clear that telling me no isn't a bad thing. I'm not going to be disappointed or turned off by it. That's how negotiations work. You meet somewhere in the middle."

"Okay," she said softly. Her fingers curled in my shirt. She was nervous. Given what had already happened with Joel, it made sense.

Circling her wrists with my fingers, I held on to them so she'd have the feeling of being lightly restrained in her mind. "Tonight, I would like to restrain you with rope. No handcuffs or anything else this time. I might use your wrists and ankles, maybe your thighs. And blindfold you.

"I intend to take you with my fingers, mouth, and cock, in various combinations, using *your* mouth and your pussy. I'm going to lick, suck, and taste anywhere I want on your body. And because you like it, I'm going to make sure that my words are filthy." She blushed at that. "Anything else, we can talk about another time."

She'd gone tense on my lap. "That's…very specific."

"Yes."

"I don't want to be blindfolded. Not the first time."

I nodded. "Fair enough. No blindfold."

Cori relaxed. It had been a test—one I expected even though I'd already told her I wouldn't be upset. "What kinds of things do you mean when you say next time?"

Smiling, I pulled her in to kiss her. "Getting a little ahead of ourselves."

"I still want to know."

"Sky's the limit," I said. "I could tell you that you weren't allowed to talk. Or not allowed to orgasm without permission." She moved unconsciously when I said that. Interesting. Sliding my hands around, I cupped her ass. "Maybe you'll let me play here."

Cori's eyes were dark and wide. She was aroused, and I fucking loved that. "I can't believe this is happening."

"It's happening," I said. "Unless you tell me to stop. And tonight, just telling me to stop will be enough. No special safe words. Just tell me to stop, and I will."

"Yeah, I highly doubt I'm going to want that."

"You never know," I said. "But I *do* want to know everything about this fantasy you had. Where were you?"

She swallowed, and I could tell she was going back and forth about whether she actually wanted to tell me. "In a bed."

"Tied up?"

She nodded.

"How?"

Blood rushed to her cheeks, and she gripped my shirt again. "My hands were above my head. My legs were…open."

"Good. Thank you for telling me." A breathless moment passed between us. "Is there anything you need before we start?"

She laughed. "It sounds so formal."

"I know." I smirked and shifted her off my lap. "Come with me."

I held her hand all the way up the stairs into my bedroom. It was as plain as the rest of the house—something I was more aware of now that I'd been in hers. But I had a very large bed, and it had convenient posts at the corners, though I hadn't done anything like this since moving to Garnet Bend.

I turned at her slight resistance coming into the room. She was staring at the bed, and I pulled her against me. "There is no such thing as too late to change your mind, you know."

"No," she said quickly. "I want to. I just didn't expect to be nervous. Is that weird?"

"Not at all. Nerves are good. They mean you're paying attention."

"Okay." She smiled, and I kept her close.

I kissed her slowly, enjoying the feeling of her body relaxing in my arms. I didn't think I'd ever get tired of that feeling. It was fucking beautiful.

Moving lower, I pushed her hair off her neck and tasted her skin. Now that we were doing this, I felt like an addict. I couldn't get enough of her.

"I'm going to take this off, okay?"

"Okay." Her voice was nothing but breath as I unhooked her bra and let it drop to the floor.

I stepped back, drinking in every curve. The way her nipples were already hard. A deeper shade of pink than her lips. She was beautiful. Incredible.

"Get undressed," I told her. "I want to show you the rope first."

"You have it up here?"

I smiled, watching as she hooked her fingers into her jeans and shimmied them off. "I do. This isn't ranch rope."

It was in the closet since I hadn't used it in a while, in a box, organized into neat bundles. Some was pretty and colorful, smoother, but more slippery. The rest was natural fiber rope. Made for tying but not made for normal ranching purposes. That was the rope I grabbed.

Cori wanted the *feeling* of being tied up, and this was the most authentic rope for that experience.

I held out the rope to her when I returned. She was naked, and the fact that she was standing there without fear or shyness was amazing. Especially given everything.

She wasn't some wilting flower, but I knew what it took to give up control like this. It wasn't easy, even if it was a fantasy. "See?"

"Wow." She ran her fingers over it. "Very prepared."

I undid one of the bundles of rope and took her wrist, winding the rope around it, and then catching her other one and adding it, pressing the vulnerable insides of her wrists together before tying them off. Tight enough that she wouldn't be able to move her hands, but not so tight that it would harm her.

Cori's breathing sped up. She was looking at her wrists, completely focused on them.

"Cori?"

Her eyes snapped to mine.

"All good?"

There was a sparkle there now. "Yes."

Her tone made me smile. "Good. Sit down for me."

I kept hold of her wrists as she sat on the edge of the bed, and I lifted her to the center. Laid her out underneath me like a fucking goddess. My headboard had rails. I lifted her arms and looped the top around those rails, tying off the rope so that she couldn't move them down.

She immediately pulled on the ropes, struggling. Her fight-or-flight was kicking in. "Cori." Coming to stillness, she looked up at me. Realized that I was on top of her and her hands were tied. I watched her pupils dilate and the softness of arousal slip through her body.

"Holy shit," she whispered.

Leaning down, I kissed her softly. "I like this."

"Do you?" She was squirming underneath me, which was making it very difficult to take my time with her.

"Yes, I fucking do." I dropped my mouth to her skin, taking one nipple between my lips and sucking the already taut peak and feeling it grow harder under my tongue. "I like that you can't stop me from licking you any place I like."

Cori moaned. The sound went straight to my cock, and I was barely thinking straight.

I dragged my mouth down her skin and farther, passing where I knew that she wanted me, and across her hip. Down her leg. She jumped when I grabbed her ankle. The next rope was in reach, and her leg was secured in seconds. Then the other one.

Her breathing sped up again as the idea of being completely at my mercy hit her. Cori didn't struggle this time, instead relaxing into it. "How do you feel, Cori?"

"I feel good." Her voice was dreamy. "Really good."

"Mmm." Coming around the bed, I dragged my

fingers over her leg, all the way up her body, watching goose bumps form and the way that she arched into my touch—as much as she could the way she was tied.

I'd never been as much into kink as some of my friends. But this? I loved this. The ability to have someone in the palm of my hand. Control that pleasure. It was a heady feeling. I was already so hard that it was nearly uncomfortable.

"Look at you," I said quietly. "All spread out for me. Nothing to do but feel whatever I want to do to you."

Cori's eyes were glazed and hazy. There was no fear. Only trust, and a healthy dose of heat.

I stripped off my shirt and pants, letting her watch me do it. No condom. Not yet. But I dropped my hand to my cock, stroking it. Cori's eyes followed my hand, naked desire burning me up.

Sliding between her thighs, I kissed the flat plane of her stomach. "Talk to me."

"I don't know what to say. It feels…weird. Incredible. I —*oh*." Her voice cut off as I slid my tongue directly over her clit. It was a whole-body reaction, hips trying to arch toward my mouth, but that was nearly impossible.

"This pussy is mine right now," I said. "All spread out for me to play with."

The sound she made when I sealed my mouth over her made me blind with pure need. This woman was going to be the end of me. If I wasn't careful, any pretense of slowness or deliberate intention would go out the fucking window. I would be head over heels for her before I realized.

In this moment, with Cori bound in my ropes, in my bed, squirming under my tongue, I failed to see how that could possibly be a bad thing.

"You know what I like about this?" I asked, pulling back far enough that I could crawl up her body.

"What?"

I settled over her, my knees on either side of her chest. "I can taste you if I want, and I can have you taste me."

The tip of my cock rested near her lips, and I didn't have to tell her to open her mouth. It already was. The feeling of sinking into that heat was nearly enough to make me come. The way her eyes closed as I pushed in deeper, completely embracing my control… *Fuck*, she was perfect.

"I love the way your lips look stretched around my cock," I said, feeling her arch under me. Dirty words were easy. Just describing what was happening in detail was enough to add to the image already in someone's head.

Quickly, I leaned forward and swept a finger under the rope on her wrists, checking that it wasn't too tight. But the movement had another purpose, allowing me to sink deeper between her lips. There wasn't any hesitation, even when I hit the back of her mouth. She could take more of me, but I pulled back and let her breathe for a second before plunging back in.

It was the hardest thing I'd ever done to pull away from her lips completely and slide back down so I was lined up with her body.

"I'm going to fuck you," I whispered in her ear. "You won't be able to move an inch until I say you can."

She shuddered, a groan escaping her. But I had to ask. "Are you with me?"

Chapter 19

Cori

Grant was everywhere. His body was over mine, completely overwhelming, even more so because I *couldn't move.*

"Are you with me?"

I processed the words, and at the same time, I couldn't fully hear them. My mind was distracted by the scratch of the rope on my wrists and ankles, the further feeling of being pinned down by his weight, the taste of him still on my tongue, and the fact that he'd just told me that he was going to fuck me and there wasn't anything I could do about it.

Something about hearing that—even knowing that he would stop instantly if I asked him to—opened up my mind so I felt like I was falling through space. Floating. Flying, even though I couldn't move an inch.

This was what I'd wanted. So much better than the fantasy. The safety and comfort of knowing that I wasn't crazy or wrong to want the feeling of belonging to someone else for a while. I didn't have to worry about what to do, because there wasn't anything for me to do but feel and listen.

My whole body shuddered, reacting to the heat and pressure of him even before my mind fully did. I pulled on the ropes, not because I wanted to escape, but because even though it felt strange and wrong, I loved the feeling of knowing that I *couldn't.*

"Cori." Grant's mouth was at my ear. "I need you to talk to me, sweetheart."

I was too far out of my head for words. What did words matter when things felt this good? I searched for them, tried to find my voice, and barely caught it long enough to speak. "I'm good."

He laughed softly, and his mouth brushed across mine. "Glad to hear that. Because you're fucking gorgeous all spread out for me."

Heat rolled through my body—made me wet. The way his words hit me in the gut was impossible. They made everything bigger. More intense.

Grant lifted off me, and I opened my eyes to see him rolling on a condom. He was beautiful. I loved the cut angles of his body and the worn places. The scars. He was just Grant, and I didn't ever want to stop looking at him. But I would definitely let him blindfold me next time.

The idea that he could tease me and I wouldn't know where he was going to touch next made me shiver in the best way possible.

Fingers brushed under the ropes at my ankles. "That tickles," I said, a small laugh bubbling up from the misty perfection that was clouding my mind.

"Have to make sure the ropes aren't hurting you."

"They could never hurt me," I said. "They feel too good for that."

Grant swore before his mouth crashed down on mine. Deep, possessive, and merciless, this kiss was. It wasn't the gentle easing into being bound. This was taking what he needed and wanted, and I loved that. Because I trusted him to give us what we *both* needed.

That dream—the vague image of being tied like this—flashed into my head. Nothing compared to the true reality of this.

I felt him at my entrance, easing in, and I moaned into this kiss. Holy *shit.* It didn't matter that we'd only been together once before. Having Grant inside me felt like coming home. He filled me up that much tighter because I couldn't move to help him or shift positions. Every time I remembered that I couldn't move, a rushing sensation washed over me that was too big to contain. It made me squirm and writhe and wordlessly beg for more of what he was already giving me.

"Fuck," he said under his breath when he slid home. All the way. His lips were against mine as he spoke. "Do you feel that? You're all mine. Tied right where I want you and impaled on my cock."

I couldn't even form a thought in response. Grant pulled back and slammed home again.

I chanted his name like a prayer every time he thrust until the words no longer had any meaning and were just the sounds I was making because of the pleasure flowing through me in waves.

Higher. They carried me higher and higher still until I was crashing over a peak and tumbling down into an orgasm that was sharp and deep, intensified by the fact that I couldn't move. I was shuddering on Grant's cock. Moaning and arching. Nothing I did was a choice. I was my rawest self, stripped away from everything because I didn't have those choices, and it was perfect.

"Hmm," he said with a smile. "I think we can do better than that."

Still inside me, Grant knelt between my thighs and reached for more rope. I felt the strands wrap around my thighs before he slipped out of me and started untying my ankles. "No," I said quietly. Not yet. I didn't want it to be over.

The sensual chuckle shivered over my skin and made everything tighten and tingle. My nipples hardened all over again, and my eyes fluttered closed. I couldn't seem to keep them open.

"I'm not finished with you yet, sweetheart."

Sweetheart. I loved that. So much better than "babe." There was something tender about it. Hell, there was tenderness in every touch and every question that Grant asked. In the way he made sure that I knew and understood everything before crossing any lines.

Emotion bubbled up in my chest, and I took a long breath. I was still floating in that delicious place, but everything was so close to the surface. I didn't want to cry—I wasn't someone who cried during sex—but if I did, they would be good tears right now.

Grant released my ankles and ran his hands over them, rotating them and massaging them briefly before moving. The ropes on my thighs were suddenly tight, and one at a time, he lifted my legs so they were high, open, and wouldn't come down. "*Oh.*"

The bed dipped as he knelt in front of me again, palms skimming my inner thighs before stopping just short of where I wanted him. I wiggled, trying to get closer, and couldn't.

"Much better," Grant said, locking eyes with me. "You're just a feast for me now."

He meant it. His mouth was on me again. *Again.* Grant was so good at this, and every time he rolled his tongue over me and groaned like I was the best thing he'd ever tasted, I flushed hot with arousal. Which just made him lick deeper. I'd never been with anyone who enjoyed this. But Grant was pressing my already-spread thighs even tighter against the ropes so he could absolutely ravish me with lips and teeth and tongue. Well and truly fuck me with his mouth.

I was shaking against the bonds, so close to coming again that I couldn't breathe. I whined when he pulled away, so far past words that it was all I had. "This is where, another time, I would tell you that you didn't have permission to come unless I gave it to you," he said.

I felt the strain of that already. How it would be nearly impossible to obey, even though I would want to do it. How it would make everything that much more focused, examining every touch and lick and kiss to make sure that it wouldn't send me over the edge. I would drown in it, happily.

Grant's mouth sealed over me again, drawing pleasure almost to the peak. "But since we didn't agree to that this time, you can come as much as you want. Whenever you want," he whispered against me. "Like when I suck your swollen little clit. Or lick it." He did. "I think I've figured out exactly where you like it."

He swept his tongue up to one side, where the pleasure always spiraled out of control almost too quickly. That one single spot was where he focused all his attention, thrusting me over the edge before I saw the orgasm coming. I sank into it, falling, shuddering, trusting it. It was slow and rolling, something that felt as if it wasn't going to end.

That was when he rose up and drove himself deep. Pulled open, tied for him, I was so much fuller, so much tighter. I couldn't stop the way I cried out as the next wave of pleasure burst over me like a shooting star. He'd driven me higher so that every movement felt like another orgasm, and I was helpless to do anything but feel them.

Another way that I was bound and tied.

Knowing that just made the next wave more powerful. I threw my head back as far as I could, arching against the ropes and letting everything go.

I was lost to the feeling of him driving into me. Pleasure and the tension of ropes biting into my skin. The sound of him groaning as he sought and found his own pleasure, dropping his mouth to my neck and whispering words that I barely registered but that somewhere my mind knew were dirty. Filthy. Everything I wanted and more.

One final firework burst in my core, seconds before Grant's voice echoed off the walls. He buried himself deep and held there. We both shuddered together, Grant's forehead on mine. My eyes were open now, and still, I liked this feeling of being surrounded and taken. Cared for in the strangest way.

For a single moment, I felt a wave of uncertainty. Was it really okay that I liked this? That we both did? What did that say about me that I was *tied to Grant's bed* and was the happiest I could remember being in a long time?

He smiled. "How do you feel?"

"Yeah." That was the only word I had. "Yeah."

"Hold still." The words were gentle. "While I get you out of these."

I missed the feeling of him when he pulled back. That fullness and the warmth of being covered by his body.

He was out of view for a moment before coming back with a washcloth and cleaning me. Even with him just having been inside me, this felt more intimate. My voice came back for that. "I can do that."

His smile was teasing. "How? You're still tied up."

"I—"

"This is part of it too, Cori. You don't feel it yet, but being tied up is harder on the body than you realize. I'm going to take care of you. That's part of the commitment I make when I agree to do this."

"Oh."

He cleaned me and disappeared again before slowly untying the ropes from around my thighs. Not only that, but stroking and massaging the muscles just like he had for my ankles. He stretched out my legs before straddling my body again to release my wrists. "Careful," he said, gently releasing them but keeping hold of them.

It was all very intentional and precise as he lowered my arms. My shoulders ached. Not in a bad way, but I could feel it.

"Shoulders?" he asked.

"Yeah. It's not bad."

His fingers dug into the muscles there, loosening them before he moved to the side. "One of my favorite parts of rope," he said, helping me to sit up.

Across my thighs, I saw the impressions the rope had left. An imprint that would fade quickly, but he was right. It was *sexy*. The same marks were on my wrists. "Wow."

Slipping a hand behind my neck, he tilted my face up so he could kiss me. Slow and gentle and with no less heat. "Stay here, all right? I'm going to get your phone so you can call Lena, and some water."

"You could have left me tied up a little longer while you did that," I said with a laugh.

"You're right," I could have. "But I won't. I would

never leave someone unattended like that for longer than it took for me to step into the bathroom."

Right. That made sense.

Grant pulled on a pair of black sweatpants, leaving his entire gorgeous chest on display before he went downstairs. Goose bumps were still on my skin. I was cold away from him. Quickly, I pulled down the comforter on the bed and snuggled underneath it. He wouldn't mind, right? My mind was still floaty in a good way, and I felt tired. That was a good thing, too. Tired in the same way you were after you'd done something satisfying.

Satisfying was an understatement.

He laughed when he saw me buried in blankets. "You're one step ahead of me. Here."

The glass of water disappeared faster than I thought it would. "Wow."

"Almost always, you'll be thirstier than you expect."

"You know so much about this."

He smiled and handed me my phone. "I had good teachers. But I haven't had anyone I wanted to do it with in years. Before I even moved here."

Hearing him say that soothed a little friction inside my chest. Even though I had no right to say anything because of Joel. It wouldn't have been a bad thing for Grant to have someone. But now that he was mine, I didn't want to think about that.

Was he mine?

I wanted him to be. Fuck slowness.

He caught the look on my face. "You okay?"

"Yeah."

Lena's number was still there from my earlier call, and Grant got into bed beside me while I listened to it ring. "Hello?" Lena's chirpy voice answered.

"Hi," I said. "I'm not dead."

Grant's soft laughter vibrated through me and had me leaning toward him out of pure instinct.

"I'm glad you're not dead, girl. You're okay?"

"Oh yeah."

"Good," she said. "I better be hearing about every bit of this as soon as possible. Got it?"

I nodded before realizing she couldn't see me. My head was still fuzzy. "Got it."

"Have a good night," she said, laughing as she ended the call.

Grant placed my phone on the nightstand before pulling me close. As good as the sex was—and it was absolutely everything—this almost rivaled it. The utter closeness and care that he was offering like it was just a thing that was expected.

Because in a normal relationship, it was.

"Thank you," I said.

"You're welcome. But you don't need to thank me. I didn't do you a favor. It's not like I didn't *very thoroughly* enjoy myself."

Curling into him and closing my eyes, I let myself relax. "It's still strange."

"Why?"

"Because it shouldn't feel that good. I shouldn't like that."

Gently, Grant shifted us so he was leaning over me. "Again, why?"

I pressed my lips together. "I don't know how to explain it."

"Are you worried about what Joel said?"

"No. I know it's not like that, but it still feels…strange. And maybe wrong to enjoy being tied up like that. What does it say about me?"

Grant let his hands drift across my skin. "What does it

say about me that I like seeing you that way? We enjoy what we enjoy, no matter what other people might think of it. And as long as everybody is on the same page about what's happening, then there's no problem."

That made sense. I was going to have to let that settle in my brain a bit more. "How did you learn about this?"

"I got interested in college," he said with a laugh. "But I didn't have a clue about what I was getting into. There's so much more to that lifestyle than I'm interested in. For example, sex is the only aspect of anyone's life that I like to have control over. Outside of that, I much prefer things to be a level playing field."

"I like that too," I admitted. "That was…just what I wanted. Not having to think about it. Just feeling it."

He leaned down and pressed a kiss to my temple. "If you enjoy something, there's nothing wrong with that. And if you want me to take the lead as far as sex, believe me, I'm more than happy to."

I shivered. It felt dangerous and subversive to say yes to that. But I did want it. Especially knowing without ever having to ask that if I changed my mind, he would be fine with it. "I would like that."

A real kiss then, his mouth covering mine and teasing it open, tangling our tongues together. Showing me exactly the way he could and would take control. I was breathless all over again when he finally released me.

"But to answer your question, I found what I was interested in and found people to teach me. Simple as that."

That tiredness was creeping up on me, threatening to pull me down into sleep. I felt mumbly and soft and warm. "So you'll tie me up every time?"

"Maybe not every time," he said softly. "There are plenty of ways that I can take control and make you feel good without the ropes. But you'll be in my ropes again," he promised.

I wrapped my arms around him and rested my head on his chest, listening to his heart beat. There was still a tiny part of me that was waiting for him to shift me away so that we could sleep next to each other instead of entwined. But he didn't. Grant pulled me closer, and I dozed off to the steady sound of his heart in my ear.

Chapter 20

Cori

My phone chimed and then chimed again.

The morning light was still pale and gray in the room. Barely past dawn. Who the hell was texting me this early, and could I kill them?

I reached for the phone and stared at the screen with blurry eyes. A name I hadn't seen in forever. Kevin Bridges. Frankly, I'd forgotten he even had my number, but he was one of the vets I'd emailed yesterday about Sunrise.

The text was just one sentence.

Check your email.

I did, still sleepy and bleary. His reply was at the top of my inbox.

. . .

Cori,

Good to hear from you, but I'll spare the pleasantries for later. If you suspect even for a second that the horse is being poisoned, you need to get a blood sample. Now.

There have been rumors for years about the Pearsons and the way they treat their horses. And more rumors about other people they might be involved with. You already know the amount of money that's involved with racing. It leaves the way open for fraud.

At this point, I don't want to put anything more in writing. But get a blood sample if you can. Because this could go a lot deeper than the one horse, and you could help a lot of animals. But please, be careful.

-Kevin

Shit.

I'd known that it was bad. Deep down, I'd known. But there was a fraction of my brain that was hoping that I was overreacting and that Sunrise simply had some kind of wasting illness I hadn't encountered before.

It was early enough now that if I went, I could get the sample and get out before anyone ever knew I was there. Grant was behind me, arm draped over my hip. I didn't want to leave. Being warm in bed with him was complete perfection. But this was important.

Slowly, I started to pull my body out from under his arm, and he tightened it around me. "What's going on?"

"I didn't know you were awake."

"Light sleeper," he said. "Something most of us Resting Warrior guys have in common. Are you okay?"

I sighed. "I have to go. Even though I don't want to."

"Come here." He tugged me back toward him, rolling me under his body. In seconds, my wrists were pinned to the bed, the rest of me pinned with his body. Though his hair was tousled with sleep, his eyes were clear and his smirk was enough to bring me all the way awake. "See?" he asked. "I don't need rope to make sure that you can't move."

He kissed me, every bit of me melting and going liquid. I was sleepy, but I wasn't *tired*, and I wanted more of what he'd given me last night. *More.* I wanted to see what else he could do—how far he could take me.

"Mmm." Grant made a sound that was pure lust. "I should eat *you* for breakfast."

"I wish you could," I said. "But I need to go. It's a bit of an emergency."

All playfulness disappeared. "What happened?"

I explained the email. "I need to get that sample. And now is the best time to do it."

Grant still had me pinned under his body, and I felt how hard he was against my stomach. I had no chance to move, and I wanted nothing more than to just stay here and let him have his way with me. But he nodded. "Then I'll go with you."

"You don't have to," I said. "It's early. It will be fine."

"Cori," he said. "I already agreed that I would go with you whenever you needed me to, and at the moment, I don't feel like letting you out of my sight. Especially with something that's dangerous. Now on multiple levels. I am going with you."

Relief flooded me. I wanted him with me. "Thank you."

"You need clothes from home?" he asked.

"Yeah." The shirt and shoes I'd worn last night wouldn't work for going to the ranch. "It won't take long."

He released me after kissing me one more time. "Ten minutes. I'll meet you at my truck."

"Okay." I was still reluctant to move, but I did. My clothes from last night, my phone. The shirt was still on the couch where he'd tossed it last night.

Now that I was away from Grant and the intoxicating feeling of his touch, I was moving faster. I didn't need much. I grabbed my medical bag—we'd need to stop fast at the clinic for what I needed. But I put on clothes that would work, threw my hair into a ponytail, and was out at the truck in eight minutes.

"We need to go to the clinic first," I said.

"Sure." Grant opened the passenger door of the truck and helped me up into it. The way his fingers grazed me, the small extra touches, they weren't lost on me now. My stomach gave a tiny thrill.

Other than that, we were quiet. He reached over and held my hand all the way to the clinic, and he was a solid, silent presence as I gathered what I needed.

"Thank you again," I said as we got back into the truck. "I know it's early."

He laughed and laced our fingers together. "There's almost nothing worse than what I've already done when I was a SEAL. Hell, this is still better than BUD/S training. Waking up early with a beautiful woman in my bed is not a hardship."

My cheeks turned pink. I expected that was exactly what he wanted.

I gave him directions when he needed them, and soon we were pulling near to the ranch itself. "I don't think we should actually take the truck in."

"Agreed." Grant kept driving until we found an

adequate patch of trees to park the truck where it wouldn't easily be seen, but it would also be easy to hop one of the fences.

God, I hoped everyone would still be asleep. I knew the Pearsons had guns, and if they were into some kind of deep shit, knowing what I knew about Joel, I didn't think they would hesitate to use them. At least I had Grant. He knew how to be stealthy. Right?

"You know how to do stealth?"

He grinned. "Yes. Though if we were doing real stealth, we'd need more camouflage and less daylight."

"Right."

Opening my door, he hooked his arm around my waist and swung me to the ground. "I would like you to let me go first."

"You won't know where to go."

"You'll be right there to tell me. But the fact that this is serious enough for us to hide?" He took my face in his hands. "I don't want to take chances with you."

My stomach swooped. No one had ever said anything like that to me before, and I didn't hate it. Even in my own mind, that was an understatement.

We were standing there, wrapped up in each other, and it was so easy to get lost in him. The words bubbled up, and I couldn't hold them back. "Can we stop pretending that either of us wants this to be slow? Deliberate? Whatever the word we're using."

"God, yes." There was fire in his eyes seconds before he backed me against the truck and kissed me. A raw, hungry kiss that was everything both of us needed. I didn't want to hold back with him, and I didn't want him to hold back with me.

"Let's do this," he said, voice ragged. "So we can get through it and I can have you back in my bed."

"Yes. Please."

It took effort for both of us to separate, but there was no chance I was letting go of him. There was a simple, small comfort in holding hands that I hadn't felt in ages. Joel and I had barely gone anywhere together. When we did, he "wasn't the hand-holding type." He thought it made him look weak.

Grant was holding my hand as firmly as I was holding his.

The sun was about to peek over the mountains, but in the cool morning, mist still hovered above the ground. That was an advantage as we walked toward the fence. Right now, I was grateful that ranches—with Resting Warrior being the exception—didn't put a high emphasis on security. At least in terms of fencing.

It was nothing for Grant to hop over it, take my bag, and then help me hop over too. This field was empty, which was good. I knew enough about the layout to know this wasn't used much. The very edge of the property. I thought that I'd walked out here once on one of my visits.

"That way," I said quietly. "Next field should connect to the stable."

"Got it."

The mist let us move more freely. It was getting late enough that ranch and stable hands might be showing up. We would have to be careful. The adrenaline I'd felt last night was coming back to me, and I was a little shaky.

I doubted Joel would be awake at this hour, but I was hoping against hope that we wouldn't run into him. Grant wouldn't hesitate to protect me if Joel tried anything, and I wouldn't be angry about it.

"Are you armed?" I asked softly.

He looked over at me sharply. "Should I be?"

"I don't know." It was the honest answer. "I figured I'd ask."

Grant squeezed my hand. "I'm not carrying, no. But in most situations, I won't need to."

He was so gentle with me that it was easy to forget he was practically a living weapon. All the Resting Warrior guys were. And given what had happened with my friends already, I was glad they had all the training that they did. Even if each of them had demons they wrestled with.

The next fence was as simple as the first, but this field wasn't empty. A couple of horses were being walked at the far end of the field—I could see the silhouettes through the mist.

"Hurry," Grant said, pulling me behind him. We skirted the field, Grant somehow choosing a path that made us nearly silent. "Where now?"

I glanced inside the stable. The place was huge, and we were at the opposite end. "All the way down and to the right."

He looked in every direction before pulling me behind him. My hand was pressed up against his lower back with the way he was keeping me close to his body. His entire aura was bigger now. Every corner, he looked around, not taking a step until he was sure that we weren't going to be seen.

There was one breathless moment when he held us in place, and I heard crunching footsteps come closer and then retreat. My heart was pounding and my breath was shallow, just like the last time. But Grant at my side made me feel better. Safer.

Turning the final corner, Grant released me when he saw there was no one there. But he was still watching. I ran as quietly as I could to Sunrise's stall and pulled it open, freezing.

"What is it?" Grant whispered, coming up beside me.

The stall was completely empty. No horse, no hay, no feed. It was clean, as if a horse hadn't been here in months. "She was here yesterday," I said. "I swear."

He looked around. "And this is the right place? One hundred percent?"

"One hundred percent."

Horror filled me. Last night, she had been so sick. I shouldn't have left. I should have done something. Should have come back with Grant to get the sample right then.

Because she was gone, along with any of the proof I was hoping to find.

Chapter 21

Grant

A week passed, and though it seemed like hyperbole, it was the best week I'd ever had. There wasn't a night that Cori and I didn't spend either in my bed or in hers. Now that we'd both admitted that we didn't want to hold back, and that what we wanted in the bedroom lined up exactly, we couldn't get enough of each other.

It seemed too good to be true, the way we fit with each other. But waking up next to her made me happier than I'd been in a long time. Even when the pain came back in force. Which was why I was currently driving all the way to Bozeman to see a specialist. I hadn't seen the doctor in too long, simply because I could be a stubborn ass about it.

The long drive wasn't comfortable, but it would be worse if I didn't do it now. My pain often cycled, and it would probably escalate tomorrow. That wasn't particularly fun to think about, so I was pushing it aside.

Dr. Peak was former military too. Army Rangers. He

had a good understanding of the work we did at Resting Warrior and knew what it meant to live with the consequences of being a soldier. He told it like it was, but he knew how to soften the blow just enough.

He also got plenty of shit about being named Peak and living in the mountains, but he was a good sport about it.

The medical campus was so familiar, I barely had to look where I was going to find his office. There had been a time when I was here every week, looking for a solution to the pain. That was before I'd decided to just deal with it. Clearly, that wasn't working anymore.

If I was going to have a future with Cori—and every minute I spent with her confirmed that I wanted that—I didn't want it to be marred by pain all the time. So I needed to get my shit together and try. The guys had been practically bursting with *I told you so* energy when they found out I was seeing the doctor and why.

At least when they found out about Cori and that we were now together, the teasing hadn't been completely unbearable. That would probably change as we got more serious. I could just see the ways they would try to embarrass me for having wanted her for so long from a distance and finally sealing the deal.

But they would never know how relieved I was. It was one thing to imagine what it would be like with a person—even so much that you craved it. Actually being with that person, no matter how well you knew them, was different. So far, being with Cori was far better than I'd ever imagined. Just thinking about her put a smile on my face.

That same smile was reflected back at me when I went into the office and saw Edith, Dr. Peak's receptionist. "Mr. Carter. Been a while since we've seen you in here."

"Yeah," I said. "It has. But you'll probably be seeing me a little more often now."

She smiled and stood. "We're having a slow day today, so things are ready. Come on back."

We didn't go to his office, but to the radiology suite. Another place I'd spent a significant amount of time. Getting onto the MRI table wasn't easy today, pain sharpening with that particular movement. The one nice thing was that my head didn't have to be inside the machine, and I didn't have to deal with feeling like I couldn't breathe along with everything else.

Hell, facedown like this? Give me a pillow, and I could take a nap.

The tech handed me the headphones that would keep me sane for the remainder of the scan. "Any music you want?"

"Anything but country," I said. "Please."

He laughed. "You're living in Montana, and you don't like country?"

"I don't mind it, but it's not what I want to have covering up the kinds of sounds the monster behind me makes."

"Fair enough. We have a good rock station I can throw on for you."

"Thanks."

Generic rock came through the headphones, and it helped block out the screeching sounds that still came through the noise-canceling headphones. They were burned in my brain at this point.

I did actually drift off during the procedure, the music cutting off in the headphones the thing that woke me up. The way I jumped tweaked my back, and I grunted against the pain. "Fuck."

"You all right?" the tech asked as I took off the headphones.

"I'll live." I eased myself off the table. "Thanks."

He led me out of the suite and into a very familiar office. "Dr. Peak will be with you in a couple minutes. You can get dressed."

Nothing like being in someone's office in only a hospital gown. I cursed again, stepping back into my pants. It was getting worse. The drive home wasn't going to be fun. But at the very least, I was taking action.

I'd just sat down when the courtesy knock on the door came before he pushed it open. "Nice to see you, Grant," Dr. Peak said. "Been a while this time."

"I know. Believe me, my balls have already been busted about it in case you were wondering."

"Good to know," he chuckled. "But I'll need to do it a little too. Monitoring this is more important than you've made it. I know that you know that, but it needs repeating."

I sighed. "Yeah. It seemed hopeless, and I let it get the better of me. I'd like to try again."

"That's a good thing, because you need to."

Saying nothing was an excellent way to make people fill the silence, so I kept quiet.

"Your scans are…concerning, Grant. The shrapnel is a lot closer to your spine than the last time I saw you. The fact that it's moving that quickly isn't a good thing. If we don't keep monitoring you, and you don't keep going to physical therapy, it could paralyze you."

I swallowed the punch of adrenaline and fear at the idea of being bound to a chair. When my mobility was limited from pain, I already struggled. In a wheelchair? I would go insane.

"There are surgical options, but you know that comes with its own risks."

"Is it a done deal?" I asked.

Dr. Peak folded his hands in front of him. "How do you mean?"

"Is the shrapnel paralyzing me an *if* or a *when*?"

"That's hard to say. Depends on a whole bunch of factors."

Raising an eyebrow, I stared at him. "You don't have to sugarcoat it for me."

"I'm not."

"Then give me your gut feeling. I don't do well with 'it depends.' If you were in my position, would you be throwing your energy into stretching and physical therapy, or would you be looking at the surgery before it's too late?"

He inclined his head. "I would be looking at the surgery. If only because the sooner you do, the easier it is. The closer that shrapnel works itself to your spine, the more risk the surgery carries, and the more likely that you end up paralyzed anyway."

Shit. That was both the answer I expected and the one I least wanted to hear. No one wanted to know that an incredibly dangerous surgery was really the only way they could have a normal life again.

"All right. How do I investigate that?"

"I'll set you up with a referral to a surgeon. She's based out of Arizona, but she comes up north for consultations regularly, so I'll see if she has room for you soon."

That was good. I had some time to wrap my head around it before I spoke to the doctor. "That sounds good."

"Grant, I want you to know that this isn't hopeless. I'm optimistic about your possibilities, and I don't want you to think that I just handed you some kind of life sentence. We'll find a way to fix this for you."

"I appreciate that." I put more enthusiasm into the

words than I actually felt. "Anything else I need to do before I go?"

He smiled. "Promise me that you're going to go back to physical therapy?"

"How did you find out I wasn't?"

"I took one look at you. And even if I hadn't, they followed up with me months ago, wondering where you'd gone since you wouldn't answer their calls. Or mine, after that."

I winced. "Yeah. Well, I promise I will call them."

"That's all I ask." He stood and held out a hand to shake mine. "Whatever happened to turn your mind around on this, keep doing it."

"Not a what," I said. "But a who."

That made him smile wider. "Then she must be one hell of a woman."

That she was. I made sure I had another appointment scheduled in a couple of months before I left the office, though I hoped I would have made contact with the other doctor before then.

As I walked outside, I dove to my right, flattening onto the grass. It took me seconds to realize that I'd reacted to a sound before my conscious mind registered it. A car drove by. Backfire. Fucking shit.

My heart raced, and pain seeped in as the burst of adrenaline wore off. This was the part I hated the most. Dealing with my injuries always brought it all back up. My reactions were off, and I jumped at nearly nothing. I would be lucky if I didn't have nightmares.

"Hey, you okay?" The question came from a man walking into the building.

Of course he would ask that, since I was currently flat on my back, looking at the sky. "Yeah. I'm good. Thank you."

He gave me a look that told me he thought I wasn't telling the truth, but he kept walking. Good. The last thing I wanted right now was anybody looking at me.

Slowly, painfully, I got myself up off the ground and over to my truck. It was a four-hour drive home, and I wasn't looking forward to it with my mind like this. Already, I was seeing flashbacks and images that I'd worked hard to eliminate from my mind.

The sun bright that morning, everyone smiling as we loaded up to head back to base. Our mission was over, and we were going home.

The highway stretched out in front of me, and I tried to focus my mind on the here and now. But the mind was a funny thing when it came to trauma. All my work at Resting Warrior, and my own personal work with it, already knew that. It didn't want to be here in this moment.

I dozed in the back seat of the Hummer, hands still on my gun. This was a safe area. Or safe-ish. We didn't expect any trouble on our drive. Just the locals we'd been interacting with for a few days.

Nothing on the radio helped. Not even the abrasive honky-tonk country station that I found and was so awful that I thought it would knock my memories clear from my head.

One second I was looking through a tinted window at a desert sky, and the next, everything was motion and sound. Metal screeching and my body being hurled like a rag doll through the air. My head slammed into the glass—thank fuck for combat helmets.

We were under attack.

Get out of the car. Get out of the car. Get out of the car.

I managed to free myself from the seat belt and climb up and out of the vehicle that was on its side. Nothing came flying toward my head. No bullets or grenades. Everything was suspiciously quiet.

The rest of the Hummers in our line were fine, SEALs spilling out of them quickly.

"Carter. You okay?"

"I'm fine." I was pointing my gun at the open desert, willing there to be an enemy for me to identify, but there was nothing. "I'm not sure about everyone else."

The only place anyone could be hiding was an outcropping of rock fifty yards away. "I'm checking this," I called.

Guys were behind me on my six, backing me up. Nothing on the ground, nothing on the other side of the road. This could just be a trap left to kill anyone who got close. Or any Americans who got close.

I circled the rocks, and I found nothing. Just empty air.

Finally, my body relaxed. "It's clear," I said. "Nothing."

Walking back toward the tipped cars, Simmons shook his head at me. "Didn't expect that. There's not even that many people who know we're here, and no one was pissed off."

"They don't need a reason to be pissed off at us," I said.

The bomb specialists were closing in on the pieces of the explosive on the side of the road. Only charred remains. Stepping closer, I waited for them to clear it. What the hell had they put in that thing?

I heard the whine of a primer at the same time the shout came through. "Move, move, move!"

I barely had time to turn my back before the wave of heat and pain struck me. There was no way to tell how far I flew, but I knew as I did, something was wrong. My whole back was on fire. Like a creature from hell had raked its claws entirely down my spine. White-hot lava pierced through me, and everything went dark.

My mind settled back into the present, and I realized I was already over halfway home. Memories like that one had a way of doing that. Stealing time that you thought you had.

After that memory, I'd woken up in a military hospital in Germany. My back was torn to hell, and I had shrapnel cozy with my spine. Right then, they didn't know whether I'd ever walk again. Thankfully, the swelling went down, and I managed to get my body to cooperate.

Nothing much had changed. I was still in limbo, not knowing if I'd be able to walk, still trapped by a single moment that had nothing to do with me.

I flinched, the sparkle of sun off the chrome of a passing truck startling me. This wasn't going to work. If I was going to do this, then I needed help. All the way.

Pulling out my phone, I slowly made my way through my numbers until I found Rayne's, the therapist in Garnet Bend that Resting Warrior worked with. I hadn't been to see her in months.

My mind was going to be all over the place for the next few days. I didn't need to make it harder by being stubborn. Taking a breath, I made the call.

Chapter 22

Cori

"I cannot believe it," Lena said. "Seriously. I mean, I am so happy for both of you. But I honestly didn't think it would happen, you know?"

I laughed and took a sip of my coffee. "Why?"

"I don't know. You and Joel just broke up, and Grant has been on the sideline for so long…" She shrugged. "I just didn't think it. And when you called me? *Girl,* I need more details after what you told me about how that dick dumped you. *How was it?*" Her eyes were practically glowing.

I flushed with warmth. Made even warmer because of the cup of coffee I was curled around in Deja Brew. We were waiting for Grant to come pick me up. Because I had another appointment at the Pearson Ranch, and especially after last time, I wasn't going alone.

Not to mention the fact that we couldn't stay away from each other. Every moment that we hadn't been at work, we'd been with each other. Mostly in bed. With me pinned under his body in the most delicious ways.

Grant was everything I wanted and more, taking control when I wanted him to and backing off when we both needed it. I loved sinking into that heat and that place where I didn't have to decide anything. Especially since I still hadn't actually made a decision about the trust. One more thing that was hanging over my head.

"It was…amazing." That was a totally inadequate way to describe it. "Every second that I spend with him, I recognize how awful everything with Joel was. From the sex to how he treated me. I don't miss him. At all. And Grant—" I cut off, unable to stop my smile. "He just makes me really happy."

Lena squealed, jumped up, and danced in a circle before nearly tackling me in a hug. "I am so freaking happy for you! And okay, I want details, but I'm not going to force them from you. I just really need to know, given I have the same…curiosity. Would I like it?"

"Hell yes." My response was immediate. "If you have a person who wants it too? Treats it seriously? I can't imagine that you wouldn't. Because it's awesome."

She smiled. I knew she was thinking about Jude, but I didn't say anything. I had no way of knowing if that was something he was interested in, but for Lena's sake, I hoped he was. If the two of them ever managed to come together in any capacity.

No wonder she hadn't expected Grant and me to move forward.

"That's good," she said. "Good."

"I hope it happens for you." Lena's eyes focused behind me, and my skin tingled. "He's behind me?"

"Mm-hmm."

I turned, and the overwhelming happiness that swept

through me hit me like a wave. It felt like I was radiating sunshine as he came toward me. He was moving stiffly—something you wouldn't notice if you hadn't completely memorized the way he moved. But he was still smiling at me, too.

I hadn't even realized that I'd stood to meet him until he'd reached me and was kissing me hello, not bothered at all by the fact that Lena was right there or that anyone could pass and see us. Our friends knew about us—there was no hiding it—but we hadn't done anything in public.

There was a fraction of a second when I worried what people might think about me suddenly being with someone new. Then Grant slipped his hand behind my neck, moving me so he could kiss me deeper, and any concerns I might have had melted away under his tongue.

Last night, his pain had been growing. And instead of the intense, deep sex we'd been having, it had been soft and slow. Somehow almost deeper. No control or rope, just the two of us getting lost in each other.

"Hello, beautiful," he whispered when he let me go.

I could feel how pink I was, and I didn't care. My fingers were gripping his shirt for dear life. Behind us, there was a sound, and I looked to find Lena staring at us, hands over her mouth to keep in her excitement.

"Hi," I whispered back.

"Ready to go?"

"Almost. Let me put this coffee in a to-go cup."

He released me so I could do just that. "Hey, Lena."

"Grant," she said with a grin. "Good to see you."

"Is this the part where you tell me that if I hurt Cori, you'll come after me?" he asked. I heard the amusement in his voice.

"Oh, I don't need to tell you that," she answered. "Because if you're asking, then clearly you already know."

Grant laughed. "Fair point."

I pushed the lid onto the coffee cup and went back to them. "All ready. I'll see you soon, Lena?"

"You better," she said with a grin.

Honestly, she was probably hoping I'd give her more details. And I was tempted. But I didn't just want to tell people about Grant and me without asking how he felt about that. What we'd done together was too intimate for me to treat it carelessly.

His truck was parked outside, and he opened the door for me. I heard the small sound he made helping me up into the cab. "Are you okay?"

His smile didn't reach his eyes. "My pain is high today."

Oh no. "If you can't go, I can reschedule."

He reached up and brushed his fingers across my cheek. "I'll be fine. Don't worry about me."

"That's the thing," I said. "We're together now. I get to worry about you."

Smiling, Grant leaned up and kissed me again softly. "I'm okay. I promise."

Right now, going to the Pearson Ranch was the last thing on my mind. It took effort to pull back from him and let him shut the door. And I hated that I saw the pain in the way he walked. Even if he said he was okay, it was clear that he was suffering.

But he took my hand across the bench seat when he cranked the truck, and we started the drive. "I know you're okay, but is there anything I can do to help? With the pain?"

"This is helping," he said, squeezing my hand. "Being with you helps."

Pleasant warmth built in my stomach. I scooted closer to him and leaned my head on his shoulder. We hadn't talked much when he came back yesterday. I knew he'd gone to see one of his doctors, but I didn't want to pry either. We were together, but not yet to the place where I could just ask what his doctors said about his injury.

I liked being close to him. It was so comfortable that I nearly fell asleep on the way to the ranch. I opened my eyes as we were pulling in under the metal sign with the Pearson logo.

"Wow," I said.

Grant laughed softly. "You fell asleep."

"Must be someone keeping me up at night. Wonder who that could be."

"I mean, I could stop that."

I sat up. "I didn't say that. I'm awake."

"You're making it very hard not to turn the truck around."

"Do it." I looked over at him. "Believe me, I won't complain."

He pulled the truck to a stop near the stable. "Do what you need to do, and then we'll go home."

"I like the sound of that. Do you want to stay here? For the pain?"

He hesitated. "Are you sure you'll be okay?"

"I can come straight back to you if I'm not," I said, grabbing my bag.

"Longer than twenty minutes, and I'm coming to check. For my own peace of mind."

Leaning over, I kissed him. "I'll be back in nineteen."

It might take longer than that, but there wasn't any reason I couldn't come back to the truck and check in. Both times I'd been in this stable since my encounter with Joel had been tense. I would be ready for a breather.

I wasn't here to see a particular horse; this was just one of the regular checkups where I walked the stable and checked anything I saw that bothered me. Or if a single horse needed attention, I would give it a look. Mr. Pearson hadn't specified anything, but a stable hand waved me down when he saw me inside. He'd been around for a while—I was pretty sure his name was Gene. "Hey, Doc."

"Hi there."

"Mr. Pearson wanted me to show you a horse. Said he'd be out to talk with you when you got here."

I frowned. "Okay." Usually, he called me. Maybe after my insistence at wanting to take Sunrise to the clinic before she disappeared, he didn't want to give me a chance to prepare?

"What's going on?"

"Not sure," Gene admitted. "Just a couple days ago became really lethargic. It's Hazelwood."

A stallion. Large and gray. I'd, of course, looked him over more than a few times in my tenure as the Pearsons' vet on call. But he'd always been a healthy horse. He was still standing, which was a good sign, but he was also on edge, whinnying when I got close.

I smelled that odd, spicy sweetness on his skin. "Hi there," I said quietly. "Not feeling well?"

He tossed his head but still allowed me to stroke his neck. "Thank you, Gene. You can let Mr. Pearson know that I'm here."

"All right."

He disappeared, and I moved quickly. This was the same. I wasn't going to lose another horse because I wasn't prepared. I'd brought more than enough for what I needed.

"Here," I said. "Be good and don't panic, all right?"

In this circumstance, I wasn't above bribing an animal, and I let him eat a sugar cube out of my hand. I had the syringe all ready to go, and I eased the needle into a vein at the juncture of his shoulder and neck. He made a sound, but I spoke to him softly. "It's all right. I promise. I'm trying to help you."

"Cori?" Mr. Pearson's booming voice echoed across the stable.

Shit.

I pulled the rest of the blood into the vial and eased the needle out of Hazelwood in time to cap it and drop it into my bag as he turned the corner. "Over here, Mr. Pearson."

"Ah." His stare was intense. "Good to see you."

"You too," I swallowed. "Gene told me that Hazelwood was having trouble. Just checking him out, but he looks fine. Just a little tired." I pasted on a smile. Right now, I wasn't going to give any hints of my suspicions.

"That's what I thought," he said with a sharp nod. "Figured I'd have you check it out, though."

"Yeah." I closed my bag and stepped out of the stall. "No problems."

He gave no sign that he knew I'd taken the sample. Good.

"Any other horses you have concerns about?"

"I don't think so," he said. "You keep us all in good shape."

Except for Sunrise. "I do try. I'll just finish up my rounds, and I'll be off to my next appointment. Of course you have my number if you have any concerns."

I felt him watching me as I made my way down the row of stalls until I turned the corner. It wasn't until I was out of sight that I realized how fast my heart was beating or the amount of adrenaline that was rushing through me. It was fine. He had no reason to think anything strange.

The rest of my rounds were quick, and I was coming up on that deadline to get back to the truck so that Grant didn't have to be in more pain looking for me.

"Cori."

Joel was behind me.

Oh no. He wouldn't do anything with his father here, right? Would his father care? It didn't matter. Three minutes and Grant would be looking for me. On top of that, I knew what a coward he was now. He thought he was a man, making all these rules and trying to make me bend to his vision of who I should be.

He couldn't be more wrong.

"Joel." I stood in the middle of the aisle, far from either side, so he couldn't corner me against a wall or in one of the stalls.

"What the fuck are you doing here with that piece of shit?"

I looked him up and down. "I don't have any idea what you're talking about. The only piece of shit I see here is you."

His face went red. "Your neighbor. The pissant who tried to threaten me—"

"Who tried to stop you when both of us thought that you were going to hit me? For something as simple as wanting to try something new in bed? Yeah, Joel, can't imagine which one of you that makes the pissant."

One step closer. And another. I hated the fact that my body locked up with fear. But I kept myself calm. I could turn and run if I needed to. No matter how much pain he was in, Grant could and would protect me.

That was the thing, though. Being with Grant made me realize that I could defend myself. Joel had no rights to me.

"You're with him?" he asked. "I heard you went to the wedding together."

I didn't answer. It wasn't any of his business.

Joel scoffed. "Guess I was right about you. Never

thought you were such a whore to go to someone so fast after we broke up, but the truth always comes out."

A laugh bubbled up and out of me. Once it was there, I couldn't stop. It was so ridiculous. How had I ever thought I'd loved this person? The truth did always come out, and the truth was that Joel's soul was ugly.

"Grant is amazing, Joel. And I don't care what you think about it. Because in the short time since you *dumped me*, he's given me more than you did in all the time we were together. I don't miss you, and I certainly don't give a shit what you think about my character after what you've tried to do to me."

He opened his mouth, and I cut him off. "No. You've said and done enough. I don't care how close our families are—if you ever touch me again, I'll have you arrested and I'll sleep like a baby. Do me a favor? Stop talking to me. Pretend I don't exist. It's better for everyone."

I turned on my heel and left him looking after me. His hands were fisted tight and he had a thunderous look on his face, so I walked a little faster. There was a piece of me that was terrified he was going to follow me and that my bravery would all come crashing down, but he didn't. I made it out of the stable just as Grant was opening the door of the truck to come looking for me.

Even across the yard, I saw his relief. And then his whole body went tense as he looked behind me. I didn't have to turn to know who was there. Grant reached out and pulled me to him. "You're all right?"

"Yes."

"Did he try?"

I shook my head. "No. I roasted him with my words before he could think about it."

Grant's eyes danced. "Well done."

"Only because I knew you were out here and I could run to you."

"You still did it," he said. "I'm proud of you."

"Kiss me."

His hands slid down my spine. "He's staring like he wants to kill us both. Are you sure? I'm not afraid of him, but I don't want to make things worse for you."

"Joel is a spoiled child who misses his toy. He's never going to believe it's gone if he doesn't see it," I said. "Kiss me. Please."

"My pleasure."

As soon as his lips met mine, I faded away, and somewhere in the distance, I heard the sound of angry footsteps on gravel, stomping away.

Chapter 23

Cori

He was poisoning the horses.

There was no other explanation, and it was right there in the test results. Something that you wouldn't ever see if you weren't already looking. Coumarin.

Now that I knew what to look for, the evidence was obvious. A substance found in spices that, in low doses, wasn't fatal—especially not to humans. But in high doses could destroy the liver. If you didn't know what was happening, the death would easily be written off as something else. Accidental. A rare virus. They just "got sick" with no other indicators.

It built up in the system gradually, which would explain the multiple times I saw Sunrise when she was getting worse. Easily introduced through food or even injection.

Maybe it was some kind of fraud scheme, but it was still baffling to me that someone with that much money could need more. Enough that they'd want to kill a racehorse for it. It wasn't like the animals weren't valuable. They were. Possibly more valuable alive. So why?

I rubbed my temples, trying to soothe the ache that was growing there. It was past closing at the clinic, and this was my last task before I went home. I needed more information on this, so I emailed the data back to Kevin. Hopefully, he knew how we could use it. Right now, I wasn't sure what we could do other than to tell Mr. Pearson that I knew he was poisoning his animals.

Something told me that wouldn't be enough to stop him from continuing.

A knock sounded on my office door. Probably Jenna telling me she was leaving for the day. "Come in. I'll lock up, Jenna."

"Funny, I told her the same thing."

I whipped around to find Grant leaning in the doorway with a smile. "Hi. Did I know that you were coming to see me?"

"No," he said. "But I wanted to. Because I have to drive down to Missoula and stay overnight. Seeing a doctor. I wanted to see you before I left."

"Oh." A small wave of disappointment hit me in the stomach. It was the first night we'd spend apart since we'd started spending them together. Which was fine. But I knew that I would miss him. "Is everything okay?"

"Should be," he said. "I promise I'll tell you all about it when I get back. But I needed to see you. Since I won't see you tonight."

I smiled. "I appreciate that."

"And I wanted to give you these." He closed the distance between us and took my hand, pressing two keys into my palm. "One is the key to my house. If you want to sleep there, you can."

My heart skipped a beat. "Because of Joel?"

He grinned. "Yes. Or if you missed me. But mostly because of him."

I loved that he thought about that. The idea of sleeping in his bed, even without him there, felt nice. "I might take you up on that. What's this?" It was a much smaller key, silver. Not like any key I'd ever seen.

"That is for what's next. Close your eyes."

As soon as I did, his hands were on me, lifting me out of my chair and up onto my desk so I was perched on the edge. "What are we doing?"

His hands circled my wrists. "We may not be spending the night together," he said. "But that doesn't mean we can't have some fun before I go."

His pain must be better today. My whole body thrilled at the way he was touching me. Strong and confident. Cold metal surrounded my right wrist, and he lifted it, the sound of metal clicking before it circled my left, and I couldn't lower my hands.

I opened my eyes. Handcuffs bound my wrists, looped through the handles of the cabinets above my desk. Heat sank through my body. "Handcuff key," I said quietly.

"Yes."

Outside, the sun was setting, painting the office with orange through the window.

"Is this all right?" he asked with a grin. The flush on my skin and the way I was breathing were obvious. But he was never going to do anything without me saying yes.

"Yes."

Grant's hands slid under my shirt, lifting it along with my bra so I was exposed to him. "It would have been a shame if I didn't get to see these before I left."

"It would have been," I said. The air was cool on my skin as he leaned forward, his lips touching between my breasts. I arched forward, chest rising toward him. He moved with almost aching slowness and flicked his tongue against a nipple. "Grant," I said. "Please."

I pulled on the handcuffs. I wanted to touch him and couldn't, unlocking that impossible lightness. The sensation of falling through weightlessness.

"Please what?"

"Please."

"You'll have to be more specific than that," he said. His gaze was locked on me as he lowered his mouth back to my skin. I cried out as his teeth caught my nipple, biting gently. Close to being too much, but never too far. All I wanted was to feel his mouth all over my body. "Grant."

It was as if his hands hadn't been all over me last night. And this morning. The way need rushed to the surface and made me desperate. Even more so with my hands locked above my head.

He unbuckled my belt, lifting me off the desk long enough to force my pants over my hips and lower. Down below my knees. They were a restraint of their own, locking my legs together enough so my hands and feet were bound and he could push my knees apart.

"I should make more plans for things out of bed," he said quietly. "I like this."

If there was one thing I'd learned about Grant, it was that he liked to move slowly. So that he could savor every move he made. Tease me until I couldn't contain myself anymore. Today? I couldn't wait.

"Please don't go slow," I begged. "I need you."

Grant's eyes went dark, and his hands dropped to his belt. There wasn't any slowness now. The condom was on, and I had only seconds to admire the way his hard body shone in the dying light.

Stepping close, he fit himself against me and pushed

in, kissing me as he did so that all I felt was him. Inside, outside, hands gripping my ribs.

"Oh my God." The words were strangled with pleasure as he began to move. Grant shifted his hands under my ass, pulling me to him as he drove himself deep. Hard and fast. Relentless, delicious pleasure that swirled through me. Up and out. Every time we did this and that kind of trust was built between us, it became easier to let go. Because he was safe. Because he would take care of me and only wanted pleasure for both of us.

I lost myself in the way his tongue danced around mine. In the way he fucked me, rattling the handcuffs and cupboards, dragging pleasure up through every movement until I was begging for more of it.

Grant broke away from our kiss to whisper in my ear. Dirty words that he knew drove me crazy. Made me latch on to that pleasure even harder, and then let go completely.

My vision went white, and I came.

The office echoed with the sounds of my cries, and they were joined by Grant's voice signaling his own orgasm. My whole body was shaking and limp, racked with the orgasm as it worked its way through me. I gulped down breath, letting my head fall forward onto Grant's shoulder.

He didn't pull away from me as he unlocked my hands and let them gently down around his shoulders. "Now I don't want to leave."

"Agreed," I said, still leaning on him. "But you should go. Your back is important. At least, I'm assuming that's what it's for. Sorry."

Grant chuckled and pulled me upright so that he could kiss me. "I like it when you're drunk on orgasms."

"I am not."

"Are too. And it's adorable." He separated us gently, making sure that I wasn't going to fall off the desk before he cleaned himself up. "Tomorrow, I'll make up for the fact that I couldn't take you to bed. Promise."

"That was a pretty good start. But I will be sleeping in your bed." I made the decision right that second. "So you can think about me there."

"Cori, there won't be a second that I'm gone when I won't be thinking about you."

I blushed, and he helped me off the desk to put myself back together. "When you say things like that, I still can't believe it."

"Really?" he asked.

"I'm just not used to it."

"Having people say nice things?"

I shrugged. "Being complimented at all."

The look on his face…I wasn't sure what it meant. Grant locked his eyes on mine and deliberately stepped into my space. He slid one hand around my neck and up into my hair. He tangled his fingers in it so I couldn't look away. "You, Cori Jackson, are kind, beautiful, and one of the best people I've ever met. Waking up next to you makes me happy, and I'm going to miss you, even though it's only going to be one night. And I'm going to make sure you hear enough compliments that you finally believe them."

He captured my lips in a kiss that stripped me open. My stomach spun with a thousand butterflies, and I realized that this was the moment I might be falling in love with Grant Carter. No matter how fast we'd moved or how long we'd been together.

The knowledge hit me, and I couldn't breathe.

When Grant broke the kiss, all I could do was stare. "I hope you believe that," he said.

"I do."

He smiled. "I have to go. I'll see you tomorrow, okay?"

"Okay."

I was still in a daze as he left. Holy shit.

The glow that I felt was everywhere. It made the room and the sunset brighter, my thoughts easier. And it was because of him.

No response from Kevin yet. There probably wouldn't be until the morning at the very least, so there wasn't any point in me staying here. I would go home, grab some things, and head to Grant's house. I loved my house, but I did feel safer in his place.

And there was the added benefit that his whole house smelled like him. I could sleep in one of his shirts, completely wrapped in his scent. Just the thought made me smile. Everything about him made me smile.

This was the happiest I'd been in a long time. Since I was in veterinary school, actually.

That made everything simpler, didn't it?

I still had a few days until my birthday and the deadline, but I'd made my decision. It would be harder without the trust, but I could do it. I'd already been doing it.

Four years away from this place, for essentially nothing, was out of the question. I was going to fight for this life that I'd made here. With Grant. With Lena and Evelyn and all the other people in the Resting Warrior family. They were more my family than my own had ever been, and that was worth a hell of a lot more than money.

The day after my birthday, I would tell my parents my decision. I was staying here.

Chapter 24

Grant

I wasn't expecting the specialist to have an opening so soon. She did, but it was the earliest doctor's appointment of my life. Early enough that if I didn't want to get up at three o'clock in the morning to drive to Missoula, it was easier just to get a hotel for the night.

Leaving early had given Cori and me the chance to have sex in her office. I couldn't get it out of my head. The memory had helped with the fact that I missed being in the same bed as her.

It was shocking how fast I'd grown used to it. In the middle of the night, I'd rolled over and reached for her, instinctually wanting to feel her warmth and her curves, and it had taken me a moment to realize that she wasn't there, and why.

The sun was just barely lightening the sky beyond the mountains that ringed Missoula. I didn't know what Dr. Peak had said to her to make her fit me in on such short notice, but I appreciated it since time was a factor with that shitty little piece of metal in my spine.

I wasn't familiar with this medical complex, but they were all kind of similar. It wasn't hard to find where I was supposed to go since it was five in the morning and far fewer cars were on the road than there would be in a few hours.

Even the hallways of the building were dim, still on nighttime lights. Only the doctor's actual office was at full brightness, with a very tired nurse behind the desk.

She managed a smile. "You're the early one."

"I am. Sorry."

"It's always like this when Dr. Keyes is in town," she said, managing a smile. "I'm used to it. Here, need the basics."

I grabbed the clipboard that she handed me and retreated to my seat. They already had my info, but it was my first time at this office. Between all the doctors I'd seen over the last couple of years, filling out this kind of form was almost like meditation. It was always the same, over and over again.

"Good thing about being this early. There's no wait," she said when I handed her the clipboard again. "Come on back."

She led me into an examination room. "Dr. Keyes will probably want to do an examination. There's a gown on the table."

"My favorite part," I told her.

At least she laughed. I didn't think anyone's favorite part was the gown, but I'd been proven wrong before.

I heard the courtesy knock. "Come in."

"Good morning," the tall woman said, stepping into the room. "I'm Dr. Amanda Keyes."

We shook hands. "Nice to meet you."

"Thanks for coming on short notice."

I waved a hand. "I'm eager to find out. Definitely worth the trip."

She sat on the stool and opened the file she had in front of her. "I have all your MRI results. Everything, actually. Thanks for approving that. It's been fascinating to look through."

"Hopefully an interesting read."

"It was, actually," she smiled. "I like the challenging cases."

I tried to hide my wince and failed.

"I am optimistic about your case," she said. "May I look at your back?"

"Sure." My mouth went dry. I'd gotten used to this part, but it didn't change my feelings about it. The bone-deep terror of people's responses when they saw the scars. Cori's reaction had been perfect. She didn't see the scars as a detriment. When I'd given her permission to touch them, she'd explored them, tracing the lines with her fingers.

Under her hands, I didn't mind it.

Dr. Keyes was used to things like this. The scars wouldn't faze her. But stretching out on the exam table was an effort. I heard her put on gloves before her fingers touched my skin, light and clinical.

She gently prodded right around where the shrapnel was buried. "Does this hurt?"

"Not today," I said.

"But it does hurt regularly?"

I confirmed it. "It comes in waves. Good days and bad days. The good days, there is no pain, the bad days range from a low ache to pain severe enough that I can barely do anything."

"Mmm." She pressed a little harder. "I do feel it. That's a good thing."

On any given day, I made a point to never press there. Because I could feel it too, and it always split me between emotions. Rage that a thing so small could affect my life this deeply. Freaked out by feeling something foreign in there. Desperate to fix it.

She felt around the base of my spine a little more before stepping back. "Okay, you can sit up." Returning to my chart, she made a couple of notes before looking at me. "I think that you're an excellent candidate for surgery."

Relief flowed cold through my body. "That's good news."

"I think so. But I'll be up front with you about the risks. Dr. Peak was correct. The shrapnel is working its way closer to your spine. It's closer than it was before, and it will continue to move. So, the longer you wait to have the surgery, the riskier it will become.

"I'm confident that I can remove the shrapnel with no loss of motor function, but I will never promise that one hundred percent. We're dealing with an incredibly delicate area of the body. There is a risk."

I nodded. "What kind of percent are we talking about?"

She made a face. "That's tough. In the shrapnel's current position, I would say I'm at eighty-five percent."

"If I'd come to you sooner?"

"It would have been higher. And if we wait any length of time, that percentage will go down."

Nervous energy coursed through my body. "How soon could we do the surgery?"

Dr. Keyes shrugged. "As soon as insurance approves it. Given that your injury is thoroughly documented, that will be fast. I do have surgical openings."

"I need to take some time to think about it. Discuss it."

"Of course. The risk, even a small one, is worth

considering. But I'll say I do think that sooner is better than later in this case. The position of the shrapnel will decay."

"Understood." I reached out a hand, and she shook it. "Thank you for taking the time."

"I'll start putting through the approval for the surgery either way, just in case. That way, if you decide to go ahead, we won't have to wait longer for it."

"Thank you."

I got dressed quickly, my whole body buzzing with a mix of hope and apprehension. This was good news—and also terrifying. Anything with the risk of leaving you paralyzed would do that. But if I didn't do anything, I'd be there anyway.

Now, there was another factor. I had to talk to Cori. At this point, this wasn't a decision I wanted to make without her. The knowledge settled in my chest. Cori…

I was falling hard and fast.

Scratch that—I'd already fallen.

I was completely in love with Cori Jackson. She *fit* into my life. Every day, every minute I spent with her was more evidence. And because of that, I couldn't make this kind of decision without her. I could end up in a wheelchair, and that wasn't the kind of life she'd signed up for.

Coffee was the only thing I stopped for on the way home. It was still early when I pulled into Garnet Bend. Barely time for Cori to be getting ready for work. I wanted to talk to her now. Right away. No waiting.

Her truck was parked in front of her house, but my curiosity was piqued. Had she used the key? I'd drop off my suitcase, and if she wasn't in my house, then I'd go next door.

As soon as I walked in, I knew she was here. The light perfume that was a combination of vanilla and cinnamon hung in the air. Her shoes were near the front door, and her coat was on the rack.

I set down my suitcase and toed off my shoes so I could be quiet. Not to sneak up on her, but she was probably still asleep.

The morning sun was coming through my bedroom window, painting her with light. Cori was perfectly asleep, sprawled over the pillows in one of *my* T-shirts. It was huge on her but had pulled up in her sleep so I saw her panties underneath it.

That sight did things to me that I couldn't explain. Seeing her in my bed and my clothes like she belonged there. She did belong there. My chest swelled with satisfaction seeing her like this. Cori felt safe here because of me.

The sight of her spread out like that made me more than happy. It turned me on. I was harder than a rock. But she would have to go to work soon, and I needed to tell her everything.

Slowly, I sat on the bed next to her. She stirred, sensing the movement. Drawing my hand down her arm, I enjoyed the feeling of her skin. It hadn't even been a day, and I was still craving her. The smile on my face…I couldn't stop it.

Holy fuck, I was in love with this woman.

"Cori," I said softly.

Stretching, she opened her eyes and startled before realizing it was me. "You're here." She relaxed.

"And you're in my shirt."

She flushed pink. "Is that okay?"

"Okay?" I laughed softly and leaned down so I could kiss her. "If I had my way, I'd throw out your entire wardrobe so you could wear nothing but this."

"I don't know if that's very practical."

My hand drifted lower, over the bare skin of her hip,

where I let my thumb curl under the fabric of her underwear. "I don't know, it feels pretty practical to me."

Her body arched under my hand. "I see the appeal."

"As much as I want to follow this path, I need to talk to you."

Cori's eyes cleared of the haze of lust that had been in them. "Is everything okay?"

"Yes," I said, squeezing her hip. "Everything is good. I saw the doctor this morning. About my spine."

She bit her lip. "I thought it might be, but I didn't know if it was okay to ask."

"You can always ask me anything. I promise."

Her hand fell on mine, and I resisted the temptation to move my hand to her ass and dive headfirst into making her scream. "The doctor I saw was a surgeon. I haven't been handling my spine properly. Nothing was helping, and I didn't want to deal with it. I'm changing that now."

Cori met my gaze hesitantly. "Because of me?"

"Partially. And partially because the piece of shrapnel I have in my body is moving. Eventually it will bury itself in my spine, and that could paralyze me."

She froze, squeezing my hand.

"This surgeon is one of the best in the country, and she's confident that she can remove the shrapnel. But there's always a chance that things could go wrong, and I end up paralyzed anyway."

Slowly, Cori sat up and ran her hands through her hair. She was adorably messy, turquoise hair everywhere. "If you want to get the surgery, you should," she said. "Obviously, I understand the urgency of it, given my family. I just… I don't want to lose you." Her cheeks were aflame, and she was looking down at the bedsheets. "Don't get me wrong, I know that surgery doesn't have a high probability of death, but that thought is terrifying because I'm…" She slowed to take a breath. "I'm in this with you."

That was as close to a declaration as she could make. I tilted her face up to mine, stealing a kiss. She was breathtaking.

"The reason I'm telling you this, Cori, is because I'm in this too. With you. I told the surgeon I needed to think it over, mostly because I wanted to discuss it with you." I lowered my voice. "Because of how important you've become to me."

Cori looked everywhere but at me. She was fidgeting nervously, and that felt a little off. But then, given that I'd just told her I could be paralyzed, it was to be expected. It wasn't easy news to hear.

"I want you," I told her. "All of you. I want to be with you, and I want to take this as far as it goes." Now I made her look at me. "I mean that."

Her breathing sped up. I hoped she understood what I was trying to tell her. "But until after the surgery, I'm not going to make any true commitments."

"Why?"

I shook my head. "The last thing I want to do is to drag you in too deep and then leave you alone. Or suddenly make you a caretaker for a partner who can't move. That's no kind of life for you."

"That's my choice, Grant."

"It's my choice too," I told her. "And I don't want that for you."

She smiled. "It won't matter. Because everything will be fine. Nothing bad is going to happen."

"I hope so."

I kissed her again and savored the way she melted beneath me. So fucking perfect I couldn't stand it.

"Nothing bad," I whispered. It was both a prayer and a promise. "How long until you have to be at the clinic?"

"I don't have anything until eleven," she smirked. "Figured I'd sleep in a little. Eat some breakfast."

Pushing her back onto the bed, I covered her body with mine. "I don't think sleeping in is on the agenda."

"No? That's too bad. I love sleeping."

I made a sound low in my throat, kissing along her neck and drinking in the scent of her. Her breath was short when I reached that spot where her neck met her shoulder. That spot drove her wild. Already, she was arching into me, gripping my shoulders and pulling me closer.

"Do you want to go back to sleep?" I asked roughly.

"What happens if I say no?"

Reaching between us, I grabbed the hem of my T-shirt and pulled it up. Over her head so her arms were tangled in the fabric. And I left it there. "I'll make up for the fact that I wasn't in this bed with you last night."

Her words were breathless. "I thought that was what the office was for."

"No reason there can't be both." I pulled my own shirt over my head and tossed it aside. "Because I woke up reaching for you, and you weren't there."

Cori stilled underneath me. "Really?"

"Really."

She swallowed. "Suddenly, I'm feeling very, *very* awake."

I laughed and lowered my lips to her skin. It was the only thing to satisfy the craving, and I was going to take my time.

Chapter 25

Cori

The sun was setting earlier, but everything still felt bright in my world. I was leaning in to the happiness that being with Grant brought me, and now that I'd made the decision to stay in Garnet Bend no matter what, my whole soul felt lighter.

There was only one dark spot, and that was the Pearson problem. Kevin confirmed that the poison could definitely be used to kill. Not enough people knew to look for it, so it was almost always ruled a death by natural causes.

Convenient, if what you were trying to do was to get money from an insurance company.

Kevin was quietly reaching out to others he knew to see if there was anything we could prove. We had the blood test results, but this wasn't like dealing with a straightforward crime. The Pearsons had money and power. One blood test wouldn't be enough.

"Cori?" Jenna called.

"Yeah?"

"Someone here to see you," she said, stepping into my office.

I had no more appointments left today. "Okay, be right there."

It was almost time to go home anyway, so I started to wrap things up. Grant wouldn't have waited out front, and Jenna knew him now. So, it was someone else.

My body froze when I stepped into the waiting room. "Mr. Pearson. This is a surprise."

He smiled. When he did, he reminded me of Joel. They both had smiles that could charm people when they needed to. "A good one, I hope."

I looked at Jenna. "You can go. I'll lock up."

"You sure?" She looked between Pearson and me. "I can stay."

"I'm sure. I'll see you tomorrow, okay?"

"Okay."

We both waited until she'd pushed out of the door before I turned back to him. "I'm shocked to see you in Garnet Bend at all, let alone my clinic. Is everything okay?"

I needed to tread carefully here. My phone was in the office, so I couldn't text Grant. But it was Mr. Pearson and not Joel. At least there was that. I didn't think I had anything to fear from him. Not while he didn't know what I'd done.

He looked around the lobby. "I've always been curious about your clinic," he said. "It looks like it's in good shape."

"Thank you." I wasn't sure that was a compliment.

"You seem to have a good thing going here. And all the years you've taken care of my animals, you've done well."

This time, I didn't say anything. I could tell he wasn't done.

"I'd hoped that it would work out between you and my son," he said with a wan smile. "Free vet care, you know?"

There wasn't any point in telling him it still wouldn't have been free.

"I should have seen it coming, that you would figure it out," he said. "You were so persistent about that damn horse."

"I don't know what you're talking about," I said, my throat going dry. Now this, *this* was dangerous territory.

"Don't you?"

I shook my head, hoping there was a chance he'd believe me.

"Funny." Mr. Pearson sat in one of the waiting room chairs, looking as comfortable as if he were in his own living room. "Because Kevin Bridges told me you'd run a blood test on Hazelwood. And that you knew I was using coumarin to poison that horse."

My jaw nearly fell open. He'd admitted to it. Kevin had told him? The betrayal stung. But the Pearsons were legends in the racing world. The reach they had was far and wide. I needed to remember that. "And you're here to do what?"

"Congratulate you," he said, giving me a round of applause. "You figured it out. I'm glad, too. Because doing that? Every day? It's frankly more work than I'm willing to do long-term."

"Why are you doing it at all?"

He gave me a look. "You're a smart girl. Surely, you've already figured out that all of this has to do with money. But I'm not going to give you ammunition against me either."

I swallowed. "Then I don't know why you're here, Mr. Pearson. You don't seem bothered by the fact that I know."

"Bothered?" He chuckled. "I'm ecstatic. Like I said, dosing those horses every day was a lot of effort. Now that you know the truth, you can do it. That's far easier and preferable."

Now my jaw did actually drop. "Excuse me?"

"Which part wasn't clear to you?"

"The part where somehow I'm involved in insurance fraud. If you honestly came here for that, you're in the wrong place."

Pearson rolled his eyes. "This is very simple, Cori. I need the money for those horses. And I can't get that money while they're still in my stable. You're the best person to execute—pun intended—this plan. I'll even cut you in for a percentage of the money. Maybe you can use it to make this place less of a dump."

I ground my teeth together, not taking the bait. Just a few minutes ago, he'd said it was in good shape. This whole thing was a game to him—one I had no interest in playing. "If you'll excuse me for a minute."

"I will not," he said. "Stay here. I don't want to have to force you. I don't want you calling that new boyfriend of yours. He's not going to know about this visit."

"And I'm not going to help you murder horses," I said. "Doing that would go against my oath as a vet, not to mention my morals as a person. And though you clearly already know, what you're doing is a crime. The very idea that I would ever help you with this is absurd."

"Is it?" He pulled out his phone and typed something.

Movement in the corner of my eye suddenly had my body frozen in fight-or-flight. The door of the clinic opened, and Joel strode in. Why the hell didn't I have Jenna lock the door? Now I was in here with the two of them, and I was no longer sure that the elder Pearson had no intention of hurting me.

"Hello, Cori."

I didn't move. The odds of me getting to my office and grabbing my phone were slim to none with both of them in here. The only door with a lock was my office, but it wasn't the kind of lock that would stop someone determined. As I knew Joel could be.

"Why don't you show Cori what will happen if she doesn't help us?"

Us. It was an us. Joel was involved in this, too. Of course he was. The further I dug down into who he was, the less impressed—and more terrified—I became.

He came closer, and I fought the impulse to shrink back. The last thing I needed to do right now was show them I was afraid. What would Grant do in this situation?

Probably, he would come crashing in and show them what he thought of them. But I wasn't him, and there was no way I could fight two men even if I had those kinds of skills. If he were in exactly my position? He'd tell me to stay calm and make sure I got out alive.

Joel brought out his phone, the look on his face one of disgust. "I said before that you were a whore for your perverted tastes, and now I've got the proof. I also warned you that you were mine, so consider this part of your punishment. Know that these aren't the only copies."

Holding the phone in front of my face, he began to scroll through an album of photos. My stomach plummeted. It was me. In my office. With my hands handcuffed above my head while Grant and I had sex.

If I weren't being blackmailed with them, I'd say that the photos were hot. You could see the way Grant held me under his command in those photos, and you could also see that I was having the time of my life. No wonder Joel looked so disgusted. There wasn't ever a time when I'd looked like that during sex with him.

But he'd been there. Watching. Or he'd hired someone to do it. So that private moment was now tainted by knowing we'd been watched.

"If you don't help," Mr. Pearson said. "These photos will be released."

"Not released," Joel nearly growled. "Plastered. They'll be printed and put on every bulletin board. Emailed to your friends. To your *family*. Have fun trying to explain that. Oh, and I'll tell them all about how you tried to have that same kind of kinky sex with me in the stable."

My cheeks flamed with mortification and embarrassment. I was overwhelmed by the instinct to hide. And not have any kinds of photos out there. *Breathe*. I held in the breath and counted to five, releasing the impulse. My friends loved me. My friends didn't care that I liked kinky sex—some of them already knew it.

"Do it," I said. "I don't care. There are worse things than liking bondage in bed, Joel, despite your weird reaction to it. And I don't think you want to bring up the stable. Unless you really think people will take kindly to the fact that you tried to rape me for revenge."

"Your word against mine, babe." His smile was sickening.

Strong. I had to stay strong. "If you think that your word is worth more than mine in this town, you have another thing coming."

His smile died then. I could feel satisfied that I'd hit my mark later.

"Fine," Mr. Pearson said. "I told him that wouldn't work on you. He was convinced you'd cave at the idea of showing your tits to the world, but I always knew you were made of stronger stuff than that."

"I would like you both to leave my clinic. I will be filing a restraining order against both of you."

Mr. Pearson stood. "This can't come as much of a surprise to you, Miss Jackson, but I don't actually give a fuck about what you'd like. You are going to do this for me, and you're going to do it gladly."

I copied his words from earlier. "What part wasn't clear to you?"

Pearson laughed as he approached me. "You're spicier than I realized. No wonder this one has been a mess since you dumped him."

"I didn't dump him," I snapped. "He dumped me and nearly became violent. And as previously stated, your precious son tried to rape me on *your* property. I have enough for an assault charge if I wanted. Now. Get. Out."

"I have it on good authority that Grant Carter was in Missoula yesterday morning," he said evenly. "He had an early morning appointment with a Dr. Amanda Keyes, regarding the spinal injury he suffered while serving in the military."

Chills ran down my spine. "How do you know that?"

"I know lots of things. Someone like me? I have people everywhere."

"Congratulations," I whispered. "You're very impressive."

"Glad you think so," he said cheerily. "I didn't want to have to do this, you know. I hoped that you'd go for our first offering, even though I suspected you wouldn't. But since you already passed on that, I'll lay out the second offer.

"Amanda Keyes is an incredibly talented surgeon. And she's worked hard to get there. But unfortunately, she doesn't come from a background of wealth like us. There was no way she could ever pay for college and medical school. Especially at one of the elite medical centers. Luckily for her, her father did some work for me."

My stomach was in knots, dread seeping into my chest. He was so confident that I was terrified. Mr. Pearson was always confident, but he was acting like he'd already won. Which made me wonder if he had.

"There are a great many reasons why it's convenient to have a surgeon in your debt," he said. "This is one of them."

I didn't want to ask. "This?"

"If you help us, then everything is fine. Grant Carter will schedule his surgery, and chances are, it will go well. Amanda really is talented. Your boyfriend will be whole and pain-free. Congratulations."

"And if I don't?"

"Then Mr. Carter will schedule his surgery, and you'd better make sure that you say your goodbyes. Because once he's put to sleep, I'll make sure he never wakes up."

Chapter 26

Grant

I was nearly late to my own meeting. A cow got stuck in the road on the way from town, and when that happened, you were at the mercy of their temperament.

Mara was cleaning the kitchen when I walked into the main lodge. “Hey, Mara.”

She smiled, waving once. In the almost three years that Resting Warrior had existed, I’d heard her say maybe ten words. She was sweet and did her jobs around the ranch well. But I hoped that we could help her progress more.

I walked into the conference room and heard footsteps behind me.

The only person who walked in after me was Liam, and that was pretty much expected at this point. There wasn’t anything Liam wasn’t almost late for, except for missions. Which meant he was almost always late.

“Nice of you to join us,” Daniel said.

“Sorry. Cow in the road.”

Liam dropped into a chair. "Something that you'll literally only hear in Montana."

Noah sighed. "You know that's not true."

"No, but hyperbole is funny," Liam shot back.

"Hyperbole might be," Noah said with a grin. "But you're not."

Liam put his hand over his heart. "You wound me. How will I ever get the ladies if I'm not truly funny?"

"You're getting the ladies now?" Jude asked. "News to me."

Noah pointed. "See that? That was funny."

Daniel chuckled and held up a hand. "All right, all right. This is Grant's meeting. Let's not spend the whole time trying to prove Liam needs to go buy a joke book."

I smirked, hiding the laugh that was building in my chest. "Thank you."

"So, what's up?" Liam asked.

Everyone was looking at me now, and I was a little nervous. I hoped that they would be happy—sure that they would be—but this was still a big thing.

"I had a doctor's appointment down in Missoula yesterday," I said. "A surgeon, recommended by Dr. Peak."

"Oh shit," Lucas said. "Is everything okay?"

"Yes." I nodded. "Very okay. She's optimistic that she can remove the shrapnel on my spine."

Universal cheering erupted. Liam was on his feet and hugging me, shortly before Noah did the same. "Congratulations, man."

"It's not without its risks."

"Of course," Daniel said. "What do you need us to know?"

I laid it all out for them. Everything about the placement of the shrapnel, the percentage of risks, and the fact that the sooner I did this, the higher chance that it wouldn't have a lasting impact on my mobility.

"Well," Liam said. "Kind of convenient that we're a place that helps people after that sort of thing, huh?"

"Hopefully I'll be able to recover at home," I said with a laugh. "But yeah, it crossed my mind."

Daniel cleared his throat. "I hate to have to ask this. But what if it goes wrong?"

He was right. It was something I needed to think about. What would I do? As much as I didn't want to lose my legs, I wasn't about to say that a life in a wheelchair wasn't worth living. It would be an adjustment. But one I didn't want to think about until I had to.

"I'll deal with that if it happens," I told him. "I don't want to invite those kinds of thoughts at the moment."

"Fair enough."

"That's all I wanted to say. I just wanted to tell everyone at the same time. I'll keep you posted if I need anything with it." They were all still smiling. "And I expect to see every single one of you at Cori's surprise party tonight."

Lucas grinned. "If I didn't come, Evelyn would never let me hear the end of it. We'll be there."

Noah stood and nodded toward the side of the room. I joined him. "What's up?"

He looked at me carefully. "Have you told Cori?"

"As soon as I got back from Missoula."

"So she's okay with this?"

I slid my hands into my pockets. "She's more than okay with it. But I told her I wasn't going to commit to anything until after the surgery."

His eyebrows rose. "Why? Are you—"

"I'm so fucking gone," I told him. "You never really know if a crush is what you think it is, but…everything is amazing," I admitted. "I'm in love with her. But I'm not going to tell her that until I know if I'll be able to walk on my own."

"You shouldn't hold that back, Grant," Noah said. "Cori is an adult. She can make her own choices. And she deserves to have all the information when she makes those choices."

I saw where he was coming from, but something still sat uncomfortably with me. I'd seen men who came back wounded. Partially paralyzed. Sometimes, it was fine. And sometimes, their relationships fell apart.

"I know," I said. "But I have choices too. I want Cori to be my partner—maybe my wife—I don't want her to be my caretaker."

Noah looked at me for long moments. "All right. But if that's something that she wants? To be a part of that journey with you? Don't completely shut her out because it's not what you think she needs."

Not exactly what I wanted to hear, but something I probably needed to. That was the good thing about Noah. He cut straight to the heart of a matter and was willing to kick your ass if you weren't seeing straight.

"Yeah," I said. "Yeah, I'll keep that in my head. Thank you."

He smiled. "So, a surprise party?"

"Lena just told me about it. She kept it from me too. Probably didn't think that I could actually keep the secret from Cori."

"Was she wrong?"

"I can keep a secret," I protested. "Asshole."

He nodded. "Sure you can. Whatever you say."

I punched him in the arm. "Anyway, her birthday isn't for a couple of days, so this is the perfect time for a surprise because she won't actually see it coming."

"Better get there," Noah said. "I'll be right behind you."

Hopefully there wouldn't be a cow in the road on the way back to town.

Apparently, the party had been in the works for a while. Lena was brilliant at this sort of thing. If she ever decided to leave Garnet Bend for a bigger city, I had no doubt she could make a name for herself as both a force of nature in the baking business and event planning.

With her personality and talent, I wouldn't be shocked if she ended up with her own TV show at some point.

I parked several blocks away from Deja Brew. We didn't want Cori to think anything was up when she came over to the café. Some of the guys had already beaten me here.

The kitchen was decked out with decorations so there wouldn't be any hints. A big green banner that read "Happy 30th!" was on the back wall, streamers hanging down. A giant cake sat on one of the worktables, along with an assortment of cupcakes and cookies and drinks. Everything you would expect if it were Lena Mitchell hosting a party.

"Good! You're here!" Lena called when she saw me. "I wasn't going to call until you were here. I'm having everyone in the kitchen."

"How are you getting her over here?" I asked.

She smirked. "I'm going to pretend that a pipe burst and I need help."

"Cruel."

"Better than saying the building is on fire. Fire is something I would never joke about." The deadness in her eyes with those words gave me pause. Jude too. He was watching her, though she couldn't see that with him behind her.

Lena was a bright and shining star in the community. She helped everyone, loved everyone, and she took care of them when she could. But at some point, she was going to need someone to return the favor.

Of course I knew—everyone knew—who should be the one to return that favor. If the stubborn man would get his head out of his ass. But I couldn't exactly judge. Jude had gone through hell and come back alive. It was frankly amazing that he was standing and walking around, let alone doing everything that he did now.

I just hoped he could let her in. Based on that look in her eyes, they both needed it. I didn't doubt that look had everything to do with what had happened to her and Evelyn.

"Well, good," I said with a smile, realizing I'd been silent too long. "I'm sure she's going to love this."

"Okay, everyone shut the hell up so I can make the call," Lena called.

Evelyn was here, too. All the Resting Warrior guys. Jenna, Cori's vet tech. Even Grace and Harlan, back from their honeymoon. Though you could see that in their heads, they were still on vacation.

"Oh my God," Lena said into the phone. "Cori? I need help. You're the first one I thought of in town who I could call."

A pause.

"No, I'm fine, but a pipe burst in the kitchen, and there's water everywhere. I'm calling everyone I know. Come as quickly as you can. Thanks!"

She hung up and grinned. "Now, we wait."

"Can we get coffee while we wait?" Liam asked.

"Right there."

A huge carafe of the stuff was sitting on the worktable.

"You know, as a former SEAL, you're supposed to be more observant than that," I told him.

He laughed. "This is Lena's kitchen. I don't know what I'm allowed to touch, and I'm really not interested in dying today."

"That's a smart choice," Lena confirmed. "But you can help yourself to the coffee."

She turned back to me. "How's it going?"

"With Cori?"

"Yeah."

I raised one eyebrow. "I'm assuming she's already told you plenty."

"I want to hear it from you."

Quickly, I glanced around to make sure we weren't being eavesdropped on. I wasn't ashamed of my feelings, or of Cori. In fact, I planned on kissing the hell out of her in front of all these people when she got here. But our business was still our business, and small-town gossip was a real thing.

"It's going really well," I said, not sure how to put it. Honesty was important, but I didn't want Cori to hear what I wanted to say to her from anyone but me. "Cori is…very important to me."

"Good. She should be."

She glanced out the kitchen door. Garnet Bend was the epitome of a small town. It wouldn't take Cori long to get here from our houses, and faster if she'd still been at the clinic when Lena called.

"She's coming!" Lena said. "Quiet!"

The bell chimed over the outside door. "Lena?"

"Back here," she called, grinning at all of us like the Cheshire cat.

"Are you okay? I hope nothing—"

"*Surprise!*" We all shouted at the top of our lungs.

Cori froze, looking at all of us, her face going through panic and fear to sudden understanding. I stepped forward, tugging her into a hug so she'd have a chance to recover without being watched. "Happy early birthday."

"Thank you." Her voice was quiet, but she sounded miserable. Down deep in my gut, my instincts told me that something was very wrong, and this wasn't a place I could ask about it.

Chapter 27

Cori

I threw up when they left.

Of course, they didn't leave without telling me the thing that I was afraid of—that I was being watched, and I wouldn't know when or by whom. That if I told anyone about their threat, they would know and make sure Grant died anyway.

The very thought made bile rise in my throat again. I was almost home, and I barely made it to the kitchen sink before I threw up again. This was what I'd asked Grant about yesterday. What if he died? The terror just thinking about that was like nothing I'd ever felt.

But this had nothing to do with his surgery. This had to do with me and fucking up. Had there been any signs that I shouldn't have trusted Kevin? I'd looked up where he was working now briefly to make sure he didn't have any connections.

I guess I didn't look hard enough.

Running cold water, I rinsed out my mouth before sinking down to the floor and leaning against the cabinets. This was my worst nightmare. Honestly. It was. I thought it was bad being blackmailed by my parents for money? That didn't even hold a candle to this feeling. Money didn't mean shit when someone's life was on the line.

I could tell Grant not to get the surgery. But he would want to know why I'd changed my mind, and he didn't deserve to be in pain for the rest of his life.

There was no way I could do what they asked. I couldn't kill animals. Not like this. This wasn't mercy; it was murder. But I loved Grant too much to let him die.

My whole body froze.

I loved him.

On any other day, in any other moment, realizing that would have been amazing. I would be jumping up and down and spinning with joy. Right now, it brought tears to my eyes. Because it was going to make things so much harder.

I loved him so much that it hurt to breathe, and it didn't matter to me that we hadn't been together long, or that this was still new. When you felt that connection with another person, you understood it. I'd always been told that was the case, but I'd never believed it until now.

A sob made its way out of me. What could I do?

My phone rang in my pocket. I begged the universe for it not to be Grant. He'd know something was wrong, and I wouldn't be able to tell him.

It wasn't Grant. It was Lena.

"Hello?"

"Oh my God," Lena said. "Cori? I need help. You're the first one I thought of in town who I could call."

Panic spiraled through me. "Are you okay? Do I need to call the police?" I got myself off the floor, grabbing my keys from where I'd dropped them in my hurry to get to the sink.

"No, I'm fine," she said. "But a pipe burst in the kitchen, and there's water everywhere. I'm calling everyone I know. Come as quickly as you can."

"I'm on my way." I pushed out the door, brushing the tears off my face.

"Thanks!" The line went dead.

This was good. This was exactly what I needed. It sucked that a pipe burst, but I needed a couple of hours focused on anything but myself and the shit that was rattling around in my brain. If I stayed in my head too long, it felt like my thoughts would drown me. Lena's disaster was my relief.

It only took me a couple minutes to get across town. In the evening darkness, Deja Brew looked cheery all lit up like it usually did. We would get all the water cleaned up, call a plumber, eat some cookies, and get the shop entirely back to normal. Maybe by the time we did that, I would be able to think straight and figure out what I wanted to do.

"Lena?" I didn't see her when I went inside.

"Back here."

Of course, Cori. Jeez. "Are you okay? I hope nothing—"

"*Surprise!*"

I blinked, fear rolling through me for a second before I realized what was happening. There was a giant banner that was telling me happy birthday, and basically everyone I knew was crammed into the Deja Brew kitchen. This was a surprise birthday party. For me. I barely kept myself from dissolving into tears.

Grant was at the front of the crowd. He pulled me into a hug, and I was glad I could hide my face for a second.

Get it together. But it was almost worse, knowing that he was at the center of it all.

"Happy early birthday," he said softly.

"Thank you."

Pulling back, he kissed me. Not shy or hesitant, he kissed me the way I saw Lucas kiss Evelyn, even when they were at community dinners. The way Harlan kissed Grace—like she was the only thing in the world that mattered to him.

Grant was kissing me in front of all our friends and family. It was a moment I wanted to remember forever, and at the same time, all I wanted to do was go to the bathroom and cry.

I put on a smile instead. As best I could. "You did this?" I asked him.

"No," he said with a laugh. "No, I have other plans for your birthday. This was all Lena."

"Of course it was," I said, looking over at my friend. "That was very sweet of you."

"It's not every day that you turn thirty," she said, bouncing over to give me a hug.

Liam leaned close. "I have to point out that today is also not the day she turns thirty."

"Oh, shut up, Liam," Lena said. "I know."

At the very least, that made me laugh. I would try to enjoy this. While I could.

"Seriously, though," Liam said, stepping closer, "happy birthday."

"Thanks."

"Did you have any idea?" Lena asked.

I shook my head. "Not a clue. I might have had a little bit of a heart attack back there."

She grinned. "That's the surprise party sweet spot. A little bit of a heart attack, but not a full heart attack. Now, I know it's cooler outside, but I think it's still nice enough to be out back. The lights are on, and I'll recruit some of the guys to bring out all the cake."

"Okay."

Jenna pulled me aside as I walked to the door to the patio. "Is everything okay? With that guy? He gave me really weird vibes."

"Of course," I lied, pushing down the anxiety that was making me shake. "That's Mr. Pearson."

"Oh." She made a face with understanding. "I guess I can see the resemblance now."

Jenna had worked for me long enough that she was familiar with Joel. But she'd never met his father.

"He can be a bit of an odd duck, but he was in town and had some questions about one of his horses that I treated the other day."

The patio was beautiful like this. Lights strung over the top of the small, bricked space lit it with a warm, welcoming glow. The tables scattered around had tablecloths and candles. Music played from a portable set of speakers. This was so beautiful. Lena had done this for me, and…

I didn't deserve it.

"Well, I'm glad everything's okay," Jenna said. "For whatever reason, I was really worried. That guy just gave me the creeps."

"Thankfully I don't think he'll be a regular at the clinic."

"Happy birthday." I turned to find Evelyn on my other side, smiling.

"Thanks."

"Do you want something to drink?" she asked. "We've got all the normal stuff, and I'm pretty sure Lena has some vodka stashed around here somewhere."

The last thing I needed tonight was vodka. The last time I'd been truly drunk was ages ago, but I wasn't going to take the chance that my friends wanted to get me quite that drunk. I didn't want to end up weeping and telling Grant everything.

"I'll just take some tea if that's okay."

"You got it."

An arm came around my waist, and in the dim light, Grant took the opportunity to lean around and kiss my neck. I was glad that he couldn't see my face and how conflicted I was. Every second that he touched me was precious now.

"Would you like to know about my plans for your birthday?" he asked quietly.

The words were so low, so full of heat, they made me shiver. "I would."

"You, me, and a blindfold," he said. "Add in rope, ice, and a vibrator and see where your imagination takes you."

My mind was instantly filled with images of what he described, and I wanted it. "Ice?"

"Hell yes."

"That sounds nice." Gently, I pulled away from him. My resolve was hardening, and I couldn't let anything take that away from me. Not when I wanted to save Grant's life. Even if what he was teasing me with was so fucking hot that it made it hard to breathe.

I felt more than his surprise at my reaction. But before he could ask, Lena burst out of the back of Deja Brew. Jude followed her, cake in hand. The top of it was lit with what I was sure were actually thirty candles.

"Okay, everyone. Get over here so we can sing and eat this cake. I don't know about you, but I could use some cake today."

Lena had no idea that was the understatement of the fucking year.

She grabbed my hand, pulled me close to the table where the cake now sat, and grinned. "'Happy birthday —'" She forcibly started singing the song so that everyone else would join in, and they did.

For a moment, I let myself feel it. The happiness of being surrounded by the friends I'd chosen and the place I'd decided to stay. This was perfect. Tears pricked my eyes, and I was glad that people would think they were happy tears and not ones of absolute terror. Because they were all in danger to some degree now.

If Pearson had Grant killed, he'd need more leverage over me to force me into whatever he wanted. So which person would he pick next to prove that point? Evelyn? Lena?

It wouldn't end—it would only get worse. Right now, I didn't see a way out of it. Except one, and that was the most painful one by far.

Grant stood next to me and put his arm around my shoulder. I gave in to the weakness and let it happen. God forgive me, I needed these last moments with him. Otherwise, I wasn't going to make it through.

The song finished, and everyone cheered. Hauling in a breath, I made one useless wish. That both Pearsons would mysteriously disappear, and I wouldn't have to make this choice.

I blew at the candles, aiming true, hitting every one so that they all went in one go. More cheers, this time for my victory. "Did you make a wish?" Noah asked.

"I did," I confirmed. "But you know I can't tell you what it is."

"Maybe I could guess," Grant said with a chuckle.

I managed a smile. "Maybe you could."

Lena started organizing plates and forks, commandeering Daniel to be in charge of cutting up the massive cake.

Noah pushed around the table to get to Grant and me. "So, you've been putting up with this loser for a little while, and you're still in it? Impressive."

"Thanks for the vote of confidence, man," Grant said.

Noah smirked. "I'm just saying. She's got a whole host of cowboys to choose from, and she got you. Not sure she got the best deal."

He was teasing, and we both knew it. Right now, though, I could tell the truth. "I feel lucky that I got to spend the time I did with him. It's been great."

Grant's hand tightened slightly on my shoulder. But if he caught the slightly strange phrasing—and there was no way he wouldn't—he didn't say anything.

The cake was delicious. Of course it was. Lena was a master of all things baked goods. Her cake was going to be amazing no matter what, but it was my favorite, red velvet.

Everyone wished me happy birthday, and I caught up more with all the Resting Warrior guys than I had in a long time. But in my head, I was still trying to forget.

Grant didn't stay by my side the entire time, but I felt him watching me. He wasn't stupid, and on top of that, he was one of the most observant people I'd ever met. He knew something was wrong.

Finally, when everyone was full of cake and coffee, Grant came up and hugged me. It was soft. Hesitant. "Want to go home?"

"Yeah." My stomach dropped. "I'll see you there."

I made my rounds and said goodbye, dragging my feet. Because even though I knew what I needed to do, as I started the drive home, all I knew was that I didn't want to do it.

Chapter 28

Cori

Grant was behind me the entire drive back home, and it felt like a ticking bomb. As soon as we reached our houses, the fuse was going to blow and destroy everything.

There was no way I was going to make it through this in one piece. Because the only way I could guarantee to save Grant's life was to break his heart. If we weren't together, there was no reason for the Pearsons to be interested in him. Or to hurt him. I would hurt both of us in the short term so that he could *have* a long term.

I pulled into the driveway slowly. Grant pulled into his. I shut off the truck but didn't get out. He was going to come over here, and… I couldn't do this. My eyes were already wet, but I held back the tears. I needed to at least try.

As I predicted, Grant came over to my truck and opened my door. He helped me down, and I started walking toward my house. It was wishful thinking to believe I could make it inside.

"Are you going to tell me what's wrong?" he asked.

I swallowed. "What makes you think there's something wrong?"

"Cori," he said with a huffed laugh. "I can tell when something's bothering you. And I can tell when you're hiding something. You were off during that whole party."

He pulled me into his arms, and there was nothing I wanted more in that moment than for him to kiss me. But I couldn't let him do it. If he kissed me, I would melt and I would let him take me inside and love me, and it would make all of this so much worse.

I pulled away.

"Cori…"

Tears flooded my eyes, blurring everything so that I couldn't see. Thankfully, it was dark, even with the ambiance from the streetlamps. "I can't do this," I said, my voice breaking. "It's over, Grant. I'm sorry."

There was nothing but silence.

The tears started to spill over, and I managed to make myself look at him.

Grant's face was blank. "Why?"

How could I make him believe it? He knew when I was upset. He would know I was lying. "Because I can't."

"That's not an answer," he said gently.

"I know."

Sliding his hands into his pockets, he looked at the ground. I got the feeling that he was choosing his words carefully. "I wasn't going to tell you this until later," he said. "Not until after the surgery when I knew exactly what I could offer you. But…I love you, Cori."

My heart stopped beating. He loved me too. Fresh, hot

tears rolled down. I wanted that. I wanted him. Inside, my heart was ripping itself apart.

"I love you so much that it hurts to breathe."

A sob worked its way out of me, and he pulled me close. I let him. I couldn't not let him. That scent of fresh pine and clean air laced with snow surrounded me. My sheets were still going to smell like him. He had things in my house, and I had things in his. This was going to be completely impossible.

"Tell me what's going on," he said.

"We can't be together."

I felt him shake his head. "That's what you're saying, but it's not the real reason. Because yesterday, you told me that you didn't want me to wait for commitment. That you were in this with me. What changed?"

My chest hurt. "I thought it through."

"What does that mean?" He was still being careful with his tone. His words. Trying to find the truth, and also, I knew, trying not to frighten me with any kind of reaction. Because of Joel. Which was why this man was so perfect for me.

"It means that I can't handle it," I said. "All of this."

"All of this."

I forced myself out of his arms, swiping at my eyes. "Not knowing how it's going to turn out," I said. He wasn't going to let me go easily. Nor should he. What I was saying didn't make sense, and he could feel it. If this was going to work, I needed to hit him where it hurt, and that just made the tears come faster.

"We can wait and see," he said. "We don't have to end it now."

I took a breath. "I can't be with someone who's broken."

As soon as I said the words, I knew they couldn't ever

be taken back. He flinched as if I'd hit him. And in a way, I had. I'd aimed right for where it would cause the most agony.

"If you go into surgery and come out paralyzed, I know I won't be able to handle that. The anxiety is just too much to even think about. It's better to end it now."

"Cori—"

"Don't," I said, my voice barely a whisper. "Please don't. Don't make it harder than it already is."

He shook his head. "I'm just trying to understand."

"I'm not strong enough. I can't take it." The lies were rolling off my tongue hard and fast now. "I need it to be over. I'm sorry. I'm so sorry."

I flung myself at him, taking one more kiss. Something that I could hold on to when I was breaking apart. He held me. Kissed me back. It was almost enough to crack my resolve. Almost enough to make me tell him everything.

But I couldn't. I just needed him to stay alive. And this was the only way I could think of to make that happen. Pain crackled in my chest, and I broke away. "I can't. I'm sorry, I can't."

"Cori."

I could barely see my way to my steps. Fumbled with the keys in the door, knowing that he was staring after me. He didn't yell or scream. Didn't try to do anything but watch me go.

The door shut behind me without me looking back. Because if I looked back, I would go to him. But I didn't have the strength to move farther. I sank down against the door and let it all go.

Sounds came from me that I'd never made in my life. This was the sound of *grief*. Never in my life did I think this would happen to me. Did anyone? Were there people who imagined having to take their own heart in their hands and crush it? Because that's what this felt like.

I buried my face in my hands and wept.

In nearly thirty years, I didn't remember ever crying this hard. Or this long. I lost track of time, sitting against the door. My face was a sticky mess, and my eyes were swollen. But I couldn't stop.

Even when I managed to get myself off the floor and up the stairs, I was crying. In the shower, too. It was only after I wrapped myself in a towel and sat on the bed that it seemed as if I'd cried myself dry.

That didn't make it better.

The bed felt empty and cold. As I'd thought, I could smell Grant on the pillows.

How could something be both comforting and painful at once? That's what his scent was. I lay down, not bothering to dress. I wasn't crying, but tears still leaked out of my eyes and down into the pillows. That was something I would have to get used to, I imagined. This pain wasn't going away anytime soon.

My phone vibrated in my bag across the room. I ignored it.

If it was Grant, I couldn't answer it. If it was anyone else, I really didn't want to talk. It wasn't as if I could tell anyone the truth anyway.

It was a long time before I fell asleep.

Chapter 29

Grant

Something wasn't right.

I stayed standing in that spot, staring at Cori's house for long minutes, trying to figure out what the hell had just happened. My instincts had been spot-on—something was wrong, because that wasn't Cori.

It wasn't that I was arrogant enough to think she couldn't change her mind, but yesterday, she'd been the one convincing me that I didn't need to wait until the surgery for some kind of commitment. I didn't see how she would make that drastic of a switch in only a day unless something had happened to cause it.

Knowing that it was wrong didn't make it hurt less.

I walked forward, not really knowing why until I was at Cori's steps. I wasn't Joel. I wasn't going to force her to be with me or fight what she wanted. But everything in me told me that this wasn't what she actually wanted.

One more step, and I stopped.

Cori was crying. Not crying like she had when she'd walked away—this was crying like I'd never heard before. She was crying like someone had died. Those sounds… I would never forget her sounding like that.

Everything in me wanted to go to her. She shouldn't be alone right now. I wanted to wrap her up and let her cry until she'd gotten it all out—even if the reason she was crying at all was me.

It tore me up to back away. It hurt, almost as much as the pain that I was desperately shoving down. I'd always been afraid that my back would be the reason someone would push me away. That fear was spiraling down my center and trying to tell me that I was worthless.

But I didn't buy it.

I knew what I felt. And yesterday, Cori had been in the same place that I was. Last night, she'd slept in my bed. Cried out my name and kissed me goodbye when she went to work, looking at me like I was the sun in her sky. Things couldn't change that fast.

Could they?

There was no way I could just go into my house and be without her in there. Not now. I'd be trapped in my thoughts, going in circles, and I would drive myself crazy.

Instead, I got straight back into my truck and pulled away. Distance was the only thing that would ensure I wouldn't go and check that she was okay. And I needed to get out of my own head.

That was the nice thing about Resting Warrior. It was the same as having a twenty-four seven gym membership. Thankfully, there were no cows in my way this time. I sprayed pebbles coming to a stop in front of our gym facility behind the main lodge.

Changing, I pushed myself. First, with a sprint on the treadmill to warm myself up. Then, I put on gloves and started beating the hell out of one of the bags. This was exactly what I needed.

Pain started to bloom in my back, but I ignored it. I needed the pain. Let myself feel it. It was more concrete than the pain that was pulsing in my chest. Easier to deal with.

The sound of the doors behind me startled me, but not enough to stop me from punching my invisible enemy. "What are you doing here, Grant?"

That was Noah's voice. One more hit, and I turned to find him and Jude walking far too casually toward me. Liam was hanging back by the door. "I'm not allowed to work out?"

"That's a stupid response, and you know it," Jude said.

"By all means, tell me what kind of response I'm supposed to have."

Noah held up his hands. "Hold on a second. Liam just told us that you came screaming into the driveway and nearly burned rubber stopping in front of the gym. Given the fact that we all assumed you would be having some very private birthday celebrations with Cori right now, we wanted to make sure you were okay."

I glared at them. "I'm fine."

"A phrase that is well-known for being basically a lie," Jude added.

Irrational anger rose in my chest. "Did you wake up this morning and decide to become a comedian?" I said to Jude, taking a step toward him. "Because you should rethink that choice."

Jude was a giant of a man. He towered over most of us by six inches and had easily sixty pounds of muscle on me. That didn't matter. Right now, I'd beat him with pleasure.

"Grant," Noah said. "What happened?"

I didn't look at him. "None of your business."

"It is when you're taunting fellow team members."

"Nothing," I said. "Nothing happened." Back to the punching bag. The only sound in the gym was the sound of my gloves hitting the canvas. "You guys just going to watch me do this?"

"Grant," Noah said. "What's going on?"

"What's going on is that I need to be left alone," I said, punctuating my words with strikes. "And I'll see you all tomorrow."

I didn't turn around to find out if they were leaving, but I finally heard footsteps retreating and the door close. They'd find out soon enough. Right now, I needed to be here exhausting myself, not spilling my feelings about it. That was something that would inevitably come later. Probably during one of my sessions with Rayne.

It was late when I stopped. I couldn't force myself any further. My back hurt like a bitch, and I was limping. That was fine. It was what I needed. It made sure that when I got home, I would fall asleep. Tomorrow, I'd deal with the guys and figure out what the hell was really going on.

Or at least I hoped that I would.

Morning didn't bring any clarity

Thankfully, the work that I'd done on myself hadn't put me into one of my worst pain days. It was bad, but it was bearable. I'd do it again, too, for the ease with which I fell asleep.

Even with that, the bed still smelled like Cori. The blankets felt empty, the bed cold. When I forced myself up and to the window, Cori's truck was already gone.

I had to do something. Every instinctual part of me said that something wasn't right. Hopefully the guys wouldn't think I was overstepping my bounds. But every passing minute was a minute that I was fighting panic.

Showering quickly, I hopped in the truck and went to the ranch. Jude was in the kitchen making coffee. Perfect. He leaned against the counter.

"I'm sorry."

Jude inclined his head. "You already seem better."

"Not really."

Pouring the coffee, he grabbed another cup and poured one for me. "Care to talk now?"

Of all the guys, Jude was probably the best one to tell it to. Not out of any kind of miraculous sensitivity, but because he was the quietest and least likely to spread the word quickly. This was already going to be hard without that.

I sat at the table and painted the broad strokes for him. "I don't have the actual words to explain it, man. But this isn't coming from her. Something happened, and she felt like she had to do it."

"And you're absolutely sure you didn't do something to piss her off?" He said it with a teasing smile, but his eyes were hard. I couldn't get mad at the question—it was the same one I'd be asking.

"I swear," I said. "I said goodbye to her in the morning, and I didn't see or talk to her again until she walked in for the surprise party. And when we said goodbye? Everything was fine."

He nodded slowly. "Let's talk to Daniel. I'm not going to dig into Cori's life without giving him a heads-up and letting him weigh in. But that does sound off. And I trust your gut."

Daniel was upstairs in the office, and the conversation was much the same. I told him what had happened and explained. He sat back in his chair and looked at me. "What aren't you telling me?"

"Nothing. That's all."

He raised his eyebrows and waited. There was a reason he was good at what he did. Interrogation had been one of his specialties.

I sighed. "I love her."

"Is that a surprise?" Jude asked.

"No," Daniel admitted. "But I have to ask the question about whether you're just more invested than she is." He held up a hand before I could protest. "I'm not doubting you. You know I have to ask."

"I know." I crossed my arms. "And I know how this looks. But I can't help the feeling that something is really wrong."

Daniel looked at Jude and nodded. "Do it. After everything that's happened, I'm not going to take chances. Cori is family now, regardless of whether or not she's with you, Grant. We need to make sure she's okay. But if she is—" he pinned me with a stare "—you need to back off."

"I'm disappointed that you think I wouldn't."

"I know you would. Still have to say it."

I sighed again. "Yeah."

Jude clapped me on the arm. "Let's go."

We went down to the security office. I felt weird about doing this—Cori's privacy was hers. But if she was in trouble, it would be worth it.

"How long will it take?"

"Give me a few minutes. I'll pull up what I can. Is there anything you can think of that would put her in danger?"

I thought through everything. Of course the Pearsons and the horses came to mind, but I didn't want to assume anything. Not until we knew more.

While he ran his searches, I dropped my head into my hands. I'd slept, but I wasn't rested.

"Her family is impressive."

"I know they're wealthy. The whole family are doctors. They're actively trying to force Cori into going back to medical school—for humans—even though she doesn't want to."

Jude paused. "How are they forcing her?"

"Money. She has a trust that she was supposed to receive at thirty. Told me she wants to use it for the clinic. But they don't approve of her being a vet."

"How far do you think they would go? Did you get the impression that they'd force her with more than money?"

I shrugged. "I've never met them. But no. My gut says that's not it. She was bothered by it, but more bothered by the fact that they weren't respecting her choices. When we talked, she wasn't afraid of it."

Turning, Jude looked at me. "Okay. I have to ask you something, and I'm not asking for details. Try not to be offended. The…preferences that you and I share. Any chance that scared her off?"

He was the only other Resting Warrior who had any interest in kink. And from what I knew, he was deeper into it than I would ever be. Though, he hadn't been with anyone in years. It was a logical question, given what he knew.

"No. I promise." I shook my head. "For obvious reasons, I'm not going to say more than that. But that wasn't the reason."

"Anything else?"

"She was looking into a client. The father of her ex. One of his horses was sick, and he was really cagey about it. I went with her to take a blood sample from the first horse, and it was gone. The second time, she got it, but she didn't tell me the results."

Jude's face went hard. "This is the same ex who nearly hit her while dumping her?"

"You heard about that?"

He nodded. "Doesn't exactly give me warm and fuzzies. What kind of horses?"

"Huge stable out there. I didn't ask, but seeing those horses? They're racers."

"I'd bet a lot of money that's where the problem is," he said, turning back to the computer.

I sat with it. My instincts didn't say it was nothing. "It's worth looking into. But why would that have to do with me?"

"I don't know yet," he said.

Pacing back and forth, I winced. My back was starting to feel worse. It had been stupid of me to push myself like that last night. No point in beating myself up about it now. It was done. But it wasn't the best decision I'd ever made. Lesson learned. I was paying the price.

"Holy shit," Jude said under his breath.

"What?"

He waved me over. "Graham Pearson is a piece of work," he said. "Never convicted of anything but connected with a bunch of shady people and implicated in a lot of crimes. Especially around racing. He's on top of his game in that world, basically a legend."

"Okay. That's a good start."

"His list of known associates is about as long as my arm."

I sat, groaning. "Anyone we know?"

"Looking. And there's a shit ton here about his son Joel too—all of it bad news. Guy put two separate boys in the hospital when he lost his temper and attacked them in high school. Parents paid them off. Was also accused of sexually assaulting a woman while he was in college. That charge mysteriously went away."

"Fuck." Cori had been lucky to get out of their relationship without physical violence. "Keep looking on Graham Pearson."

There had to be something. My gut had never failed me, and I didn't want this to be the first time. If I was wrong, I would swallow my pride, but I knew I wasn't. There would be something, and we would find it.

Jude went still, staring at the screen.

"Find something?"

He cleared his throat. "What did you say the name of the surgeon was? The one you saw?"

"Keyes. Amanda Keyes. Why?"

"Because," he said, pointing at the screen, "she's on the list. Amanda Keyes is a known associate of Graham Pearson."

My stomach plummeted through the floor. There was the connection, and it was worse than I ever imagined.

Chapter 30

Cori

I was sick to my stomach. The medicine I'd taken to try to help the nausea wasn't actually helping. Not a surprise. This sickness didn't have to do with anything I ate.

As soon as I got to the Pearson Ranch, they were going to want me to poison horses. Who knew how many? I couldn't do that, but I had a plan. A Hail Mary, just in case. At the clinic, I borrowed Jenna's phone and sent an email to one of my vet friends I *knew* wasn't attached to the Pearsons. No connection to the racing world whatsoever. I told them to email Resting Warrior and to tell them what was happening and where I was.

If I really was being watched, then I had to assume they had the power to monitor my phone and email. If they had eyes on me, they could see if I made any calls. But I was able to grab Jenna's phone and take it to the bathroom quickly. It was a risk, but it was one I had to take.

All I could do was pray that my friend got the email and passed it on in time. Because the Pearsons weren't going to be happy about my saying no. Again.

Dread seeped down my spine as I pulled into the drive of the ranch. After this was over—however it ended—I was never coming back to this place. They could find another vet. Or maybe they wouldn't, because like hell was I going to let anyone I knew work with them ever again.

They were waiting by the stable. Joel leaned against the barn, arms crossed, glaring at me. Mr. Pearson looked less angry, but that didn't mean he was less dangerous. He was more.

The feeling of them watching my every move as I got my medical bag and crossed the gravel to them only added to the nausea swimming in my gut.

"Good to know you're punctual," Mr. Pearson said. "I don't have all day."

I took my breath and braced for the lie. "I'll do this, but hurting Grant is off the table."

"Is that so?"

I looked him in the eye. "We're not together anymore. He's not leverage. And no more blackmail pictures either."

Joel laughed. "It was quite the performance you gave, dumping him. Far better than the one you gave when we broke up."

I rolled my eyes. This wasn't a conversation I was going to indulge. I hated that he'd been watching our breakup—that he was watching me at all. But there was nothing I could do about that right now. I looked at the elder Pearson again. "Promise me that you won't touch him."

"Your insistence on it doesn't make the argument that using him won't hurt you," he mused. "But fine. As long as you follow through, soldier boy is safe."

"Good," I said.

Please, let Jane have seen the email. Please let Grant and the Resting Warrior guys be on their way. Please.

I hoped that Grant would forgive me for last night. That once he understood, he wouldn't hate me for hitting where it was meant to hurt.

"Let's go," Mr. Pearson said, walking into the stable. "You have a list of horses to infect today. We're going to pass it off as a fast-moving virus."

"I still don't understand why you need me to do this," I said. "You have two hands."

He looked over his shoulder at me. "You're smarter than that, Cori."

I was. He needed someone to take the fall in case the authorities found out that the horses were murdered. The country vet with a point to prove. They could twist it any way they wanted.

"Why are you doing this? If I'm putting myself on the line, I want to know."

Joel smirked. "You don't get to ask that."

"There's nothing she can say, Joel. If she reveals what we need from it, she incriminates herself. At the very least as an accessory. So I don't mind telling you that it's about the money. The horses I'm disposing of aren't winning. Not nearly enough. At this point, they're worth more to me dead than alive.

"When they're gone, I'll use the money to invest in better horses. To win more."

"So, you don't *need* the money? You're not in debt or something?" I tried to contain my utter horror and failed.

"We always need money," Joel said. "Not that you would know that. Did you know she's giving up her trust because she won't go back to medical school?"

Mr. Pearson started to speak, and I interrupted. "You gave up the privilege of having an opinion on my life choices, Joel. Multiple times now. Shut the fuck up."

His father laughed. "It's a pity it didn't work out, Cori. You would make an excellent Pearson."

"I'd rather not."

We ended up next to Hazelwood's stall. He was still breathing, but barely. "You'll start with this one. Here."

He gestured, and Joel handed me a pouch. Inside were vials of clear liquid and syringes. "What is this?"

"It's what we've been using. Coumarin. A much more intense dose. It should be effective within a few days."

Where were they? It had been long enough that they could be arriving any second. Please. If anything in the universe was listening, I needed them to show up. I didn't want to kill this horse.

I took my time checking Hazelwood's vitals. Doing busywork things. Cleaning the injection site. Cleaning the needle. Slowly filling the injector with the liquid—something that could have taken seconds. I made it last.

But there was only so much I could do. The needle was resting against the horse's skin. All I needed to do was push the needle in to finish this, and I couldn't do it. There was never a chance that I was going to, but I'd hoped that they'd get here. I'd hoped that the Resting Warrior crew would swing in like heroes and stop it before I came to this.

"You know I can't poison this horse," I said quietly.

"Excuse me?" Joel's voice was loud.

I looked up at him, pulling the needle away from the horse. "I can't poison this horse."

Mr. Pearson sighed. "We hoped it wouldn't come to that, but we expected it. That's why there's a Plan B."

Pain exploded through my head, and suddenly I was sprawled over Hazelwood's body. My vision blurred, and I couldn't get to my feet. Dizzy. I was dizzy. They pulled me to my feet together, each holding an arm.

No. Whatever this was? This couldn't happen. I'd thought they would force me with the needle. What was this? I thought about Grant. He would tell me to fight it. So I did. I kicked out at the two of them, and I heard the grunts as my feet made contact with them, but they didn't let me go and didn't let me regain my feet. They dragged me through the dirt. "What are you doing?"

Did I want to know?

Joel's laugh echoed through the stable. "This was my idea, and I think you'll like this, Cori. I saw the pictures, right? You weren't joking when you said you wanted to be tied up, and from what I've seen so far, you fucking love it."

My head was ringing from where they'd hit me. I couldn't quite make my vision clear or the world stop spinning. Being dragged wasn't helping. "Where are you taking me?"

I was slammed up against a wall, knocking the breath from me. Not a wall. A pillar. One of the pillars in the center of the stable, where paths crossed.

Joel had my arms, pressing them so hard into the surface that they ached. I kicked him and instantly regretted it. New pain bloomed across my cheek. He let me go only long enough to hit me again.

"I figure since you enjoy being tied up so much, you'll enjoy this. One last time. With me."

"Never with you."

Joel's hand wrapped around my neck, tilting my chin up so I couldn't look away and couldn't breathe. Around my body, I felt rope slither into place. Panic burst through me. No oxygen and no way to fight. I didn't know what they had planned, but I wasn't sure if I was going to survive it.

"Oh, Cori," he said, pressing harder. "You were with me long enough to know that I always get the last word. Always." More rope was wrapped, and I felt Mr. Pearson's hands in passing as he circled, securing my shoulders and my hands.

Air. I needed air. None was getting past the strength of Joel's hand.

"Getting rid of you at the same time is a bonus," he said. "If I can't have you, then no one gets to. Especially not some worthless soldier with an attitude problem."

I couldn't speak. The world began to fade as I struggled for air. Panic receded as my brain started to shut down. Oxygen was the only goal. There was no move I could make. The ropes bit into my skin, keeping me against the pillar. I was going to die.

"But I won't kill you. Can't have your body looking like it was dead beforehand."

He released me, and color rushed back into the world. I breathed so fast that I choked, coughing. My lungs and throat burned. "What are you doing?" I finally managed.

Mr. Pearson came to stand in front of me. "All of it needs to be an accident. That fire that destroyed all the horses at the Pearson Ranch. Such a pity. It caught too quickly. There was absolutely nothing that could be done." He smiled grimly. "And the poor local vet who was in the area and ran in to try to save the animals? That was such a tragedy. No one will ever question the fire that killed the beautiful and perfect Cori Jackson."

"No." My voice was rough, throat struggling after what Joel had done to me. Where was Grant now? Did he hate me? Would he get the email too late and feel regret? Did the Pearsons find out about the email and get to Jane, too?

"I'm sorry that it came to this," Mr. Pearson said. "I

really am. I would rather have had us be on the same side, but you're not leaving me a choice."

They walked away, passing by the pillar so that I couldn't see them anymore. "*Wait,*" I called. "Please don't do this."

Joel stepped into my line of vision. "Feel free to scream as much as you like. There's no one here. Every employee has the day off."

"Joel!" I yelled after him. "You're not this person, Joel. Please."

I heard the heavy doors of the stable close. More than one set. The stable had something like seven entrances, and I heard them all shut one after another. This was really happening. Oh my God, *this was happening*.

Fighting against the ropes was useless, but I still tried. They were so tight, they would leave bruises. If I survived. No way to move or slip out from under them.

All this was a mistake. The risk that I took didn't pay off. I should have just told Grant the truth, no matter the consequences.

Now, I was here, and I had to wallow in the fact that I broke his heart before I died. They weren't here, and if they weren't now, the chances—

I cut off the thought.

No.

Instead, I focused on Grant. I should have told him that I loved him, so that he knew. Maybe he would have been here with me. Maybe we would both be about to die.

I shook my head, trying to keep the panic at bay.

The scent of smoke in the barn made that completely impossible. I saw it at the far end of the stable, the horses already murmuring in response to the smell. I only had so much time before the smoke made me pass out. And I wasn't going to give up. I wasn't going to just let myself die.

So I screamed for help. Maybe there was nobody here, and they'd given everyone the day off, but stranger things had happened. I needed a miracle, and I would wait for it until the last second.

I kept on screaming, making my throat raw as the first flames licked up the walls. It was too fast. Too soon. Now the horses were screaming too.

The guys had to know. Jane had to have sent the email. They were on their way. Grant was on his way. I had to believe that.

The sound of burning swallowed up my screams.

Chapter 31

Grant

Jude and I heard the frantic footsteps before Daniel burst into the room. "You were right."

"What?"

He pushed his laptop onto the table. "Just got an email on the main Resting Warrior account from a vet named Jane. Says she's passing on information from Cori about Graham and Joel Pearson poisoning horses. Cori's being blackmailed, and she needs help. This was the only way to get us the information."

The vilest curses I knew came out of my mouth, and I was already on my feet, grabbing my keys. "We should check the clinic. If she's not there, she could already be at the ranch, but it's on the way."

They were with me and on my heels. The pain in my back was growing, and I didn't fucking care. If they touched Cori…

I jumped into the truck. "Give me your phone," Jude said. "I need her number."

Daniel slammed the back door to the truck, and we were spinning out of the driveway. "Do we need to call anyone else in?"

"I'm not waiting," I said, stepping on the gas and tossing my phone across the seat to Jude.

"At the very least, I'm telling them what's going on. They can be en route." Daniel was talking on the phone then, letting the others know.

"Don't bother with the clinic," Jude said. "She's not there."

I swallowed, focusing on the road. "Please tell me she's at home. Or Deja Brew. Anywhere but there."

Out of the corner of my eye, I saw him shake his head. "She's at the Pearson Ranch."

"How far is that?" Daniel asked.

My words could barely make it out through the tension in my jaw. "Thirty miles."

Daniel swore. "Go as fast as you can without killing us. I'll call Charlie and let him know. Tell him to meet us there and to make sure that none of his people pull us over."

I sped up.

Now it made sense. Something was clearly wrong last night at the party and before she broke up with me. "Fuck, they must have used me."

"Explain," Jude said.

"The surgeon." We hadn't had time to dive into that before Daniel had burst through the door. "Think about it. They must have some kind of leverage on her. Maybe they used that to pressure Cori. Threatened her. Maybe that's why she ended it, because in her mind, it was the only way to get out from under that pressure and help me."

I shook my head, glancing over at them. "The way she

was crying after she went inside…" The emotion of those sounds would never leave me. "I've never heard anything like that."

"Well," Daniel said. "One thing's for sure. I wouldn't trust the doctor to do the surgery after this."

"We don't know her side of the story," I pointed out. "She could be pressured, too. I don't think Peak would have recommended her if he didn't trust her."

Jude looked forward down the road as I made a sharp turn in the direction of the ranch. "Worry about that later."

"What are we afraid that we're walking in on here?"

I tightened my hand on the steering wheel. "What did Jane say in the email?"

"Only that they were poisoning horses and that Cori felt like she was in immediate trouble. That she was being watched and needed help."

"Cori was onto them," I said. "A horse was sick, and when we went to get a blood sample, the horse had disappeared. The next horse that got sick? We got a sample. But she didn't tell me the results."

Daniel looked at me in the mirror. "That doesn't answer the question. What the hell are we walking into?"

"I don't know," I admitted. "But she's a vet. If they're poisoning the animals, maybe they want her help. But Cori's never going to kill an animal. Not voluntarily. And…" I hesitated. Because I wasn't sure if it was something Cori wanted anyone else to know. But in this case, they needed to. I sighed. "After they broke up, the next time she saw Joel, he tried to rape her. A stable hand walking in is what saved her. So, no, I have no idea what we're walking in on."

"Jesus." Daniel scrubbed a hand over his face. "Okay."

Every mile that passed, the pain in my back grew. It felt

like the shrapnel had moved. I didn't know if it was just time or if I'd accelerated that process. All I knew was that it had never felt like this before.

But it didn't matter. Cori was the only thing that mattered. And if the bastards were willing to kill horses, humans weren't a huge step.

"The guys are on their way. Charlie too."

"Call them back," Jude said. "Tell them to bring an ambulance."

My heart skipped a beat. "Why?"

He pointed straight ahead. "Think it's a coincidence that there's smoke from right where we're headed?"

Oh my God. In the distance, over the hill, curls of smoke rose in the sky. And it was only getting darker, thicker, and more visible the closer we got. "Shit. Hold on."

I pushed my foot down on the gas.

Images of Cori dead were flying through my head. Of the explosion, too. Of my unit mates lying dead in the aftermath. I couldn't stop them, and I couldn't slow down.

I had to get to her.

I *had* to.

We swerved into the ranch's driveway so fast I felt the truck deciding whether it wanted to roll. The universe was on our side that it did not. But the black smoke rolling just past the trees…

The entire stable was engulfed in flames. Horses were screaming. I got the truck as close as I could without it being a hazard before getting out.

Cori was in there. I knew it. Every bone in my body knew it. The roof was already collapsing.

My body screamed in agony, but I forced it back. I would take the pain—and the injury—if it meant that Cori was okay.

I launched myself into the stable.

Daniel and Jude were behind me, frantically opening the stalls that weren't on fire and trying to get as many horses out as possible.

Where was she? Where would they have put her?

"*Cori!*" I shouted her name, but it was lost in the sound of roaring flames.

A piece of burning roof fell, and I dove out of the way, shouting in pain. My back didn't want to function. Even my survival instinct told me to curl up and not move because it was so fucking overwhelming.

No. This wouldn't be the way it ended. For me, or for Cori.

I forced myself to my feet and kept moving. They would have put her in a place where they could be sure that she wouldn't make it out. In the middle. I opened stalls as I went. The horses deserved a chance, even if they didn't make it.

Panic started to set in. The air was thick with smoke, and I would only last in here for so long.

Where was she?

I wasn't a praying man, but I did now.

Please. Please let me find her in time.

She wasn't in the corners—I checked, just in case. But nothing. Straight toward the center. The flames were hotter here, and I felt my body shutting down from smoke and pain.

The central beam of the stable was still standing, and there was something attached to it, swinging, burning.

Rope.

She was there. A beam was in my way, and there was another one on the other side already collapsed. This place was coming down and fast. But I saw her. Facedown on the ground, inches from flames.

"Cori." I coughed, diving under the beam and crawling to her. She wasn't moving. "Cori, sweetheart."

I rolled her over. She wasn't awake, but she was breathing. That was enough. All we needed was a chance.

Lifting her was the most painful thing I'd ever experienced. My legs shook, eyes and lungs burning. We needed to get out of here right now, or I would be passed out too. I couldn't drag her under that beam—we needed to go the long way.

"We're going to make it," I told her. "You're going to be okay. You did so good with the email. I love you."

A huge *crack* was the lone warning I got before the beam fell. The only thing I could do was shield Cori. It slammed into my shoulders, throwing both of us. I managed to get my body over hers, but at a cost.

Something was wrong. My legs weren't working right. It was as if they were on a delay. Slower. I was moving through molasses. Or honey.

The exit was around the corner, but it felt like a literal mile. I coughed again. Even low to the ground, the smoke was thick, and I was dizzy. "Come on, Cori," I said, more to myself than to her. "We're almost there."

My legs fought me the whole way as I forced my way to standing. Grabbed her arms and pulled. There wasn't a chance I could lift her now, and I couldn't shout. There was too much smoke in the air for that kind of breath.

Time zeroed down to the next movement. The effort I had to give to pull and not faint. Once more. Again. Around the corner.

Light from the outside was shining, barely visible.

I heard shouts, and Jude was suddenly there, lifting Cori off the ground and running. Daniel wrapped an arm around my shoulder, and I leaned on him until we got out of the building.

Air had never tasted so sweet.

Jude laid Cori on the ground, far enough away from the building that she wasn't in danger. "She's breathing," I said, voice rough and ruined from the smoke.

"You got her out," Daniel said. "You did good. The ambulance is on its way."

"Good." I fell to my knees beside Cori, unable to make my legs hold me anymore. The jarring movement of the fall sent one final jolt of pain flooding through my system. It was too much.

"Daniel," I said. "Call a second ambulance."

That was all I had time for before the rest of the world went black.

Chapter 32

Cori

Movement. I was moving.

Why was I moving?

My eyes felt like I'd been walking out in the middle of the desert. They were so dry. Burning.

Slowly, I opened my eyes, and I saw something on my face. Plastic? What the hell was going on?

A siren sounded outside, and it clicked. I was in an ambulance.

The fire.

They'd left me in a fire.

I hadn't expected to wake up at all, but here I was. Who was here?

Noah sat beside me, and a paramedic, but Grant wasn't here. Where was Grant?

"Where is he?"

Noah's head snapped up from his phone. "You're awake. Hey. You're going to be okay."

"Where is he?" I asked again.

"We got your message, and they got there just in time. Right now, everyone not headed to the hospital is tracking down Pearson and his son. We're going to get them. Charlie is going to meet us at the hospital, and you'll have to make a statement."

I pulled the mask down off my face, immediately noticing the difference the oxygen made. "Noah." My voice was barely a croak. "Where is Grant?"

He was all that mattered to me right now, because I was fine and he wasn't here. I wasn't stupid. Even if I ripped his heart into shreds, he would still come for me. And he would be in this ambulance with me—wouldn't let anyone else take his place—unless there was something wrong.

Noah looked hesitant, and my stomach flipped. "Please, just tell me he's okay," I begged.

"He's alive," Noah said. "They took him in the first ambulance because you were stable. It…doesn't look good for his back. His legs weren't working when they put him in the ambulance. He'll be at the hospital by now, and they're getting that surgeon here. Flying her in."

"You can't," I said. "They'll make her—"

"We know about her. It's being dealt with. Believe me, Cori, we're not going to let anything happen to him. I promise."

My eyes were so dry that I didn't feel like I could cry. But my chest ached all the same. He had to be okay. If I broke his heart, and then he…

I looked away.

"We're here," the paramedic said. "Hold on tight."

They wheeled me in on the gurney, insisting that I keep the oxygen flowing. All I wanted to do was to see Grant.

Noah was with me the whole time.

"Can you find out where he is?" I asked. "As soon as they tell me I'm okay, I need to see him. I need to."

"I'll find out," he said gently. "But Grant would also have my ass if I left you here alone."

Jude walked into the room just then. "He's upstairs. You can't see him yet."

"Please."

There was understanding in his eyes, but no relenting. "Get checked out first, Cori. Grant isn't going anywhere. Daniel is with him. And Lucas."

I tried to push down the panic that was spiraling in my mind. The last thing I said to him couldn't be me breaking up with him. Not when it was the last thing I wanted.

But Jude was right. Grant wasn't going anywhere, and he would want me to get checked out. If he was awake, it would be the first thing he asked, because that's who he was. It was the only thing that held me still through the examination and the chat with the doctor that told me what I already knew.

I'd been lucky. My burns were minor, and I suffered from smoke inhalation. Despite that, it looked like my lungs would make a full recovery. I had a concussion because of where they'd hit me, but there was nothing to do for that except to monitor it.

"While you're here, please keep the oxygen mask on. We'd like you to rest for a few hours."

"Can I see him?"

The doctor raised an eyebrow. "If you keep the oxygen with you, and you promise not to overdo it, you can go see him. But I'll tell you now, he's not conscious. They've already sedated him so that there's no chance of him moving and making his injury worse."

"That's okay," I said. "I just… I need to see him."

She smiled. "Go ahead."

I practically leaped off the bed. Jude had beaten me to the door, and I followed him. Noah was behind me. "Oh my God," I said as I reached the elevator. "You're my bodyguards."

Jude nodded once. "Until we find them, you're a witness they tried to kill. We're not taking chances."

That was a sobering thought.

I didn't have to ask what room he was in—Daniel was standing outside the door, guarding Grant too. He held out his hands. "He's not awake."

"I know," I said. "I know, but I still have to see him."

"You broke up with him," he said gently.

My head was shaking before he finished the sentence. "I didn't want to."

"He knows that. But I want to make sure before I let you in there…there's a chance he doesn't come out of this walking. And I won't let you get his hopes up if you're not okay with that."

It was a fair question, but it still hurt. I didn't doubt that it would take the guys at Resting Warrior a little while to trust me again. "I was always fine with that. I think that I'm more okay with it than he is." I swallowed. "If you think that would matter to me, you don't know me very well."

"I figured," he said with a smile. "Just trying to protect my team."

"I know."

He stepped aside, and I walked into the room. Grant was facedown on the bed, not moving. His back was exposed, showing his scars. If he were awake, I didn't think he'd want that. Grant never wanted to be judged by them.

I brushed my fingers gently over his back. I remembered the first time I'd seen them so clearly. The way he'd reacted when I'd seen them.

There were new ones here, a red stripe that looked like a burn. Fresh. This was from the fire—from pulling me out.

I dragged the chair next to the bed, close to where Grant's face was. He looked like he was asleep and not unconscious, ready to have a surgery that could change his life forever.

"Hi." I reached out and ran my fingers through his hair. Gently. With his back in such precarious shape, I didn't want to touch him too much. At the same time, I couldn't stand not to touch him. "I'm so sorry," I whispered.

"This isn't what I wanted. And if you can't forgive me for last night, then I understand. But I love you."

My emotions were too close to the surface, and tears frosted my vision. I tried to hold them back. "I love you so much it hurts. I hoped that if they couldn't touch you, they would back off. But—"

No more words could come out.

I laid my head down on the bed next to his head, where I could hear him breathing. Making sure that my movements didn't shift at all, I laced my fingers through his. "I love you," I managed to whisper. "Please don't leave."

The chances of him dying were slim, but they weren't zero. After Joel and the fire, it was at the forefront of my mind. Grant had to stay, so that I could tell him the truth, no matter if I'd broken us completely or not.

Tears streaked down my face and soaked into the bed. "Please don't leave."

"Cori?"

Lena stood in the doorway. She was wearing her apron, and there was flour all over it and some on her face. I leaned forward, lowered my mask briefly, and kissed Grant. Maybe, even unconscious, he would feel it.

I barely made it out of the room before I couldn't hold it in anymore. Lena pulled me into a hug, absorbing my sobs on her shoulder. My oxygen mask was fogging. "Hey," she said. "You're okay. And he's going to be okay."

"You don't know that."

"No," she admitted. "But I believe that."

Lena guided me over to some chairs across from the door to Grant's room. Evelyn was already seated, and as I looked up, Grace and Harlan walked in. Everyone was here.

"Are you okay?" Lena asked.

"No."

She laughed softly. "Obviously not. But physically? They pulled you out of a burning building."

Lena shuddered, and Evelyn looked over at her. They both had had bad experiences with fire.

"Yeah," I said. "I'm fine. Minor burns. Smoke inhalation. Head got knocked around a little. I'll be good as new. I just hope that he is."

Grace crouched down in front of me. "Even if he's not, he'll be okay. He'll have you. He'll have all of us."

"It's not that. Being in a wheelchair is fine. There's nothing wrong with it. But movement is Grant's life. It would be…devastating." I curled my knees up to my chest and wrapped my arms around them. "I could have become a surgeon," I said. "My whole fucking family are surgeons, and they wanted me to be one too. Then maybe I could help him. Maybe I should still do that so I won't fail anybody else. That would be worth the four years, right?"

I was just talking. The words were pouring out of me uncensored, but I couldn't seem to stop.

"Cori, honey," Grace said. "Even if you were a surgeon, you already know they wouldn't let you operate on him. Can't operate on a family member or significant other."

"Yeah, but still…"

She nodded. "I know."

Grace understood. Her first husband had died unexpectedly. Even though their marriage hadn't been a romantic one, it was still devastating to lose someone like that. More so when it turned out that he'd been murdered.

Either way, in a strange sense, she related.

Lucas walked out of the elevator carrying a mountain of takeout boxes and beelined straight for us.

"I sent Lucas for food," Evelyn explained. "We're going to be here a while, and you need to eat."

"Honestly? I don't know if I could keep anything down."

She smiled and put an arm around my shoulder. "It's sandwiches, so they'll be good for a while if you're hungry later." Leaning closer, she whispered, "But I will warn you that if you don't eat at all, Lena will probably hold you down and force you."

That managed to make me smile a little.

Time passed slowly, waiting for things to happen. I'd zoned out so completely that I was nearly dozing when a flurry of commotion broke out on the floor. A tall woman in a lab coat approached Daniel, though we were all watching her now as she came over.

"Daniel Clark?"

"That's me." He shook her hand.

"You're listed as the contact for Grant Carter. I'm Dr. Amanda Keyes. I'll be performing his surgery."

I sprang to my feet and had almost made it to her when Lena pulled me back. The doctor looked at all of us carefully, especially me. "I was informed of the…circumstances under which my name was used, and I would like to clarify some things. You're Cori?"

"I am." At the moment, I wasn't sure if I wanted to hug her or punch her in the face.

"I'm sorry you were told that anyone had leverage over me. Especially enough that I would kill a patient on the table. That isn't true. I took a medical oath, just like you."

I rarely went by "Doctor." But that's what I was. Sometimes it didn't feel like it. Today it certainly didn't.

"But—" Lena squeezed my arm.

Dr. Keyes smiled. "It is true that the Pearsons paid for my education. But that was through a scholarship program. I qualified at the time because of work my father did, and we did the research. I had no reason to believe there was anything deeper to it.

"On top of that, there was nothing promised in return for receiving the money. I have all the papers I signed for the scholarship if you want to see them."

Daniel nodded. "I would, please. To verify. After the surgery."

"It won't take that long. I'll have my office fax them here now." She pulled out her phone and sent a text. "Now, this surgery is going to take a while. If you want to go home and rest, that's fine. We'll keep in contact with you."

"I think some of us are going to stay, but thank you for the offer," Daniel said.

"What are the chances?"

She sighed. "They were good when I saw him at his appointment, but I understand there may have been movement."

Behind her, Grant was wheeled out of his room, and my heart was in my throat. Lena squeezed my hand again. I was glad she was here.

"We need to revisualize the shrapnel before I go in and take it out. He's being taken for the scan now."

"Please fix it," I said. It was such a simple request, but it was the only way I knew how to say it. "Please fix him."

She locked eyes with me. "I'm going to do my very best. I promise you that." Then she looked at Daniel. "You'll have those documents within twenty minutes. Before I scrub in."

"Thank you."

She disappeared, and my knees felt wobbly and weak. "You believe her?"

"I do," Daniel said. "But I'm going to read those papers carefully all the same."

Lena hugged me from the side. "She's right. The surgery is going to take a long time. If you want to go home and sleep for a while, it will be okay."

"I would be out of my mind there," I said. "I can't."

Nobody really expected me to leave. Grant would probably tell me to go. But if the positions were reversed, I also knew that he wouldn't leave my side for even a single second. And I felt the same. "I'll stay."

"Then we'll stay with you," Lena said.

And that was that. It was going to be a long day.

Chapter 33

Grant

Sound came back to me first. Familiar sounds that threw me back in time to the last time I'd woken up like this. The soft, slow beeps of a heart rate monitor. The overhead announcements in the main halls. Squeaking nurse shoes and rolling carts.

The scent of cleaning and, deeper, the scent of worse things.

I was in a hospital.

Not completely surprising, given my last conscious memory. The surprising part was that I didn't feel any pain. Whether that was because I was full of pain medication remained to be seen.

Slowly, I opened my eyes. The lids were heavy, and my eyes still felt scratchy from the smoke. There was a window in my line of vision, the sky darkening with evening. Was it still the same day? How much time had I lost?

I took a deeper breath, and it hitched in my chest. The

feeling of smoke was still in my lungs, tickling. I coughed, and I heard a soft gasp to my left. "Grant?"

Slowly, I turned my head. Cori was curled in a chair. It was clear she'd been crying. She looked exhausted. There were bandages on her hands and another one peeking out from under her shirt.

She was the most beautiful thing I'd ever fucking seen. "Hey, sweetheart."

Her face crumpled, and she came straight for me. She lay over me gently, clearly trying to be careful. But I caught her. Pulled her to me. She felt so good.

"I'm sorry." Her voice was watery, speaking through tears. "I didn't mean anything I said last night. You're not broken. I would never think that. I love you. If it's too late, I understand. I just couldn't let you think that was real. It wasn't real."

She was speaking so fast, all the words coming out of her in a rush. "Cori."

"I couldn't let them kill you."

"Cori." I put a little more power into the word, and she stilled. "Cori, look at me."

She pulled her face up so I could see her, tears streaking her face. I reached for her, brushing my thumbs over her cheeks to wipe away the tears. "I know. I knew last night. I…" I took a breath and closed my eyes. "I heard you crying after you went inside, and it ripped me apart. After everything, I didn't want to believe it. But if it had been true, I would have let you go."

"I know," she nodded. "I'm glad you didn't believe me. I love you."

"I love you too," I told her. "And I'm not going anywhere."

Cori took a shuddering breath. "I didn't know if Jane would get you the information in time."

"She almost didn't. I almost lost you. If we'd gotten that email…even *minutes* later…" I shook my head. "I don't want to think about that."

I pulled her face down to mine and kissed her. Kissed her the way I'd wanted to kiss her last night. I wrapped my arms around her carefully, not wanting to aggravate any burns or injuries. "You're okay?" I asked in between tasting her lips. "You're not hurt?"

"Only minor. I'll be fine."

She tasted like cinnamon, and the way her fingers curled around my shoulders made me ache. I loved this woman so completely, I didn't have any regrets. "God, I wish we weren't in a hospital because I need you right now."

Cori laughed into my lips, kissing me harder. "I don't think that's going to happen for a while. You'll be here for a bit."

I'd pushed aside any questions about what my prognosis was. If I didn't know, I could still pretend I was okay. There was a needle in my arm, so I definitely had some medication in my system.

Instead, I just kissed Cori. It was the better option. And there was no doubt in my mind that I was going to kiss her for the rest of my life. Cori was it for me.

The sound of a throat clearing pulled us apart. Dr. Keyes stood in the doorway, smiling knowingly. "Mind if I interrupt?"

I glanced at Cori. If Dr. Keyes was here, then she'd gone through both Cori and the team. They wouldn't have let her operate on me if there was even a chance that she was dirty. "Of course."

She saw what I was thinking and smiled. "I've cleared the air with your team, and I can do the same with you, if you like."

Waving a hand, I shook my head. "If they cleared you, I trust them. I'm sure they'll tell me all about it."

Cori went to move away, and I caught her arm. She pulled the chair close so she could sit, leaning over the bed to rest her head on my arm.

"Very well. I'm here to see how you're feeling."

"Fine," I said. "Is there a reason that I shouldn't?"

She looked at me sharply. "Move your toes for me please."

Sudden terror gripped my stomach. If this didn't work, my whole life would be different. I wiggled my toes, and they moved. No lag. Relief was so swift and acute that I got chills.

"Now, carefully bend your knees."

I slowly bent one knee and then the other. They both felt completely normal.

Dr. Keyes smiled. "That looks good. I was able to fully visualize the shrapnel, and looking at the immediate scans, it's all gone. We'll obviously keep checking after things settle a bit, but I'm confident you'll make a full recovery."

My head fell back on the pillows. It was one thing to wonder if it could be real, and another thing entirely to have it *be* real. I didn't even know how to react.

"It was just in time. Whatever you did, if that shard had moved any more, this would have been a different conversation we're having."

"I'm glad it's not."

Cori wove her fingers through mine and held on tight. I was so happy that she was here, and that we weren't going to separate. No part of me wanted that. If anything, I wanted her closer in every part of my life.

"We're going to keep you for a few days to monitor the surgery site, but the recovery on this shouldn't be too bad. You'll have some pain for a while, and will need physical therapy. I don't want you doing any heavy lifting for a few months. But I expect that your mobility will improve quickly."

"Thank you, Doctor. Truly."

"You're welcome. If you need me, my phone is always on. But the doctors here have been briefed on your care. As has Dr. Peak." She smiled again. "I'll get out of your hair and let you visit. You have some more people who are waiting to see you."

"Thank you," Cori said as the doctor was walking away. She turned her face farther into my arm. "I suppose I have to share you now."

"Just for a little while. Promise."

Daniel knocked on the doorframe. "Ready to be overwhelmed?"

I laughed, and it turned into a cough with the smoke shit still in my lungs. "Better get it over with."

His face transformed into a grin, and as soon as he waved his hand, the room flooded with people. Every member of the team, plus Lena, Grace, and Evelyn. There were a *lot* of people in here, but they were all smiles and a mixture of nerves.

I looked at them. "Looks like I'm in the clear."

The cheers were deafening.

"That's such good fucking news, man." Liam reached out and shook my hand. Everyone was happy, and I could barely keep up with all of their congratulations and relief. There were so many that they started to wash over me.

The whole time, Cori just leaned against my arm. She drew circles with her fingers over my hand, quiet.

Lena came over to her and touched her on the shoulder. "Are you going home?"

"No," Cori said quietly. "I'll stay."

I didn't think Cori could see the way that Lena smiled

—full of genuine happiness, but also longing. "All right. I'll check in with you both tomorrow," she said.

"I'll do the same." Daniel pointed at me. "If you need anything, I expect you to call."

"I will."

They all filtered out together, saying goodbyes that blended into a chorus. Grace was last, and she pulled the door partially closed behind her.

"Do you think we'll get in trouble if you sleep in my bed?" I asked Cori quietly.

She looked up at me, hopeful. "Probably."

"Do it anyway." I savored her smile as she kicked off her shoes, and I carefully scooted over, arranging her next to me so she wasn't tangled in the IV.

Cori curled against my chest, and I felt settled. This was where she was supposed to be.

"Grant?"

"Yeah."

"Do you forgive me for last night?"

I pulled her closer, my words soft. "There was never anything to forgive, Cori. You were in an impossible situation, trying to protect me."

"Okay."

Leaning down, I kissed her hair. "If you need to hear it, I forgive you. But never doubt that I am completely in love with you, and that this—" I tightened my fingers "—is where you belong."

Cori sighed. A sound of relief and pleasure. She was probably more exhausted than I was, having been through her own ordeal and worrying through the entire surgery. Sleep was hovering around the edges for me too. I pulled Cori more firmly onto my chest, and together, we slept.

Chapter 34

Cori

"I think that's everything," Lena called from across the yard. "Minus the massive amounts of redecorating you're going to have to do. Honestly, if you were going to choose one of these houses, you're choosing the wrong one."

I laughed as she climbed the steps. "I know. But paint is a thing that exists, and Grant already owns this house."

She made a face. "I know, I know."

Grant would be here in less than an hour. The last four days had been an absolute whirlwind in the best way. Neither Grant nor I wanted any distance after this. And living next to each other made it easy.

Though my rent was great and I loved my house, the decision was simple. We would move in to his house, and I had completely free rein to decorate the house as I chose.

We picked out which furniture we'd keep from each house, and once we'd decided, the Resting Warrior guys made it happen. Moving had never gone so quickly or smoothly. The decorating would take time, but the house was completely put together. No tripping over boxes or things that didn't have a place.

Lena looked around the living room. "Not half bad for four days. You know what you're going to do yet?"

"I'm not worrying about it at the moment," I laughed. "Not until everything is a little more settled."

She pinned me with a stare. "If you end up having hot paint sex, I want to know about it."

I flushed pink, because Grant had already made it clear that was going to happen. Not that I was going to tell Lena that. Yet.

"Okay," she said. "I'm going to drop by some stuff for you guys later. I'll leave it on the porch and text you because I don't want to interrupt."

"Lena." I rolled my eyes.

"Girl, it has been almost a week since you've been able to jump that man's bones. You don't think I know that's exactly what's going to happen?"

I sighed, but it was through laughter. "You're the worst."

"And the best!" She blew me a kiss as she ran down the stairs.

I shut the door and sank down onto the couch. Noah was bringing Grant home, and I was about to go crazy. But they'd wanted to bring him to make it easier for me.

My phone buzzed, and I grabbed it, expecting a text message from Grant. But it wasn't.

It was a phone call…from my sister.

"Alice?" I answered. My sister and I were on decent terms, but I hadn't heard from her in a while. And we definitely weren't phone call people.

"Cori," she said. "Hi. I've been trying to call you. Mom and Dad are on the line too."

"Oh," I said. "Hi."

In the whirlwind of all this, my birthday had come and gone. I hadn't told them about my decision, but it was pretty clear that I'd been occupied. The search for the Pearsons and what I'd survived was national news.

Luckily, the Resting Warrior guys were excellent at keeping the press away.

Graham and Joel had been caught. They had been at a racetrack a few states away, attempting to establish an alibi for the fire. But since I'd survived, and the cops had tracked down Kevin, neither of them had a leg to stand on.

I was glad that, other than the statement I'd made to the police, I didn't have to think about them ever again.

"Hello, Cori," my mother said.

"Stellar, Mom," Alice said, sarcasm dripping. "Cori, I'm really glad that you're okay. And that they caught those assholes. I wish I could say that I can't believe it, but I can."

My father sighed. "Graham is a good man, Alice. We've been over this."

"No, Dad," I said. "He's not. He was poisoning his horses, tried to kill me, and did nothing even though he knew his son tried to rape me. So, no, Dad, I think we're not going to take that stance."

There was nothing but silence. Good.

"Yeah," Alice said. "It's been real fun over here. But I'm so glad you're okay. And Grant?"

"Yeah," I said, unable to keep the smile off my face at even the mention of his name. "He's coming home in about an hour."

"That's fantastic. Obviously, if you need any surgical help…"

"I know," I said with a laugh.

Alice sighed. "But this call is actually not about that. This call is a chance for Mom and Dad to apologize to you, even though they don't want to."

I stared at the wall in shock. "Why?"

"Because," Alice said. "No one else knew that they were trying to force you back into medical school. And even though the rest of us think you would be an absolutely brilliant surgeon, this field isn't for everyone, and no one should be forced. Let alone blackmailed."

"Oh…wow," I said. "I'd made my decision. I wasn't going to go back. With everything happening, I haven't had a chance to let you guys know."

Silence stretched over the line.

"Go ahead," Alice said.

My mother clearly wasn't happy. "We aren't changing the terms of your trust. You now have full access to it. Our lawyers will be sending over the papers later today."

"Really?"

"Really," Alice confirmed. "You should have heard the phone call where the rest of the family told them what they thought about that."

I had to cover my mouth to conceal the laughter. That would have been awkward as hell, and I was kind of glad I hadn't been a part of it.

"Thank you," I said. "All three of you. That money will go a long way toward supporting my clinic."

"If you ever reconsider…" my father said.

"I won't."

"Well, then. I guess we'll say goodbye. We're glad you're recovering."

They dropped off the line entirely. "That was awkward."

"Tell me about it," Alice said. "I nearly had to pull the same kind of blackmail just to get them on the freaking phone. But seriously, none of us had any idea, and I know you've felt pressure about that for a long time. It's not fair for them to try to force you into it."

"I really appreciate it, Alice. Truly." The grind of tires came from outside. "I think Grant just got here, so I have to go. But we'll talk soon?"

"I'd like that. Have fun!"

I ended the call and took a moment to melt into the sofa. The trust was mine. That kind of money was enough to keep the clinic going indefinitely. And Grant was here. This was one of the best days ever.

Truck doors slammed, and I went to the front door. Grant was there, walking on his own two feet. He was slow—surgery was surgery, and there would be more time to recover fully, but everything looked good.

Noah waved from the truck and pulled out of the driveway.

"He's not coming in?"

Grant's smile was so wide I thought it might break his face. "I made it very clear that staying wasn't an option."

"Aww, we could have given him coffee at least."

He came up the steps. "He has coffee at home. You and I are celebrating our first night in *our* house, and I want to get started on that."

As he finished the words, he reached out, tugging me into his arms and kissing me. My body went fluid, molding to his. We'd kissed in the hospital, wishing we could tear each other's clothes off.

Grant shut the door behind us. "I'm not allowed to lift things yet, so I can't carry you upstairs. But I need you up there. Now."

I wasn't arguing, not letting go of his hand the whole way up the stairs. We would take it slow and gentle and easy.

There would be other times for hard and fast. Other times for rope and kink, and I looked forward to it in a way that took my breath away.

But right now, it would just be me and the man I loved and nothing but slow, sweet time.

Epilogue

Cori

Three Months Later

The snow was so bright that I had to squint against it in the early afternoon sun. "I should have brought my sunglasses," I said.

A soft laugh came from behind me, and Grant tucked his arm more firmly around my waist. "I told you."

"Yes, you did. Happy?"

"That I'm right? Yes. That your eyes hurt? No."

I put my hand on top of his. "How do you feel? Are you okay?"

"Cori, sweetheart, you don't have to ask me if I'm okay every five minutes."

"Sorry."

He pressed a kiss to my hair. "Don't be sorry. I'm okay."

We were on Ginger's back. The sprain I'd checked out what felt like years ago now was fine, and this was part of getting her back up to speed.

And it was Grant's first time riding a horse since the surgery. By all rights, he probably could have been riding before now, but all his doctors were erring on the side of caution. I didn't blame them. I wanted to be on the side of caution as well.

That made me ask how he was feeling every five minutes, much to his amusement.

We'd almost taken separate horses, and then at the last minute, he declared that he wanted us to ride together. No complaints from me. Getting to be this close to Grant wasn't ever something I would say no to.

My mind flicked back to the trial, and I pushed it aside. I didn't want to think about it, but it kept popping back into my head like bad song lyrics. Round and round and round.

"Do you think I'd go to jail if I jumped off the witness stand and punched Joel in the face?"

"Maybe just overnight," Grant said. "As tempting as that sounds, I'd rather you didn't."

I sighed. "I know. But somehow, I don't think he's going to be able to keep his mouth shut during my testimony or yours, and that's going to make it difficult."

"I'll build you a dummy in the backyard, and you can beat the hell out of it any time you like."

"That sounds fun."

If he did that, it would be nice. Just as nice as every other part of our life since moving in together to his place. Our house was now just as colorful as mine had been. And I had very specific and…*vibrant* memories of the painting process.

Grant loved painting, and it wasn't always the walls that he wanted to use as his canvas.

My life with him was a distraction from the fast-moving trial and the fact that my parents were still trying to get me to go back to medical school, though without blackmail this time. He was my constant when everything else around me was a storm.

"Where'd you go?" he asked.

"Just thinking about…everything," I said. "Where are we going?"

He hadn't said anything other than that he wanted to go for a ride with me. But though the Resting Warrior property was large, there weren't a lot of places to go, and it was too snowy for us to go to their other hidden property.

"You'll see."

"I swear to God, Grant, if Lena's put together another surprise for me out here, I'm just going to kill you."

Grant's laugh rang out over the snow. "As hilarious as that would be, I can at least promise you that's not the case."

"Good."

"I thought the surprise party was nice."

I winced. It had been nice, but given the circumstances, I didn't think I would ever really want a surprise party again. Just thinking about it put a pit in the bottom of my stomach. There was nothing about that day that I wanted to relive.

A little way ahead of us, there was a small group of trees that looked familiar. And within them, almost invisible and covered in snow, was a small building. The last time I'd been here, no snow had been on the ground. Though the hail had made it kind of look that way.

"Is that the same one?"

"It is," Grant confirmed.

I laughed. "Why are you taking me there?"

Behind me, I felt him shrug. "It was really the start of everything," he said. "I just wanted to visit it."

He wasn't wrong. That had been the official beginning of everything between us. Grant made it no secret that he'd liked me before then, but that moment surrounded by shattering hail was when we'd found each other.

We pulled up just outside of it, and Grant dismounted easily before lifting me down off the horse. "Grant."

"Cori." He lifted an eyebrow, daring me to tell him that he shouldn't be lifting things as heavy as me. He'd been cleared by the doctors, but I was still nervous. No matter that every time he lifted me like that, I got butterflies through my whole body.

He smiled down at me. "Stay here for a second. And close your eyes."

"This isn't reassuring me that there isn't an impossibly tiny surprise party in there."

"Close your eyes," he said again.

I obeyed, blocking out the sun. Frankly, it was a bit of a relief since it was too bright. The air was cold, sweet, and fresh. It reminded me of Grant, and that wildness that was always there underneath the surface.

"Okay," Grant called, his voice quieter from inside the little shed. "You can come in."

I opened my eyes, squinting against the sun. Petting Ginger on the neck, I made sure her reins were tied off before pushing open the door and freezing.

"Not a surprise party, exactly," he said.

A blanket was spread across the ground in the small space, and a couple of candles had been set around the edges. On the blanket was a basket of food and a bottle of wine.

"Grant," I managed. "What is this?"

He grinned. "A picnic, of a sort."

I laughed. "You decided you wanted a picnic in a shed in the middle of January?"

"Yes," he said with absolute certainty. "Because this was the beginning of everything, I wanted to start here."

"Start what?" I took a step forward, and the door to the shed closed behind me. Daylight filtered in through the small, high windows, but it was far dimmer, letting the few candles create a cozy glow.

"Cori," Grant said. "I love everything about our life. I love waking up with you every morning. I love every color you've put all over our house. I love helping you explore every fantasy you have and finding more."

I blushed at that, disbelief dancing at the edges of my mind. Was this happening? Was he doing what I thought that he was doing? That wasn't possible, right? It was too fast?

No.

There was that quiet voice that told me that if he was going where I thought he was, then it wasn't too fast. Because I already knew, too, that this was it. Grant and I were together, and that wasn't going to change.

"There's only one thing I could think of that could make it better."

Grant sank to one knee, and I was already crying. I covered my face with my hands, trying to clear the tears so I could see him and remember this moment.

A box appeared in his hand, and in the dim light, a ring shone.

"I love you," he said. "That's not going to change. Ever. And the thought of waking up next to my wife and having it be you? Cori, it takes my breath away. Will you marry me?"

I stumbled forward, nearly tripping on the blanket that he'd laid down, to get to him. My hands landed on his shoulders and the tears were still blurring my vision, but I could see him. So happy, so hopeful, and so mine. "Of course I will," I choked out. "Yes. Yes."

Grant pulled me down to him, kissing me and wrapping me so tightly in his arms that I never wanted to let him go.

"I love you," he whispered.

I only pulled back when he did, looking down as he slid the ring on to my finger. Twisting gold with an angled diamond and little turquoise stones surrounding it. It was beautiful. Perfect.

"How long have you been planning this?"

"The physical proposal?" he asked. "Not long. But I knew that I wanted to marry you before the fire, Cori. From the second I realized that I was in love with you, I wanted you to be my wife. That was why I didn't want to commit to anything. My *wife*. Not my caretaker."

"I wouldn't have cared."

He smiled. "Which only proved my point that I wanted to marry you."

"Before the fire." I took his face in my hands. "That was so fast."

"I don't care," he said. "I knew."

In a second, I was on my back, his mouth on mine. "Careful of the candles," I laughed.

"We're getting married." He grinned.

I couldn't stop the blinding smile that spread across my face, and I let him kiss me, let us get lost in each other before we pulled back. "There's just one thing."

"What's that?"

"Evelyn will kill us both if we get married before her

and Lucas. Harlan and Grace were one thing. I think we might drive her mad."

He laughed, full and bright. "Fair enough. I don't need a fast wedding. We can wait, as long as I get to put that second ring on your finger."

"You will," I promised.

"After all," he said. "We've got forever now, right?"

"Right."

Grant kissed me again, and everything else dropped away. We had forever.

•••

About the Author (Josie Jade)

Josie Jade is the pen name of an avid romantic suspense reader who had so many stories bubbling up inside her she had to write them!

Her passion is protective heroes and books about healing…broken men and women who find love—and themselves—again.

Two truths and a lie:

• Josie lives in the mountains of Montana with her husband and three dogs, and is out skiing as much as possible

• Josie loves chocolate of all kinds—from deep & dark to painfully sweet

• Josie worked for years as an elementary school teacher before finally becoming a full time author

Josie's books will always be about fighting danger and standing shoulder-to-shoulder with the family you've chosen and the people you love.

Heroes exist. Let a Josie Jade book prove it to you.

About the Author (Janie Crouch)

"Passion that leaps right off the page." - Romantic Times Book Reviews

USA Today and Publishers Weekly bestselling author Janie Crouch writes what she loves to read: passionate romantic suspense featuring protective heroes. Her books have won multiple awards, including the Romance Writers of America's coveted Vivian® Award, the National Readers Choice Award, and the Booksellers' Best.

After a lifetime on the East Coast, and a six-year stint in Germany due to her husband's job as support for the U.S. Military, Janie has settled into her dream home in Front Range of the Colorado Rockies.

When she's not listening to the voices in her head—and even when she is—she enjoys engaging in all sorts of crazy adventures (200-mile relay races; Ironman Triathlons, treks to Mt. Everest Base Camp...), traveling, and hanging out with her four kids.

Her favorite quote: "Life is a daring adventure or nothing." ~ Helen Keller.

facebook.com/janiecrouch
amazon.com/author/janiecrouch
instagram.com/janiecrouch
bookbub.com/authors/janie-crouch

Printed in the USA
CPSIA information can be obtained
at www.ICGtesting.com
LVHW042140020524
778991LV00009B/793